To Serve Man

What Americans Need to Know,
But Don't Want to Hear

Nichole Johnson

MoorRey Publishing

Table of Contents

This work is the result of thousands of frank and honest conversations. The names and documents have been changed and or redacted to protect the trifling.

For people who learned the hard way.

Nic

I was released from prison eight hours ago. Four hours after my release, Hurricane Andrew made a left turn in the Atlantic Ocean and was now making landfall not far from my mother's house, whose floor was my temporary residence. I couldn't sleep I was excited not just because I was out but because I was alive. It was four thirty in the morning and I was watching an episode of 'Martin'.

When the Category 5 Hurricane made landfall, it was as though the heavens had just opened, as water quickly pushed against my mother's house, sending it swaying. The rain and the sustained 165 mph wind speeds must have awakened my seven-year-old sister, Rebecca. "Why is my room...shaking?" Rebecca mumbled, rubbing her eyes. She was half asleep and had wandered into the living room.

The one-hundred-gallon fish tank when empty weighed 180 pounds, but the tank presently contained 2 Sailfin Catfish, 5 African Jewel fish, 3 Mayan Cichlids, 4 Black Acaras, 5 GloFish Danios, 8 Peacock Gudgeon, various aquatic plants, gravel, stones, plastic toys, a sunken pirate ship and about 100 gallons of water and it weighed about a thousand pounds when I saw it tipping over on my little sister. I jumped up, grabbed my sister and used my back to push the fish tank against the wall. I quickly braced the tank with the couch.

A rush of oak and cypress trees snapped in the distance and then bang! The power went out, leaving only darkness. Rebecca and I huddled as best we could under the door jamb, and that's when she started crying. My mother yelled, "Stay where you are!" We didn't move until the wind died down. About five hours later we heard sirens from emergency vehicles and cadaver dogs barking.

People who haven't done much in life like to say their abuse is worse than being murdered or that their experience is worse than being wrongfully incarcerated. Unless you are those little white girls from Ohio, who were imprisoned for a decade in that dude's basement, birthing babies, your tale of abuse in a nation full of abused people isn't worse. You just survived. 65 people lost their lives in the trail of destruction Hurricane Andrew left, we survived.

My younger brother, Martin, and I were close. He had many experiences and traveled to many nations over the years but even he didn't know what to expect from me. I had been counted out and the odds weren't great that I'd make it out alive.

Here I was, the cold bars had not ended me. I am the same person but somehow everything was different. I was older, faster, stronger, and hopefully smarter and my muscles were more visible.

Debra, my mother, knew I had been through hell and back. She told me to just relax, slow down and enjoy life. My mother told me that I could stay with her as long as I wanted to. She had just had Danica, my youngest sister, nine months ago.

I was an able bodied adult, I wasn't going to infringe on their space any longer than I had to. I wasn't going to just relax, I couldn't, that's why I slept on the floor instead of the couch- I needed to feel uncomfortable.

Behind those bars, I had witnessed individuals evolve into absolutely terrifying subhuman forms. Those bars rendered insignificant my fears of needles, snakes and unleashed dogs. The problems I had with acne and uneven skin tone were now laughable, even one of my legs being slightly longer than the other wasn't worth a thought.

Cold iron bars have a way of making you accept things, in the most profoundly cruel ways. Daily, life and death hung in the balance. I was far from a hood but I understood the streets, still there were moments when I was close to breaking. All I could do is keep praying and keep moving forward.

I knew better how it felt to be forgotten— written off. I knew how it felt to lose everything. Once I understood that my anger was prompted at the root by fear, it made the business of surviving easier. All of the negatives were in play. I had to survive by understanding my fears but also the fears and motivations of others. Doing this allowed me to avoid the punches, kicks, chokes and shanks that came my way.

I knew what I was and was not mentally capable of. I did a lot of watching and thinking and I realized that most of the things you are scared of never happened. But if you sit around thinking about them they will manifest.

What emerged from that horror was this incredibly aware blank slate with a strong sense of right and wrong. I learned that people that have been known to shoot other people can't necessarily fight and that once you take away systems, the mind breaks down…it can be reset.

I could hear and see unfairness easier. I learned quickly how people only talk to or listen to you if there's something in it for them. We waste so much of our lives talking to people, who for whatever reason won't hear understand or accept anything you're saying. This realization allowed me to avoid more conflicts.

I had a greater understanding of what humans were really capable of. I saw how agendas had become more important than truth. I saw the advertisements for the mental manipulation that they were and I saw the media not working for the people but against them. I saw the world different, I thought different and fought different.

In the aftermath of the hurricane my mind buzzed with ideas, distrust and fear. Not the fear of being stabbed in the neck with a pencil while eating lunch. More like a general fear of not being wanted. Not being wanted isn't as immediately scary as a prison riot, but it permeates everything.

It was strange just being home. You haven't seen a real human being until you've seen them broken down particle by particle, stripped of every rule, every norm and every agenda. I saw humanity debased in all its forms; it's something that stays with you.

Even though I had personally gone through hell, I realized that telling the truth was my only option to maintain my sanity. There are huge psychological consequences in not saying what is true. I didn't mind the backlash that came from saying something that is unpopular, unfavorable or unpleasant. I did mind losing control of my tongue and mind by giving myself over to falsehoods.

Most people only have their individual approximation of the truth, but it's important to be afraid of the right thing— for me repeating falsehoods was the same as putting deceit into my everlasting soul thereby contaminating it.

I believed that there will come a day, after your head is filled with so much garbage, that you'll have to make a decision that counts, maybe a life and death one, and because you've compromised yourself, your judgment will be impaired.

As a society we have voluntarily told and embraced exceptional mistruths for profit and acceptance. Telling the truth takes courage— courage was the one thing I had left.

Today, I am "free"; I am both victim and beneficiary of this moment and of all the bad and good things of the past. In a way we are victimized by ourselves when we fall victim to our own susceptibilities. There are distinct parts of me that can do in spite of this, and the part of me that can't do because to this.

I quickly got reintroduced to people, I've been introduced to. I didn't have the luxury of panic attacks or feeling sorry for myself or even to complain about a lack of sleep. My four year old daughter, Nichole, needed me. Her mother demanded money, so there was a need for me to be afraid of the right thing. I needed a job and I needed to get off of my mother's floor.

My daughter eats, even if I don't. I couldn't blame the stove for what I did. I wasn't going to grab a bag and hold down a street corner, like some no-account hoodlum. A month after the storm, I cleaned sewage, power washed away toxins and I worked at an auto parts store. Four months after the storm I was working at AMC Theater.

Movies had always appealed to me, beyond the visuals and escapism. I was drawn by camera angles and performances more than explosions. For employees the movies were free and the food was half price. The popcorn wasn't bad; this was the perfect place for me to work.

For two months, I worked every shift I could get. That was enough to get an apartment. Out of necessity I needed a roommate and my best friend Anthony Johnson was the obvious choice.

Anthony, at 6'2" was two inches taller that I was, he was also thinner than I was. He had a laid back, thoughtful manner. Women loved his intelligence almost as much as they loved his height and brown skin. Anthony was my 'A1 from Day 1' as they say. I helped make his transition from the military to civilian life seamless.

He could have gone the route of private military contracting but he was done doing the wrong thing for the wrong people. Anthony had not long been discharged from the Navy when he moved in with me.

Every week Anthony would mutter, 'That 50/50 marriage shit doesn't work'. A few months ago he had been served divorce papers, so I got him a job at the theater. He was hustling to save and I was hustling to survive. We were making new friends, mostly women friends.

Neither of us had much money, but we each had a particular skill set. We were intelligent and in good shape. On the phone, I would talk to ladies until the early morning. My kisses were legendary. My massages were professional grade. When I touched, they could feel the magic in my hands. I rubbed them the right way. And I owe it all to my grandmother.

When I was young my grandmother used my brother and I as low cost dishwashers and weed wackers. We had to clear yards and fields by pulling up weeds by hand. Oh how we hated that, but when I was 15 my hands were noticeably soft and I could easily crush a soda can. She also made us rub her rough feet and bunions.

Now, I had one woman for the morning, one for the afternoon and often one for the night. One time, due to a scheduling snafu on my part, three women ended up in our small apartment at the same time, snarling at each other as they waited for their turn, but that's a story for another time. Our visitors came by whether the utilities were on or not.

To make ends almost meet, I did odd jobs, recycled cans and shook my ass... these muscles were good for something other than protection. The thing about being a hoe is that most of the time you're not sure that you are one until something not so good happens. Occasionally, I went to houses filled with drunken women and loud music and I flexed my abs, gyrated in zesty shorts and took most of my clothes off, to pay my rent.

I wasn't Chris Brown, but I would randomly break out choreographed dance moves in my living room, in my yard or wherever I was.

However, shaking my ass for cash just wasn't fun, it was a job with terrible benefits. So, I didn't do much of that because my parents raised me wrong.

I played basketball and jogged through every poverty-stricken area in South Florida. My body fat hovered near ten percent; going lower into those single digit body fat percents affects you sexually. I found it easy to keep my body fat low because I was broke. Wrongfully incarcerated or not, I was behind in life and I still had hoop dreams.

I eventually sent my highlight video to the Orlando Magic and the Los Angeles Clippers, when those teams were terrible, hoping for a training camp invite. I ended up playing for the Oklahoma Calvary of the Continental Basketball Association, when Isaiah Thomas owned it, yes that Isaiah Thomas, but that's a story for later.

In the theater, where I worked, people from all walks of life came. The people I worked with were a unique bunch. People were getting fired and hired weekly, employees opened back doors for friends, they kept the wallets and purses they found; I couldn't do those things, like I said, I was raised wrong.

I was fast at the register. I communicated well and I looked people in the eye when I spoke to them; I owe that to my dad. He taught me to always look a person in the eye when speaking to them. My dad has a Masters in Finance so he made sure that my younger brother and I had a firm grasp of mathematics.

My dad showed my brother and I different ways to be clear with our words. My dad commanded a room, 'You can't have a positive life with a negative mind', 'Never lose, just learn', 'You have to be willing to fail to be great at something', 'You don't ask your father for money on Father's Day. You ask a month ahead, be smart about it.' He'd say. My dad always has words of wisdom ready for any occasion. His guidance and positivity helped me more than I can say. I still occasionally go to church with him, 2nd row pew.

Being that I had a record; I worked many jobs, at every job there are pricks in just about every positions; working at the movie theater was no different. In between pouring sodas, selling gummy candy and malt balls, I had to kiss ass…a lot of ass.

In order to get enough money for my daughter, I had to take the worst shifts, the worst crew and the worst assignments. I thrived under pressure. I didn't get stressed easy. I didn't whine or complain. I came in on time and did my job, so management didn't give me any problems.

I wasn't aware of how my uniform made my bigger than average butt for a man stand out. Customers want extra butter flavoring and extra butter was something I had to turn around to get, that's when other employees noticed that customers would ask for extra, extra butter just so they could look at my ass. It wasn't funny to me but was a big joke to the entire staff. It was my idea to move the butter flavoring to the side of the concession stand and make it self-service. Little did I know that suggestion would make concessions more efficient and be expanded nationwide.

The worst thing about this job was cleaning the popcorn popper because it has to be cleaned while it's hot. I cleaned out theaters fast. With that air blower, I blew all the disrespect that people left on the floor right into trash bins. It wasn't long before I was promoted to staff lead. I was so proud of that metallic name tag that read Nicodemus.

I completed tasks quick and efficiently. I handed the constantly ringing telephone, long lines and screaming customers with ease. I deftly navigated the power drunk managers, the sexist, racist, and hostile work environments— I was raised by a single mom so high pressure work environments were a walk in the park to me. As someone who was recently raised from the dead, not much rattled me.

I am a new creation, motivated by my tragedy. And because of that, I am thankful for each day, so I go into work happy, always grateful for the opportunity. To my supervisors, the fact that I could count and read somehow put me ahead of the curve. To them I was that one in ten thousand. One day, the general manager approached me, "Nic, do you want to go to the Concession Olympics?" he asked.

In my head I was like, *what the fuck are the Concession Olympics?* It sounded real Caucasian. "Yes" I answered. A couple weeks later I went to the Concession Olympics. It was in Hialeah, which is about 30 minutes away from where Anthony and I lived.

The event was held at a huge state of the art, 21 Screen Theater. Dozens of employees from theaters all around Florida attended. As the company president and general managers, drank cocktails and socialized with one another, we took orders and cleaned auditoriums as part of the competition. Each competitor was timed and checked for efficiency. They even had a large digital score board in the middle of the theater.

Watching the positions change on the leader board increased the pressure on me. I was up there sweating in tight black pants and throwing popcorn with the best of them. I had the fastest transaction times, but I came in second place overall. I received a silver medal, a plaque and a hundred dollars. My General Manager was promoted to the corporate office for his innovative concession ideas.

This was the first time I had ever been recognized for doing something I enjoyed doing.

Eva

Eva Maldonado didn't talk much and she didn't smile at all. She was 5'6" with a noticeable Spanish accent, especially when she was upset. She had curly jet black hair and pale skin; she could almost pass for white. *Almost.* She wore heavy winged eyeliner, her lips were darkly lined, she had acrylic nails, gelled-down baby hairs, cut crease eye shadow and tattooed-in arched eyebrows. She had a round face and an average body.

Eva appeared to be devoid of even a basic level of kindness. She was a cool co-worker because she did her job and didn't make more work for me. She had tattoos on her arms and in the webbing between her fingers. If all of that wasn't enough to tell people not to speak to her, she had a particular way of talking to you that made you feel like you made a mistake.

One afternoon I was in the hallway walking towards the break room when I saw Eva. I heard someone say *chonga* and two unbuttoned Pendleton shirt-wearing *cholos* approached Eva. She had just finished cleaning a smaller theater.

I had never seen these dudes before, for all I know these guys had weapons or maybe they were her cousins playing around, I didn't know. I know… I know I am supposed to mind my own business, but I was raised wrong.

"Yo, what the fuck is going on?" I blurted out, walking over to them, sizing them up with my eyes.

"Who are you, homes?" one of them responded.

"I'm her boyfriend," I fired back.

There may as well have been comic bubbles of confusion over their heads. They looked at each other, as they sized me up. They paused for about four seconds.

"Oh... you're her boyfriend," The medium size guy stammered.

"He's my boyfriend…" Eva said backing me up.

"No disrespect, homie, we didn't know," the smaller one apologetically said.

"And now…" I said.

"Step!" Eva stated pointing towards the front of the theater.

They turned and walked out of the theater. I looked at Eva and gave her a head nod and went into the break room. Those guys were being disrespectful. I am sure that if Eva didn't have on her uniform, she would have taken care of the situation herself; nobody wants to lose their job over stupid shit.

That's the thing about needing to keep your job— it prevents people who need to have their ass kicked from actually getting their ass kicked. A few days later, co-workers were teasing me with "So you and Miss Maldonado are dating huh?" as I entered the break room. They must have heard about what happened in the hallway, I just ignored them.

Some people are always on standby to hear gossip or to get involved in things have nothing to do with them. A week later, I was sitting in the break room and Eva was on the other side of the table. I knew that her break was over but she lingered around. When it was just me and her in the break room, she walked over and stood over me.

"I didn't get to thank you for what you did last week," she awkwardly said as the words struggled to come out of her mouth. She had an aggressive stance, like she was going to punch me.

"Those guys were out of line end of story," I said.

"Just… thanks anyway…dasit…" Eva quickly stated and walked out of the room.

After that, Eva started speaking to me like I was a human being. She still spoke to everyone else like they were navel lint. This new found niceness actually helped us work together better. We helped each other with scheduling and clean ups. Eva was promoted to staff lead and I was promoted to the box office and the box office is the cleanest, most visible position and its two steps below management.

Anthony was dating Sharmutasha another one of my co-workers. She was from the Middle East and an aspiring actress; she had taken several acting classes. She had odd acting gigs here and there; she told anyone who would listen that her big break was coming. She lived in a downtown condo and Anthony didn't like her but she had money and a pussy; there wasn't much of a downside.

Sharmutasha got a role in one of those hair replacement commercials. She talked about it like she had just hit the lotto. For the premier of the commercial she threw a party to celebrate. Her condo was packed with people to watch this commercial. We were all quiet when the commercial came on. In the commercial she smiled and passed a file to the fake doctor and stood behind him as he pulled on the client's hair.

Sharmutasha had wine and champagne bottles, the food was catered and my youngest friend, William Davis, kept things moving with his music playlist. Anthony left early because Sharmutasha said some shit he didn't like. You know those parties where there is only one white girl…more often than not I was the one that brought her. I didn't discriminate; life was too full of information and wonder for me to do so. Tonight I was solo and I was having a blast entertaining people with my practiced disco era moves.

About two in the morning, the party had almost cleared out and since Sharmutasha was Anthony's girlfriend, I felt slightly obligated to help clean up. The condo was trashed and I liked her condo because when she was out of town we had gatherings there.

When Sharmutasha stopped yelling at Anthony over the phone she asked if I could take the last two people home. I told her that I had walked there. I didn't want to do it but I also didn't want to lie. I walked a lot, I had a car but it was a bucket. The two remaining party-goers told me they didn't live far and that no one was coming to pick them up. One was a new employee that I didn't know and the other was Eva Maldonado.

"Fine," I grumbled, placing my compliance next to my distain for their poor planning.

I grabbed a big bottle of champagne. Eva grabbed a bottle of wine and the three of us left. We weren't in any condition to be walking down the streets at two in the morning but we did it anyway. They regaled each other with hood stories and giggled as we walked ten blocks to the new girl's house.

"It's late; I'll see y'all at work tomorrow," I said, thinking that Eva was going to stay with this co-worker for the night. In my mind, I had already left the girls there.

"I think I live by you," Eva said before I could walk away.

She said that she lived a few blocks from me, so we continued on together. We walked the barely lit streets for about a mile. When we were close to my apartment, Eva asked could she use my bathroom.

So we went to my apartment. When we got there I put our bottles on the floor in the living room and talked to Anthony who was still fuming about Sharmutasha. Eva came out of the bathroom and sat on our worn brown couch.

"Ready…" I said standing near the door.

"You got champagne and I got wine, let's chill and drink," Eva softly said.

"Okay, cool," I said. I was at home and it was warmer than being outside.

We must have been too loud for three in the morning, because Anthony went into the bedroom and closed the door. We just sat on the couch looking at random music videos, drinking and laughing. When the gangbanger movie 'West Side Story' came on everything was quiet. I looked over and Eva was staring at me.

"I like you," she whispered. The flickering light cast different shaped shadows of her on the wall.

"Of course, you my work girlfriend," I responded with a drunken smile.

Eva's tone had seriousness to it; it was escapable because I totally missed it. She kept looking in my direction.

"Yeah, you're cool," I added, my eyes darted around the room as I tried not to look at her.

"I want to fuck," she said, putting down her glass.

Here is the thing about me; you don't have to tell me twice once the signal is given. Eva took off her clothes faster than I did. I nervously pulled out a condom; she took it and put it on me and there was no going back. We went at it on the couch, on the floor and then up against the wall. Her bones dug into my pelvis, but somehow even that felt good.

We cycled through all of the popular positions, but Eva preferred to face me. She whispered to me in Spanish, *Vas a soñar conmigo, Creo que somos buenas juntas and Dame más…* all I know is that it sounded good.

She fucked me like it was finally Christmas and now she get to open presents. She took everything I had with a moan. I could feel her insides twitching as she lay on top of me. I wrapped a blanket around us. Eva reached into her coat and pulled out an inhaler. She shook it, put it into her mouth and inhaled twice. She took another sip of wine and then we fucked in the spooning position until sleep overcame us. The next morning, we got up and I walked her home.

Her apartment was upstairs. The apartment was a mix of old Florida and Mexico; there were lit candles of Madonna throughout the living room. Religious Spanish plaques hung on the wall. Her father was there, he was older than I thought he'd be. He was the kind of guy you'd expect to see singing drunken Spanish songs with a guitar, only meaner.

The look he gave made me think that he might be with the cartel. His posture changed the way a cat does when it feels threatened. His movements became quick and he started looking like he was stuck on an airplane looking for exits. From his mannerisms and tone he had pictured me, fucking his precious little Eva. Every time he blinked the scene in his mind changed to my big blackness passing his daughter's tonsils. I am sure he imagined me doing things with Eva that he had done with her mother. Little did he know that his little girl wasn't to be trifled with.

Her father started shaking his head as if he was too upset to remember where his gun was. Normally, I would turn on full asshole mode and say something like, *"Señor, soy uno de los simpáticos negros"* or *"Lo cierto es que tu hija me jodió"*, but I got the distinct impression that he would not be impressed with my 8th grade Spanish or my sarcasm.

Eva said, *"Calmate papo…"* I didn't understand much else. They yelled at each other for a few minutes, then Eva smiled at me and said, "Thanks for walking me home. I'll see you later." I was already on my way out the door.

My walk home was slowed by the realization that I was holding it together, but I didn't really have it together. Currently my struggle was not only the health, safety and welfare of my child but also working and staying out of trouble. My head was filled with thoughts of, what is the right amount of pain? What is the right amount of suffering? Could someone like me be redeemed? Could I be truly loved? Was there hope?

I cried when I got to my block.

When I saw Eva at work, everything was normal. By normal, I mean we didn't walk around with the 'Hey, everybody, we just fucked' vibe. We were already pretending that we were together, only now we weren't pretending. Eva would ask me to walk her home or she would ask to come by.

She invited me over when her dad was out of town. She held up some kind of clear liquid, I think she called it *guaro*. Eva is Mexican. She said she got it on her last trip to Mexico. "This is the best thing a person can drink," Eva announced, handing me a full shot glass.

I smirked at her and confidently stated, "You don't know who you dealin' wit" then I threw two shots of the liquid down my throat. It tasted like chocolate and honey, it put me on my ass quick and that is where Eva wanted me. She wanted me to relax while she sucked my dick; she liked kissing on me which was fine by me.

She liked to suck my balls while rubbing my six-pack abs. When we fucked, she wanted all of me inside of her. Her sexual frequency was similar to mine; in the morning or late. She didn't want foreplay; she said she didn't need it. She said just thinking about me primed her to orgasm. She wanted it hard and fast. She wanted me to try to push through her body.

She smelled sweet and tasted like my favorite breakfast cereal. She wasn't into romance, candlelight dinners, or even taking showers together. She wasn't into fairy-tales, she was into real life. She was passionate and unafraid and that is its own kind of beauty.

She wasn't the type of woman that had breasts that even in a sports bra, appear enhanced. By the end of the day, her back didn't ache because bra straps dug into her shoulders. Small breasted women didn't look at her with envy.

Eva had orchid-pink lips and a pronounced jaw line, spider leg eyelashes, pinched-in cheek bones. She had orange sized breasts with a dark berry for a nipple, which elevated slightly when aroused. She wasn't voluptuous but her figure really showed in the tight dresses and short skirts she wore when she was out of her work uniform. She didn't wear high heels just to go to the store.

After a month she randomly asked if I liked her in a lot of make-up or a little, as if not wearing make-up any wasn't an option. I told her that I liked it when she wears less, from then on she didn't wear much make-up.

We watched movies and we played games. She invited me to parties in the barrios, the part of the city that was full of Spanish-speakers. At these parties, I was the only person there identifying as black. When you are in your twenties, you don't really think you are doing crazy shit, but when you look back on it you realize that you were. I knew that my sarcasm or 8th grade Spanish wasn't going to cut it here.

You know those photos where 8 to 10 people are posing holding firearms at parties, well that's the type of people I am talking about and I'm the dumbass taking the picture. The people at these parties would speak Spanish to me as a joke, and when they did, Eva would shove them and yell "English please!" I ain't no punk but from my point of view, these aren't the kind of people you yell at or push.

Eva didn't take shit from anyone. I saw her beat up a girl who looked at her the wrong way. At these barrio gatherings she wasn't out of place, the ways she seemed at work. She taught me more Spanish and she shared things about her culture with me. She made sure people knew not to fuck with me.

Eva's black curly hair always seemed damp, but it wasn't. When she smiled, her smile was surprisingly pretty. She wasn't big on going out, which was great because I didn't have going out money. We spent a lot of time visiting various parks and walking on the beach.

Little Havana is filled with Latin-inspired restaurants, bakeries, fruit stands, cigar shops, rum bars, art galleries and music venues. It is not uncommon to find residents gathered in parks, discussing politics or playing dominoes. The streets are lined with murals and mosaics. I convinced Eva to come with me to get Cuban sandwiches in Little Havana. Eva didn't like going to Little Havana.

As we drove to Little Havana, I asked her why she didn't like going there.

"It's not that I don't like other Latinos," Eva began. "I don't know if you realize this but a lot of Latinos are prejudiced. In most Latino communities, being darker is laughed at or looked at as inferior.

Cubanos are bullies; they can turn prejudice into full blown racism. My skin is light, but if I were your skin tone, I'd be invisible to them."

"Is it that bad?" I frowned.

"They be dancing to Roger and Zapp while grabbing all of the racist shit out of the closet. They use a lot of blackface..."

"What! I haven't heard this," I said, shocked.

"In our community we talk about it, but people don't understand what we are saying anyway...that's why we will always speak Spanish."

"So I can't pass?" I asked.

"Not even close," she sighed. "I just don't like being around that kind of attitude."

"So being with me isn't some kind of fetish?"

"I'm prejudice too, who isn't? My family pushed me to be with someone who has European features..."

"Well..." I inquired.

"Nicodemus, I see you, not your skin tone," she said.

When you are in Miami, the best place to get the Cuban sandwiches was Versailles on 8th street. Versailles became a gathering place for Miami's Cuban exiles when it opened in 1971. It takes Versailles 15 minutes to make a Cuban sandwich. While any Publix Deli makes a Cuban sandwich in two minutes, everyone I know would rather wait the extra 13 minutes for these tasty delights.

The Cuban sandwiches we got were made with roast pork, ham, Swiss cheese, pickles and yellow mustard pressed into crusty bread. We got our sandwiches, key lime pie and headed back home. Eva didn't want to stay in Little Havana any longer than she had to.

"With my people, either you are the light-skinned *güero*, or dark-skinned *prieto* of the family," Eva said. "My cousin is a little lighter than you. When he was young, I heard my grandma tell him that he messed up the race. Imagine your grandmother telling you some shit like that?"

"That's fucked up."

"She said it in front of everyone! My cousin spent his whole life trying to please her. Not his grades, not the way he dressed, not the way he spoke, not the career he chose…nothing was good enough. One day he just asked her *how could he fix it?* She told him to make the race better by marrying white. And that's exactly what he did."

"That's why your father went off on me like that?"

"I'm his little girl, but it's not just Cubans and Mexicans who feel like this. In most of the countries that I've been to, black is not beautiful. *No negra bella*, not even if you call yourself Afro-Latino."

"But that's popular now…" I said as she fed me a piece of key lime pie.

"They don't like it. They say it diminishes Latino. It's like here in the states when people of color say that they are mixed so they can play more than one side."

"Miami isn't just full of Cubans," I responded.

"In Miami, Hispanic means white Cubans; being a lighter skin shade around the world can make life easier. If you can pass for white or have white backing the more successful you'll be. That's just how things are.

"It doesn't matter if you've never committed a crime, are a good neighbor, a good friend or a good person, if your skin is dark. A lot of people are one skin shade from being perfect. People they don't like are labeled as invaders, aliens and criminals," Eva said.

"That kind of conditioning goes on outside of the Latino community too," I responded.

"At least here you have representatives and can push back. In my culture if going after your skin tone doesn't get them the response they want; they'll go after your education status or how much money your family has, and that's where I get hit hard."

"It's weird because we don't call an Arab an Amish because they look white, or Euro-Americans, a mixed person or mestizos because they also have Irish, Italian, German, African and Indigenous blood...right." I said.

"Because their skin is usually light. I need to get another job; I need more money," Eva sighed as we got closer to home.

"I just got promoted to supervisor, I know they'll be looking at you soon..." I hopefully said.

"It's harder for me," Eva said.

"Harder...Why?"

"Because I'm illegal," she said, sighing.

"Illegal..." I said.

"Yeah." She trembled.

"But you work at the theater with me..." I said reassuring her.

"Fake ID and fake social security number got me that job, not all companies hire illegals."

"No person is illegal," I said, and I didn't say another word for the rest of our journey home. What I knew about the United States' immigration issue was only what I had heard in the heated discussions my dad had. He said that immigration laws were not being enforced due to corporate greed, political party growth, religion and race.

Eva said she felt free and accepted when she was with me. We were spending a lot of time together and everyone at work left her alone because of the work girlfriend thing. She went to my basketball games; she even went walking with me and Nichole. I started to think of building a life with Eva.

Not long after the Cuban sandwich trip, I went to work expecting to see Eva, but she wasn't there. The managers told me that she quit without notice. I called her cell phone; it was disconnected. I went to her house. I tried to talk to her dad. He was loud and annoyed but it was enough for me to understand that she had moved. A week later I ran into one of Eva's homegirls.

"What happened to Eva?" I asked her.

"Nic, illegals move all the time…" she nonchalantly responded.

Eva had disappeared.

Window Women

The neighborhood I lived in was quiet. Nichole, my sisters, cousins and various friends from time to time would be in my yard enjoying the sun with me. Initially, I wasn't aware that women were in windows looking at us and me in particular when I came back from my morning jog or when I came back from the park or when I washed my car out front.

One warm summer day, in the middle of an arm curl set, I looked up and there was a four-year-old kid standing on my grass asking to play with my medicine ball. Before I could answer, he asked for my jump rope and then he had his dirty little hands on my soccer ball. He started touching all of the gear I had out.

"Where are your parents?" I probed, looking around. The child pointed up; I followed the direction of his finger and saw a woman two house over, looking out a second story window. I made eye contact with her and that was it.

Soon more children came to my front yard; eventually I started helping them with their homework. I showed them how to interact with others, how to make introductions. It wasn't all fun and games; I had requirements if they were to come to my yard—they couldn't fail class or be on punishment.

It took Anthony a year to get on his feet and move out. He moved to the next city over and he visited me fairly often. I was making enough money so my five-year-old daughter, Nichole, was with me most of the time, so seeing and hearing children outside was common. My yard was a safe harbor for many children. When the children were at odds with one another, it was the perfect time for conflict resolution and lessons in three-dimensional thinking.

These mothers in windows would send a kid to my yard to ask if they could go with me to the park or when I played tennis. "Where is the daddy?" and "Why don't you take them?" were now afterthoughts. Children need the sun, structure and positivity. Music, dancing, coloring, drawing with chalk, origami, painting and video games were always on the menu in my yard. The unruly and disrespectful ones got banished from the yard; they would have to watch from the window for a time.

When I needed somebody to watch Nichole, no one would. Nichole wasn't one of those bad children that grandmas and aunties don't want to watch. If you give her a book, she'll read it. If you give her a toy, she'll play with it and she was quiet. Some of the women in the neighborhood would watch each other's children, but when it came to me no such agreement would be made.

Growing up I spent a lot of time at my dad's house. I spent summers over my grandparent's house; I spent countless time at my aunts and uncles houses. I made friends and went on adventures in this way. It was a community; it was a village and it was massive. The village raised most of us, but for some reason when we became adults many of us refused to return the favor.

We have been told that cancer is the disease, but it's the symptom, in this community there were nothing but symptoms. Many of these women behaved as if they never bonded with their children, as if they were devoid of maternal love. I raised my daughter and I raised the children of the window women when they didn't want to be bothered with them. Dealing with these people I learned not to inject common sense into areas driven by emotion. These women wanted me to mentor and watch their children for free, but they really wanted me to fail.

When their children acted up at home, I got a call. When their child was cut by glass, I got a call. When their child was burned by a curling iron, I got a call. When their child needed help with homework, I got a call. Who did they call when their young son threatened them? Who did they call when the child tried to drop-kick grandma? Who did they call when they needed their rules reinforced?

However, if I were to ask if a child could go to the park or come out to play with Nichole, they'd say no. The intercity was their kingdom and they always let me know it. The thing is that these women didn't just want me to fail. They wanted all the accolades, all the celebrations, all the praise, all the benefits, all the money and all the love. If I were to succeed in raising Nichole without help, somehow it would diminish them.

My success would force them to stop calling their husbands incompetent and to stop seeing their boyfriends as idiots. In short order, I discovered the hardest part of raising a child— is you. You have to evaluate every situation, you have to change your mind set. You are the one that has to change your mind from the child being an imposition, a burden, a death to the individual— you.

I saw these mothers flirt with the high school track team members as well as the football and basketball players that walked down the street. They would say inappropriate things, touch them on the shoulders or invent reasons to go to the games. Some of these window women messed around with these high school dudes. They were fucking dudes that have P.E. tomorrow. Chasing after high school penis gave them a break from their reality shows and porn.

School boys are only available during the day, at night street urchins and drug dealers would come visit them. The older guys in the neighborhood help them with the plumbing, electrical wiring and anything else that may or may not be broken in their house. All the women had to do was wear a half-closed housecoat, maxi dress or only for show workout gear and that usually paid for the service.

'I'm a mother', or 'She has babies'. You couldn't possibly know what she's has gone through' are their go to talking points to shut discussions down. I once responded with, 'What if she doesn't have babies?' and I lost a friend. These ladies don't want discussions; they don't want to compromise, they want glory. The only thing they are willing to share is fault.

I've heard these women say inaccurate and immoral things hundreds of times and if you don't have breasts you can forget about telling them any kind of truth; they'll just disregard it. They say things like, 'Would you treat your mother like that?', 'Would you talk to your wife like that?' as if by merely having a vagina they were granted the respect of your mother or life partner.

I realized that even I was part of the problem I allowed Nichole to get away with things I would have never allowed my son to get away with. I had fallen into the error of how society reinforces negative behaviors. Sometimes when you blossom young, you are given attention and priority neither motivates a person to develop other aspects of themselves such as, interests, career paths, character or personality the things a person needs to become a well rounded adult. The very qualities needed to have good relationships, the very things that make a person interesting. Women are the least suspected and most protected, in many instances we all look the other way.

These mothers exercised control, they exercised power and they wanted the children to know it was they who authorized what they could or could not do. It was they who allowed them to go to the dance, it was they who said who can tutor them, it was they who made it possible for them to have better grades and it was they who permitted them to have friends.

The women routinely say; I wish there were more free programs for youth, I wish the YMCA and Boys and Girls Clubs were in the area, or I wish someone would take an interest in my child. Those "someones" are called their dads, I said and I lost another friend. As I said, it takes a village to raise a child. These women want the community to help raise their children but they don't want to help the community become better. They didn't want to do the work, they just want the results.

In this community there were few men in homes and fewer marriages. The ratio was three women for every man. The negatively and the sheer weight of dealing with the window women was unbearable for a normal person. If the window women had boyfriends, they didn't stay around long and if they were around, the relationships weren't healthy. So many people are so ruined that they can only have "unhealthy" relationships.

In these cities, beyond the sirens, beyond closed doors, they wield real power, they control the population, they control the violence, they control the money, they control the hurt, they control the pain and they control the abuse. They control the relationships and they'll be damned if any outsider comes in and tries to disturb their paradise. I find it funny that all these hood kings and queens can't get street lights or potholes fixed.

Some of these children were troubled, emotionally unbalanced and prone to violence. They acted out, failed in school and made poor decisions because they felt like no one loved them, like there was nothing out there for them. It would be easy to disregard them or to use their plight to advance your organization.

These children had seen so much negatively in society that it was normal. Even I was troubled by seeing a human being broken down to the smallest mental strands. I had no money, no degrees and no backing...the only thing I could do was show them that somebody cares; that there was hope. Even children with good grades and well to do parents found themselves in my front yard.

Over time the children grouped themselves by aptitude and interest, I noticed stark differences between girls and boys. The girls seemed to develop faster than the boys. They followed directions better. They were better at reading facial expressions. They employed emotional tactics when asking for items. They shared better but they were meaner and for a longer period of time.

The boys could weaponize anything and I mean anything. They took things from others that directly caused conflict. They often played alone and were sadder. The boys ate dirt a lot longer than their girl counterparts. The girls had more subtle ways of getting what they wanted.

All of the children engaged in various play routines. The ones that could read would read stories to those that couldn't. The ones that could write taught those that couldn't. The young children were more aggressive than the older ones, but they all learned to play and share. It wasn't just my rules, or my discipline that did the trick, once you get one or two people doing something, it becomes easier to get others to do it, especially children.

These children were filled with wonder and they embraced hope once they were given it. I knew what it was like to be a child and have no one care about my grades. I knew what it was to be a youth with a unique talent that no one understands. I knew what it was like to be in a family and still feel alone. I helped some of them uncover their potential and hone their skills.

I knew who my children's primary care physicians were; I knew birth dates and Social Security numbers. I didn't ask for instructions or help from the women in my neighborhood, and that seem to bothered them. Why was me raising my daughter without their help a threat to them? Why would I adopt the thinking of the miserable?

There was a problem with not asking for help and that problem was that I wouldn't get any; it also meant I didn't have any backup or supporters, no allegiances, no alliances. I helped adults too, beyond advice; I got people jobs and helped them enroll in school. I acted with the belief that the do-nothing mentality could not prevail.

I thought differently, I believed that the best way to help the homeless was not to be one of them. "If I can see it and believe it, then I can achieve it' this was a motto my dad had taught me long ago. I believed that people who have prospects usually think more about their environment and about their future and not just about their now.

I was no longer fending for myself; I have a child, so I took a CPR class. I live near the water, so I learned how swim and took a water lifesaving course. Doing these things made sense to me. I didn't need other people to save my child or me.

I had a job that paid the bills and it had potential. I worked harder than most. I went to as many school board meetings and PTA meetings as I could, and I relayed information in a way everyone could understand. It is important for community members to know what is going on in and outside of the community.

I may have had information and ideas, but it was people like Anthony that knew how to get things done. Anthony, along with others, began to devote some of their time to my growing activism. The first thing we had to do was make the neighborhood uncomfortable for trouble makers. As the community recovered from the hurricane, it became safer; no stealing, no robbing, no unauthorized late night hanging out, no gang banging and no violence. I had to make sure Nichole was safe outside, which meant other children had to be safe as well.

We were more than Teen Summit refugees. We resolved to not to allow children to be molested, not to allow guns to be pulled on 10-year olds or for a childhood to be lost at 12. Most of the people we helped were overlooked, underserved and under-represented in terms of resources. None of us had been told to care by screens.

My friend William was the social media wing of everything we did. He was two inches taller than I was and he had the lightest skin tone of all of us. William's mother is Caucasian but don't call him biracial, you'll get an attitude. He has shoulder length dreadlocks. William made sure the community had an online presence and knew how to contact various city officials.

All of my friends had a particular skill. Jerome was good at compelling people; Anthony was an expert in using finesse and I brought people together. Anthony also made sure everyone knew how to protect and defend themselves. The team was good, we didn't need a mascot.

The state of Florida has conservation issues. Miami may even be underwater in my children's lifetime, assisted living facilities are understaffed, children come up missing every week, the gap between income inequalities is widening. So in order to get from discussions to solutions, we had to find a way to be honest with ourselves and each other.

I enjoyed and appreciated nature; the children and I spent a lot of time in the sun. I didn't need the spotlight, it's easier to observe and analyze when the spotlight isn't on you. Trial and error forced me to realize that everyone is not going to get it or you for that matter. If I am going to stay here; I was going to be a catalyst for the change. I needed to get my friends involved and engaged so we can determine where train services go or which community gets a bus. Which areas to build highways through and which neighborhoods get parks.

I was regularly having gatherings at my apartment; basically we partied on major and minor holidays. On the 4th of July, my friends invited their families to my house. Sometimes these kickbacks were so big they became block parties with 50, 200, 300 people up and down the street.

Dozens of people played video and card games on lawn tables. Children ran and chased each other and bounced in the jumpers. Once, a friend of mine who worked with the fire department came by with the fire crew. They gave dozens of children rides around the block in the fire truck, you should have heard the children's excitement.

My neighbors joined us with music, entertainment and food. There were people in the streets, on the lawn and in the alley. My yard was dotted with mothers, fathers, aunts, cousins, tables, inflatable jumpers, pools, water balloons, a taco truck and a cotton candy machine. The food was great and there were no attitudes. Not bad for $100.

America has an alcohol problem and none of us were immune to it. The gatherings began as a way around driving under the influence. They were where we could drink and smoked with the subtle mind soothing lies we tell ourselves. The first time I saw truth hit someone and change their behavior in real-time, justified the development of these gatherings.

I began to cultivate spirited, insightful, honest, enlightened information laden conversations from these gathering. The irreverent responses were filled with movie, music and pop culture references. These gatherings were making people happy. For the time being, it was the only path forward for an extreme people pleaser such as myself.

I kept busy. I had fun, but I had a dream of playing basketball professionally. I wasn't physically gifted but I maximized what I was given. I had to be stronger, confident. I had to become a student of the game. I was invited to semi-pro free agent camps.

The basketball court was one of the few places where I could find myself. When I am on the court I don't think about the losses, only the wins. For me each bounce of the basketball was just more therapy. There's nothing like the way the ball bounces of the floor, the way you impose your will on another person or the roar of the crowd when your jumper hits nothing but net. The money, the prestige, the women, the fans… the lifestyle, it was all addictive.

I spent three months in Chicago, South Dakota and Oklahoma. Free agent camp was a breeze, training camp was tough. I made it through training camp and preseason—I didn't get cut. I can ball—no doubt but I had to prove myself every workout, every practice and every game.

I played with NBA hopeful youngsters that constantly missed free throws, shot air balls from deep and spectacularly turned the ball over. My anticipation was unparalleled, my defense was on point, but many of these guys were naturally gifted and they could explode off the court. I was killing myself playing against these hungry 19 and 20-year-olds. One practice I was cutting through the lane and got another elbow to the face which knocked me on my ass, still no whistle. That's when reality starting to creep in on me.

One percent of players from the top one percent make it to the NBA and I was nowhere near that percentage but I loved the game and until now it had loved me back. I had a five-year-old daughter in Florida who missed me. Hearing her voice on the phone was enough to make me want to go back to Florida.

Being undersized, the sweat, the cheap hotels, the competition, the $30 stipends, the long bus rides…weren't the problem. Not playing was the problem. The coaches knew that at 25 I was one of the oldest players on the team. The coach had to play the younger players. I was no stranger to hard work and I'm not a quitter but I had an apartment and a supervisor position waiting on me, I didn't have to play ball.

My window of opportunity was getting smaller but some of these dudes were homeless; some had no diploma and most were desperate. For most of them the stakes were high and some had nowhere else to go, it was all or nothing. Without basketball they won't survive, that's all they know how to do... it could save their life.

If I had made it to NBA I would have sat on the bench with a smile on my face but in a semi-pro league, no one wants to ride the bench. Older players like me often never getting off the bench. When you are the 11th man, the coach never looks your way and they don't call your name. You sit there the whole game, cheering and clapping but when the clock starts to run down, the bench starts talking to you and the things it says shouldn't be repeated.

I took the Amtrak back to Florida with my dream on pause. It was a giant leap of faith for me to leave my home three months ago. I may not have completely succeeded but it the experience showed me that life is more than ten square miles. I managed to get my apartment back. I came back carrying a promise that I could get my theater supervisor job back, but they had given the position to someone else. I ended up working at a competing theater chain. This theater chain was full of superior assholes. They didn't like new ideas and I was paid less than before.

I had to ride two busses just to get to work. In major cities public transportation isn't for faint of heart, but you do what you have to do. On the bus rides to work often I laughed at myself thinking...

My lack of height, my lack of natural physical gifts, my age... I shouldn't have even been able to compete at that level. I shouldn't have been invited to tryout, I shouldn't have made it through training camp, I shouldn't have made the team. I should have just taken this as a victory...I should have just kept playing ball.

I was determined to make this decision work for me, and I got a promotion in four months.

I went around Florida playing pickup basketball games at different parks and gymnasiums; sometimes I would play for money. I would have played without the money; the money just made me feel like I hadn't fully let go of my dream.

A high school friend and teammate of mine, Brian Crawford had graduated college and was an assistant coach at IMG Academy in Bradenton. IMG Academy was one of the top tier sports academies in the nation. In high school, Brian saw me work harder and smarter to earn my spot. He asked if I had graduated college. I told him that "I enrolled seven years ago, but I never attended." Brian always liked playing one on one with me. So we played and just like in high school, I schooled him again and again.

After one such on court ass kicking, Brian told me that he had spoken to the IMG Academy Director of Basketball about me and had set up a meeting. I sent an introductory email to the Director along with my highlight video and then I drove nearly 200 miles to the sprawling 600-acre student-athlete campus. I arrived 30 minutes early for the meeting.

We watched the highlight video of my high school games and a few semi-pro ones. We talked about the high post being the fulcrum of the offense, short rolls and double ball screens along the three-point line and how basketball fundamentals translate off the court. A few days after that meeting, Brian told me that the Director thought highly of me from my state title days and that he wanted me on the academy's staff.

Me, a coach! It wasn't playing basketball in Midwestern towns with a few thousand people in attendance, but this opportunity would still allow me to follow my dream. The Director called me and told me that next season I could have a coaching position but I needed to have an Associate degree. So, I enrolled into Miami Dade College summer school. You can earn an Associate degree in less than two years. I enrolled in two classes, just to see if I could do it.

The cobwebs in my brain could have been used as the set design in a cheesy horror flick, the gears just weren't turning. A fourteen-year-old Asian girl named Anh sat next to me in Algebra class. I thought it was funny that her parents forced her to go to college as summer school, until I saw that her scores were higher than mine. Her parents were visionaries.

Anh felt bad for me and she tried to let me cheat off of her test, but my parents raised me wrong. I couldn't cheat and feel good about it.

Tutor Time

My whole life, I had never really failed at anything. In high school I passed trigonometry but now almost eight years later I was having problems with algebra. My dad says that if you are going to do something, don't do it half way, do it all the way and I was all the way failing algebra.

There was a little voice inside of me that laughed at me every time I double checked my answers. That little voice knew the answers were wrong. Too much time had passed since I had opened a book to work out math problems.

I had just started summer school at Miami Dade and I was working at Publix, as a second job. Today, Shantel Davis was in Publix shopping. Shantel Davis was shorter than the average person. I knew her from around the way. I saw her a few times on the block.

I usually don't speak to friends or the tattooed people I grew up with because my Japanese boss stares at me with his mind tilting towards a narrative of "A thug works for me". Never mind that I was being paid below the wages of everyone else and there were raises not given to me, I was just glad I finally a job that I didn't have to break my back doing.

"What's up, lil' mama?" I said as I approached her. Shantel had on— wait, it doesn't matter what she had on. I only spoke to her because I vaguely remembered that she hung out with a girl I had fucked back in the day and that she was in college.

Shantel looked up from the items in her basket and stared at me for a second, "Nic…Nicodemus Johnson... from Murder Block!" she said excitedly. From the corner of my eyes I saw my boss' head pop up over the counter like raised antennae. I walked into the next aisle with her.

"You go to Miami Dade College...right?" I asked.

"I graduated two years ago. I'm at FSU now. FSU, Go Noles!" Shantel excitedly said while doing hand chopping motions. She giggled and continued to put items into her basket.

"So... you had algebra…right?" I asked.

"Everyone has to have algebra," she responded.

"Did you pass?" I asked.

"You have to pass or you can't graduate or transfer," she grinned

"Do you still have your workbooks from that class?" I slowly said trying not to reveal that I was new at this higher education thing. Shantel paused for a moment and looked at me.

"I think so," she finally said.

In my head a dim, seldom used light bulb flickered, warming some of the cobwebs. In that little bit of light I saw myself in a blue polo shirt, emblazoned with the academy's logo and I was on the sidelines coaching youngsters to the state title.

"I don't mean to pry, but how were your grades?" I said, pressing the conversation forward.

"My grades are always good, that's how you get more scholarship money." The pencil in my mind scribbled, *down good grades, equals more scholarship money.*

Shantel was a college graduate. She lived with her brother. She had a five-year-old son, Roman, who was small like her. Shantel majored in Child and Family Sciences with a minor in Psychology.

"Do you think you could tutor someone?" I sheepishly asked.

"Sure, who needs tutoring? Your sister..." she quipped, reading the back of a package.

"Me, I'm the one that needs tutoring!" I snapped back.

I would normally be embarrassed to admit this, but these were desperate times. Anh was earning a solid C and I was struggling to keep my D- from being an F+; my scores were still far and away the lowest scores in the class. The professor posted our scores on the class door. He claims that he does this for motivation; I say he does it for embarrassment. My scores were the only ones that were going down.

Shantel looked at me, puzzled.

"I mean, I would pay you of course. How much would you charge to tutor, to tutor me?" I sputtered out.

"I don't know, I have to think about it..." she responded.

I put my number in her phone and I told her to call me when she was done thinking about it. Later that night, she called me. What we worked out was that when she didn't have school she would tutor me for an hour for $10, and that's the *homie luv* price. I had to pick her up and find a place to study.

Midterms were coming up in about four weeks and this evening is going to be my first day of tutoring. I went to my tutor's house and I picked her up.

"Can we go to McDonald's?" she asked after getting in my car. Shiiittt, I would have taken her ass to Red Lobster if she helped me understand these equations.

My Tutor ordered combo meal #1, that's the Big Mac meal and I supersized it. We weren't comfortable studying in McDonald's, there was a lot of noise, people were staring and a homeless family seemed to be using the booth next to ours as a shelter. It was after 7 p.m. so we knew that the library was closed.

"Can we study at your house?" she suggested, sensing my frustration.

Here's the thing about my house; when my daughter isn't with me, I was drinking, smoking, slow song playing and most likely fucking. In fact, after this tutoring session I was planning to do all of those things. So I told her that I had some friends coming over and that we could just pick up tutoring tomorrow.

"The homies are coming to your house to chill?" My Tutor asked, surprised.

I nodded.

"Let's go to your house, we can do algebra later. I haven't seen some of those guys in a long time."

So, we went to my house. William was waiting outside my door, blasting Kanye West. William is 22 years old. He used to work for the city with Jerome but now he does social media promotion for local night clubs. He's at most of my gatherings, even if it's just him and me. He can promote and organize all from his smart phone.

William and I shook hands like an elaborate NBA pregame ritual. I quickly introduced My Tutor to William and he nodded in My Tutor's direction, I wasn't sure if he knew her.

"What crackalackin'? Buenos retardes." William said.

"There you go… You more childish than Donald Glover…" I said opening my door.

William came in and grabbed my surround sound remote control and tapped a few buttons and my apartment filled with Prince, Sean Paul, Flo Rida and weed smoke. I mean a lot of weed smoke. I didn't know how my tutor would feel about what she was about to see, so I said, "Shantel, you don't have to be politically correct here if you don't want to be."

"Politically correctness is for the weak…" William said bobbing his head.

"Don't mind him he grew up in a two parent household." I said.

"Oh." My Tutor said.

"Cohabitation is for non-broke people, co-hobo-tation is for broke people." William said in an off-handed way while rolling up a blunt.

"Where do you work William?" My Tutor said as she sat on the small couch.

"I prefer not to be a wage slave; it doesn't sit right with me to be paid based off of what I don't know, so I have a vending machine…"

"How are the vending machines?" My Tutor questioned.

"Basically it's like pimping," William responded. "You can get mad and shake the machine all you want but you won't get any more money. You get more money with better product, better locations and better—looking machines."

"Nic, you have nice collection of books," My Tutor commented as she glanced at my bookshelf. I had titles from Chaucer to Shakespeare to Poe. This year I had Nichole read Morrison, Yamashita, and Smith. Last year I helped her read through King, Rawlings, Grisham, Rice and Sorkin. The other books were poetry and financial literacy ones given to me by my dad.

There was a knock on my door. It was Jerome Jackson. His skin was darker than any glancing touch the sun could produce. Jerome was a neighborhood hero. He was 5'10" and a running back in high school. I was very comfortable at home. How comfortable, well in a fit of silliness I jumped up and said in my best Martin Lawrence impression, "Watch yo mouth... I say Jerome is da house!" Then I did a jig and fist bumped and hugged him as he entered.

JJ that's what we call him, scored 6 touchdowns in a high school football game, it would have been 7, but I got flagged for clipping on one of his run backs. The truth is Anthony clipped someone on all JJ's end zone runs; he only got flagged for one. Jerome would have made it to the NFL if he hadn't torn his ACL his first year at Florida State.

What made Jerome a legend was that he was helping us make sure a lot of nonsense missed the community. He made a difference and he helped us keep the peace. He was off and on with his high school sweetheart and now ex-wife, Sarah. They had two children, a girl and a boy. They had been divorced for almost a year. Jerome is a mechanic supervisor with the City of Miami and he was a diehard Miami Heat fan. He is usually wearing red, yellow and black, Miami Heat vintage colors when he stops by my house.

"To me, Dwyane Wade in his prime was the closest player to Michael Jordan," Jerome asserted, walking into the apartment.

"So, you just not gon' recognize Kobe..." William responded blowing out smoke.

"Kobe needed, a good low post player, a great coach and the right pieces around him to win a chip." Jerome said.

"And you are disregarding LeBron James, he played with Wade." I argued.

"I don't have anything against LeBron, but he can't play with anyone for more than 4 years and he defers too much to be the greatest. He had Kyrie and a lot of other great players on his team. Hell, Wade taught LeBron how to win." Jerome responded.

"That's asinine," William declared, passing Jerome the blunt.

"LeBron came to Miami to join him; it wasn't the other way around!" Jerome passionately stated as he puffed the blunt.

"If Wade is close to Michael Jordan then Michael is the G.O.A.T. right?" I asked.

"Ummm, Wade has Jordon on off ball cutting, pin downs and on defense; he puts fear into the hearts of players. It's close, Jordan is 1A and Wade is 1B."

"What about number 30?" I asked.

"Who Curry... he's too little," Jerome insisted.

"His game big," William said.

"Wade isn't a much taller..." I taunted.

Jerome's eyes started to bulge, his lips pressed tightly and the veins in his neck started to appear. "You niggas don't know basketball!" Jerome declared, shaking his arms.

"You Tonka Truck face fukka, pass the blunt and sit yo ass down," William said.

This is how we often spoke to each other, it's all love. When you are at my house the only attitude allowed is mine, but be prepared the quips are often sharp and fast.

"They are all great players, at least none of them were race-aided like John Stockton." Jerome said once he calmed down.

"There you go, but you right. Stockton is in the Hall of Fame and he couldn't even use the left side of the court. If another player got close enough to force him to use his left hand, the refs called a foul." I said shaking my head.

"30% of his points came from free throws." Jerome said.

"It was obvious they just didn't want all of the faces of the NBA to be brown ones. It would have scared away advertisers and some fans." I said.

"For real tho." William said.

"Positivity is a lie; I eat depression for breakfast," Jerome said as he sat in a chaise lounge pose on my big couch. "What's up, Shantel?"

"Hi, Jerome…" My Tutor said quietly.

"Are you still involved in the university football program?" I asked Jerome.

"You know it…" He said reclining. "You know nothing in Title IX requires schools to spend the same amount of money on male and female teams. Title IX requires schools to take measures to make male and female participation on sports teams is proportional to the overall numbers of men and women in the student body.

"Football players die and get injured for life. Players in basketball get injured for life and those programs bring in the most money, it's only right that those programs get the lion share of the money. Somewhere along the line the conversation got perverted and administrators got political."

William turned on Zhane and music filled my apartment and then we started drinking. The next thing I knew it was 9 o'clock on a cold Tuesday night.

My Tutor sat in the far corner of the small couch with her legs folded underneath her, eating French fries and drinking cherry coke. In between blunt rolling and video game matches, I checked on her. As William and Jerome argued, I asked her if she was ready to go home. She said no. It was half past midnight when my house began to clear out.

I figured My Tutor would say something about my study habits, or say "Dey in here smoking, he's smoking, people over there are smoking, it's everywhere and I am in here trying to breathe", but she didn't. When I drove her home she said that she was happy she got to see some familiar faces. I gave her ten dollars and I hurried back home. A late-night visitor was on her way to my house.

Two days later My Tutor called me and asked me what I was doing. I was going to be up all night; the whole crew is in here, so I said, 'nothing'. She suggested an early tutoring session, so I went to get her. She again ordered the supersized combo meal from McDonald's and we went to my house. When she finished her food, I pulled out my book, she pulled out her notes and we started going over my algebra lessons.

An hour of tutoring later, I still didn't understand it, but I felt better about not understanding it. Then there was a 'hide yo shit' type of banging on my iron security door, it was just William. I put my folder and algebra book away.

"I'm going to run her home. I'll be back in twenty minutes," I told William as he grabbed my remote control.

"You can take me home later," My Tutor offered.

This is how things went for about a week. Then one day, My Tutor asked if her son, Roman, could come too. I had activities at my house for children, so I was like whatever. I liked Roman. He showed me a picture of his father that he had never seen in the flesh. In the picture, his father was dressed up and standing next to a brand-new blue Audi S4 Quattro.

When I grow up I want to have a car just like that one, Roman vowed to me. On the days Roman came along, I put him in the room away from the smoke and drink festival and they both ordered the supersized #1 combo meal. After two weeks of tutoring I had a solid D grade.

One night, it was time for me to take My Tutor home, when she again asked, "Can I stay the night? I'll just sleep on the couch and you can drop me off in the morning." She said that her brother's wife was tripping on her. Of course she could spend the night. On a good night there were two people on my floor and couch and on a great night there were four people.

My tutor had a big bubble butt but I didn't think of her in a sexual way. She really didn't talk or reveal enough for me to get to know her; besides she was 4' 8" on a good day. Being quiet is fine, being short is okay, but My Tutor also has rough skin covering most of her body. By covering I mean head to toe, ass to elbow. It was eczema. It wasn't cracked, peeling or inflamed, but it was everywhere. It felt like the skin on a bad kid's kneecaps and it looked like the skin on your nut sack.

I remember, the girls on 'Murder Block' calling her midget and alligator skin. I don't recall anyone claiming to have been with her. The good news about her spending the night was that my gatherings could go on for another two blunts.

When I had a girlfriend, I was faithful. There may have been an occasion or two when my girlfriend and I had a girlfriend. While occasionally amazing, sexually being with two people or being in a relationship with two people for an extended period of time is a kind of like work… it's mostly not fun and vastly overrated. Girlfriend by committee is not an easy thing to consistently do.

At present I was not in a committed relationship but I had a unique roster of sexy, diverse sensual encounters. I was liked and it wasn't because of my clothes, my car, my house or my job. I had a negative net worth but every week I was breakin' in new pussy, until the sun came up and then one of us would leave.

Tonight, someone messaged me some wild thoughts, she came over, we went rounds and she left. I showered and got a solid hour of sleep before I had to drop My Tutor off and go to school. She was still asleep on the couch. I woke her up, dropped her off at home and went to work.

Hurricane Andrew destroyed a lot of communities, so it made my apartment nice and inexpensive. I adorned it with hip hop infused artwork. I lived in North Miami, one of the many middle size cities in Florida. Mind you, North Miami is not North Miami Beach. Around here the only thing that drowned out yelling mothers were the cars that screeched in the streets until four in the morning. It was the inner-city and its fifteen miles from Miami. North Miami was at the tail end of the crack and gang epidemics that had decimated so many urban neighborhoods. They weren't selling drugs they were selling trauma.

We had 'Bedrock' which covered a five-block radius; that was cut from the same cloth as 'The Enterprise' from the film 'New Jack City'. Like any other inner-city there were murders, robberies, assault and other nefarious acts being committed on a regular basis, at least that what the news reports say.

I could have decided to settle in the god forsaken Pine Hills or the cheaper Redneck Riviera but I wouldn't have a chance of surviving. This part of town was not desirable but at it wasn't Panama City or Pensacola; those cities are the last step people take before moving to the panhandle, then Alabama then dying.

This was a time before huge rent increases, fewer parking spaces, increased toll fares and a growing homeless population and the other tell-tale signs of gentrification. When I was growing up, children could play in parks, vacant lots, or in the streets if they wanted to, but not so much now.

This was the last time period when children preferred to be outside whether the grass was green, yellow, or hidden underneath a field of dirt. Still there were places people wearing certain colors just couldn't go. Streets were affectionately called 'The Dime Block' and 'Murder Block' and it's not far from where carjackings, robberies, shootings and murders are common.

It's home.

Denise

My friends and I partied in big and small groups. You could find us at beaches and parks, playing football, basketball, soccer, hacky sack, Frisbee or bike riding. We partied everywhere but we usually ended up at my apartment. Sometimes there were so many of us that I hooked up the extension cords so we could party outside. I never knew who would show up at my place. My house was populated usually by those that lived close by and sometimes by people I hadn't seen in years. These gatherings had everything from wine to 100 proof rot gut alcohol and snacks.

Anthony was now working in the Department for Children and Families. He was a year older than I was, making him the oldest of those that came by. He spent two tours of duty fighting the sons of the men we killed. He says that America tampers in its elections and the elections of other nations more than any country on the planet.

Anthony claims to have played a minor role in small shock and awe campaigns. He told me that there were times in the desert when he was alone, up against the odds with no guarantee of returning home. He doesn't go too in depth, he says that he was just doing his job, just following orders, just tying up loose ends for the nation.

Anthony didn't have nightmares, speech impediments and no options. He got out of the service before being put in a situation where he would be medically retired by taking 7.62 by 54mmR to the back of the head. It's the kind of shot that you might survive but you'll wish that you hadn't.

After living with me for about a year when he got out of the service; he got his own apartment. In his apartment, his medals weren't on display; he wasn't enthusiastic about showing them either. His desire to be left to his own vices had curdled into a kind of sour isolationism, expect for his forays to work and occasional visits to my apartment.

He didn't come back with PTSD, he went in with it. Depression and anxiety manifest as aggression and violence when you were raised in Liberty City after the riots. People say he's 'one of the lucky ones', because he wasn't so numbed by violence that he needed to see bodies exploding and torn apart just to feel something, anything.

Anthony had been places where the blood still hasn't dried. He had been spared blood splattered nightmares. When he was in the service he could quickly identify fellow service members that had not fared as well as he had. He steered clear of those subtle slasher-types waiting for something, anything to trigger the mayhem.

Anthony struggled to reconcile his peaceful isolation with his more explosive skill set, this pretense became less convincing the longer it went on. Yet for a time, here in this place, his desire for peace was temporarily satisfied. Anthony is usually ambivalent on subjects and that automatically makes a person morally repugnant. He wasn't a knee-jerk reactionary or low information social medianite, he was sensible, measured.

War didn't put him in the Hurt Locker, his wife Melanie did. Scars from military skirmishes didn't compare to the ones his wife inflicted, and those battle scars, don't look like they're fading. It doesn't look like they're ever going away. In the divorce, Melanie got the house and kids; he got the bills and that's how he ended up living with me for a year. Tonight, he was the first to arrive at my house.

"I should have listened when they told me not to add her name to the house title," Anthony sniffed. "Every time I get low, Nic, you find ways to elevate me. You accept me. You don't judge me. That's real love. I'm fortunate that we are friends. I genuinely respect you."

The serious tone of Anthony's voice caused me to stop moving things around in my apartment. I sat down across from him.

"You've never been a say green because The Wizard says green type of person. Prison changes a person, especially an innocent one. Who wouldn't become harder, less compassionate, cold and numb after going through that shit? None of us knew if you were going to turn into John Spartan or Simon Phoenix."

"Somehow I manage to align closer to Edgar Friendly." I responded picking up on his movie reference.

"I would have rolled with you even if you wanted to take dope public. I was surprised that the thankless low-wage jobs didn't make you hopeless," Anthony said. "When we lived together I watched you eat a lot of bullshit just to be with your daughter."

"I was surprised I stayed on the straight and narrow."

"You could have just been like fuck the world and no one would have blamed you. You're legitimately a good dude."

"I just don't know how to not move forward."

"That's just it though; after all that you've been through you could have given up and just streamed TV shows. You could have done nothing about injustice. You could have not cared about the youth or the future. You could have not fought for what was right. You don't take yourself so seriously. You're the only person I know that's funny enough to get paid on stage and serious enough to get elected.

"People are fickle, they'll forget, but I will never forget. When everyone is at their worst, you're at your best. They all respect you,

even if they won't say it. You really have nothing to prove, nothing."
Anthony said.

"I always ask myself, does having a job, paying your taxes and being a good father mean you are a decent person? I had done everything right. I did good deeds. I always helped others and I still ended up getting done like Cameron Poe. I don't have to prove anything to anyone and here…" I said pointing to my head. "I get it." "But here…" I said pointing to my heart. "I have something to prove to myself.

I reached out my hand; Anthony grabbed me and hugged me tight. "If you start singing *Lean on Me* imma punch you really hard," I said and two traumatized people had a good laugh.

At these gatherings, most of which turned into Smoke N' Sips, Anthony tends to ask logical questions and he could argue multiple sides of an issue. However, he could go stretches without saying anything as he engaged in a kind of conscious inertia. Still, there were times when he was sadder than the time we all stood underneath The Fairchild Oak.

William entered my apartment and sat down. "What y'all choppin' it up about?" he asked.

"How winning doesn't always bring peace," Anthony stated, arranging the dog tags around his neck.

"Mathematically speaking, let's say you are a rapper and you had sex with 800 women, and you have eight children—that's like a rate of 1%. On the other hand, if you have sex with one woman and have three children, that's like a 300% rate or something like that," William explained, sitting in his usual spot on the floor near my speakers.

"Ok…" I said puzzled.

"Well, shouldn't we aim for lower percentages? I mean, the more you sleep with the lower your percentage goes..." William said.

"This is the theory you've come up with?" Anthony responded.

"Is it better to have children earlier or later in life?" William asked.

Anthony and I looked at each other and we both said, "Earlier..."

"Yo Nic, if I suddenly die..." William said, looking up at me.

"What? Are you ok?" I worried.

"Yeah," William replied "I'm just saying if I die suddenly— I Just need you to promise that no matter where I am that you'll come and get my cell phone and destroy it..."

"Another leak has brought someone in power down." I said.

"See, I keep telling you that this stuff is part of a larger plan..." Anthony said.

"Explain?" I said.

"Leaks and computer system hacks are social weapons and public relations tools. Whatever was leaked is now out and no one really cares how or why it got out, but that's often more imported than the leak itself. Look at these entertainers hooking up and breaking up for clout, just checking their often fraudulent sexual endeavors. Most of it is just PR even the negative stuff ..." Anthony said, looking at the newscast.

"You mean those reports on 20-something entertainers being involved with each other is PR?" William asked.

"Yes. The same way 90% of news articles are just advertisements most people can't tell the different between a news report or an advertisement." Anthony confirmed, changing the TV channel.

"Ads for what?" William replied, taking wires, connectors, speakers, chargers and batteries out of his backpack and placing them on the floor.

"Tech companies, movies, drug companies, agendas, whatever... There are a lot of messaging done in articles, ads, TV and movies; if you didn't get it—it wasn't for you. Data is valuable; most companies are built on it. Your user data is turned into ads." Anthony said.

"Just because someone can sing, dance or act doesn't mean their advice, morals or child rearing methods should be listened to," I quipped.

"So I could get an article written on night club life in Miami or the best places for spring break or how a law might affect a city's nightlife and use it as an advertisement to promote my business..." William said.

"Of course, but you'll have to pay influencers to put it on their feed or claim that they use it," Anthony said.

"Fo sho." William replied. William started vibing Janet Jackson, Anne Lennox and Keyshia Cole.

"If you win the Oscar, the belt, the chip, the ring, the post, the series, the race or the match, but we as a people are losing what purpose does it serve? Record labels should be sued for focusing on nakedness, glorifying drug usage and violent lyrics." I said to keep the energy going.

"What?" William responded.

"Would you fellas agree that some of these artists are rapping about real murders and violence and the label knows it?"

"I agree that is happening, but trampling on Civil Rights with RICO cases as a way to respond to violence is wrong. Lawsuits will just tamp down business profits and that's just not going to fly." Anthony argued.

"Here's the thing, I'm talking about saving lives." I insisted. "An appetite for the death of Black people has been cultivated. One or two successful lawsuits holding the labels accountable and they'll drop all these young committers and glorifiers. Most of the people they sign are murdered or jailed within a few years, some prosecuted with their own lyrics."

"It may save lives but big business knows that violence and sex sells, so there will always be a work around..." Anthony offered.

"What's that?" I asked.

"Don't have the artist write their own lyric..." Anthony said.

"That deserves some dap..." William said fist bumping Anthony.

"See that's why I like this man...he's a thinker." I stated.

"Labels know the ignorant have a shelf life, so a major label might still sign someone that raps about guns drugs and violence, just on a smaller scale." Anthony said.

"Sue video sharing sites too..." I remarked.

"Sounds like censorship..." William said.

"It's just a little trampling." I responded.

"You're saying it like the record labels intend for people to get hurt...that would be evil." William said.

"Well, don't movie studios intentionally cast movies to upset groups of people so they can use their outrage as free advertising..." Anthony added.

"It seems like it." William responded.

"In this case, control the music and you control the behavior. I'd settle for getting rappers to stop using or mentioning shoe brands, car brands and fashion brands." I said.

"Man, man, man…that's the reason they are allowed to be put out in the first place. They are global brand reps, even if they don't know it. Take that away that and there is no industry." Anthony said.

William had just rolled up a large blunt when My Tutor arrived, someone dropped her off. She greeted everyone and sat in the same spot on the couch as the smoke started to fill the room.

"Remember when we were talking about how things get lost in translation?" William asked as he lit the blunt.

"Yeah... what's up?" I answered.

"Isn't a chip, a mark?"

"Yes."

" … and chips run computers. It is said that the rich or poor, the great and the small, the slave and the free can't speak, can't move can't buy or sell anything without the chip, right…" William said.

"That's what it says in the Book of Revelations..." I said realizing where William was going with this reference. "You are saying that where we read the word *mark*, we should be reading the word chip."

"What are you getting at?" My Tutor said puzzled.

There was a light tap at my door. I opened the door and there stood Denise Alexander with her perfectly manicured brows, wearing a red velvet blazer, velvet trousers and a lace bodysuit; looking good, smelling better, carrying a designer backpack.

As she entered my apartment, Denise greeted me with a soft "Hey babe." Her arms loosely swinging back and forth, her hips gently swiveled side-to-side. Her confident stride was electric. It made me double take and I wasn't the only one.

Denise had just been promoted to assistant manager at Publix. She is 5'5", light skinned, with brown hair down her back. She is a champagne girl that loved Hennessey, with a small, colorful Chinese prosperity tattoo on her inner wrist. A middle-class goddess, beautiful but uncomfortable with how she looked. She had the kind of face cosmetic companies put in commercials and the kind of body R&B singers sing about.

Denise used to be a pole dancer. She helped organize a strippers union to stop wage theft, stalking, racism in hiring and violence. The first time I met her was right after I got out at the 'Strippers On Strike' protest. She had a sign that read, 'Exploit the System That Is Exploiting You.'

About a year ago, during a large gathering, she asked if she could spend the night at my house. She was too fucked up to drive. She asked if she could wear my robe after her shower, of course was my response. She picked up her purse and went into the bathroom. People were still clearing out of my apartment when she came out of the shower and went into my room. I had just started to clean up. My friends took out the trash as they left. I finished washing dishes and sprayed some smell good into the air. I sat down and started flipping through TV channels.

A random movie was on when Denise came out of my room. She walked into the living room with my satin Red Dragon robe hugging her body. My eyes followed her every step towards me. I gulped hard as she slowly untied the robe and it gently opened. Her sweats had been replaced by green lace nearly see-through lingerie. Gone were her out of fashion eyeglasses. Her slightly curly brown hair was damp about her shoulders. The room filled with scent of white jasmine.

The heat from her light brown eyes melted me. I had no words; all I could do was move over. She sat down next to me, leaned back and crossed her legs so the caramel could glow in the dim light of the floor lamp. She had a look in her eyes I had never seen before. As she sat next to me, I could feel her heart beating. She turned and pinned me down on the couch, her soft body covered me. Her face was serene. I usually put out a Pretty Ricky *Grind on Me* or Bobby Valentino, *Slow Down* vibe, but this was different.

Was I turned on? Hell yeah!

I felt like Clark W. Griswold standing on the side of the pool, waving my arms back and forth repeatedly saying, 'this is crazy'. I could feel the tension in her body as she straddled me like a veteran bull rider. All I'm sayin' is that your legs have to be strong to climb a pole and spin around, performing for ten minutes.

She was putting out the Erika Banks, *Buss It* vibe; I was putting out the Khalid, *Talk* vibe. If ever there was a say-less moment, this was it. We could have fucked right then and there. There were some wild thoughts and sensations going on inside of me, one of which was Ooh, I'm about to dive in, but we spent the night talking, about life of all things. We opened up to each other. She didn't like where her life was headed. I told her to change it. Later that month, I helped her get a job at a Publix.

Everyone believes that I had her dancin' naked in my living room, which prevents the homies from hitting on her. I didn't bother to tell them that I that nothing happened because they wouldn't have believed me. Perhaps, creating that narrative was the point of her asking to spend the night in front of everyone. Sometimes, I regret us not having an epic night, month, year, lifetime of banging each other's brains out. I was nowhere near the best version of myself.

Was I frightened by her aggression, perhaps? Denise wanted more than a good time and I knew it. Like mine, her soul was always on fire, passionate. She and I clicked. I knew that she wanted to take it there, but I wasn't ready. I really wanted to say, Please, oh please don't love me. Walk away, you'll be better for it. I was a mistake she was willing to make, but she could do better. I really want to see her happy.

Denise has a two-year-old daughter, named Princess, so she doesn't drop by often. Today, she brought a lemon cake. She put the cake in the middle of the kitchen table and went into the living room. Denise attended high school with William.

"Why you still have basketballs all over your house, ain't you retired?" William sarcastically questioned as he pushed my basketballs into the corner. I ignored this.

"You bought a new couch?" William snapped.

"Do you see a new couch?" I replied. I didn't ignore this.

"What kind of man gets a new couch? And you got two kinds of dip in the kitchen. Bro... you like one step from getting married..." Anthony barked, shaking his head.

"Do you think male R&B singers are shirtless on these album covers just for the ladies?" I threw out this question to make gauge the comfort level of those gathered.

"Ummmm," My Tutor uttered.

"Ok." I inquired further. "What do you think about professional sports players flying out other players to workout in their private workout room slash basement with their shirts off?"

"Man, they training…" Anthony reassured.

"Ok, let me ask you this..." I continued. "What do you think about a person who is always rolling around on the ground in their underwear, while a 300-pound sweaty man is on their back, choking them? Not that there's anything wrong with that."

"It's not underwear... it's a costume." William insisted.

"It's draws..." I mocked.

"You always are ruinin' shit." William said.

"I know," I smiled.

"Somebody is always going at it over here." Denise said, taking her seat. "What's up William? How is it going?"

"You know I'm out here doing my thang, making moves…" William said.

"Yeah... yeah... you still ain't about shit." Denise said.

William looked at Denise and started slowly singing, "You, got me fucked up, talking yo shit, fuckin' wit me…"

"Why you parodying Whitney Houston like that?" My Tutor said smiling.

"Naw, that's Kenny Rogers…" I said.

"Debby Boone." Anthony said. William pointed in his direction and nodded his head.

"As you know, Miss Alexander has just been promoted to assistant manager, but she has more news to share about her journey," I announced.

"Her journey?" Anthony repeated, sitting down with the bowl of chips.

"I talked with my grandmother about her life before she died," Denise explained. "...and that inspired me to research my Native American ancestry. I wondered why my mother and aunts weren't enrolled in any tribes. So I checked my DNA and checked the Dawes rolls for the Five Civilized Tribes..."

"Dawes rolls..." William said, going into the kitchen.

"It's a Native American census, and sure enough my great, great, grandfather, is on there," Denise said. "My people are older than Miami, older than the United States."

"This cake is good as hell!" William hollered from the kitchen.

"So you're in the tribe..." My Tutor said.

"Not exactly. You have to have 1/16 blood and prove that you are a descendant to apply..." Denise said.

"1/16th. If that's all, then I'm Native American..." Anthony sneered, adjusting his seat towards Denise.

"Who isn't 1/16th, right?" I said.

"87% of tribal members are 1/4th or lower only 13% are higher than 1/4th.," Denise said.

"I thought the standard would be like 50%," William said, coming back into the living room.

"Let me guess the other percentages are European..." Anthony said, rubbing the small scar on his neck.

"What was your percentage?" I asked.

"32.6%..." Denise responded. "They don't require a certain blood percentage; they require that a citizen have an Indian ancestor who appears on the Dawes Rolls. I got my Certificate Degree of Indian Blood card, all the necessary certificates and all of my lineage documents and I submitted my enrollment application and I waited and I waited..." Denise sighed.

"Well, what happened?" My Tutor asked.

"I was denied."

"That's messed up," William groaned.

For a moment we were all silent. I stood up and Denise tightly embraced me. Her eyes started to water.

"You were denied by people less Indian than you are." William stated.

"Nic, you encouraged me to start this journey and I want to thank you for that. For over a year I documented everything. I went through the appropriate process and the worse thing is that I wasn't given a reason why I was denied."

"I think they denied you because you had a baby by a Black man," William fumed.

"Shut up William," I barked.

"You don't know why she was denied, so my reason is just as good as anyone else's," William roared back.

"I truly hope that wasn't the reason..." My Tutor said.

"This cake is damn good. Who made this?" Anthony shouted from the kitchen.

"Miss Alexander made it..." My Tutor responded.

"Just call me Denise. I made it for Nicodemus, don't eat all of it," Denise responded.

"If anything you should be in the tribe and getting reparations," I joked.

"Black folks didn't even get military helicopters or sports teams named after them." Anthony said.

"I've been told to get over slavery and Jim Crow, but they just prosecuted a hundred-year-old Nazis guard and concentration camp secretary..." William said.

"Slaves or prisoners of war, there is no difference." I said.

"Are you saying that the Trans-Atlantic Slave Trade was actually a world war..." Denise said and I nodded my head.

"Hmmm..." My Tutor uttered.

"All of this is real deep." Anthony interjected while plugging in the blender. Anthony liked to blend at gatherings. He came over with spiced rum, blackberry brandy and ice. I already had bananas liqueur and white rum. That was all it took for him to go to work in the kitchen. With a twist of his wrist, he splashed the concoction with orange juice and a sweet & sour mix. Then he garnished the cocktails with a lemon, lime and a cherry. He took a lot of pride and care in his alcoholic creations.

"I can tell you everything about my ancestry." Denise continued. "I can go back as far as 1810, the year Solomon-Simmons' great-great-great-great-grandfather, Cow Tom. Some black people were enslaved by Native Americans, but not my great, great, great, great—she was Seminole. A 1976 federal lawsuit made it easier for tribes to change citizenship rules and they kicked out a lot of black people."

"How you just kick people out the tribe tho?" William said fuming.

"Your Blackness nullifies your Seminole status…" I snarled.

"You are indigenous and indigenous means that your people were in a place before anyone came to this continent." Anthony said.

"Native Americans have always had this fear that by accepting black people as part of their tribe they won't be seen as Native American first. Some view African-Americans as spoiled, snotty people who squander opportunities. There are others who view the Blacks who fought in the Indiana Wars and others as turncoats." Denise said.

"It takes a while for the dominant culture to realize you're *a friendly* and now we have to convince Native Americans of that too. Why would you want to be part of a group like that anyway?" Anthony asked, disgusted.

"Pass the lighter…" William sang. Anthony tossed him the lighter without looking.

"You know what you have to do..." I said to Denise.

"Put everything where it goes and get rid of the unnecessary things." She responded.

Jerome entered my apartment fist bumping everyone. He took off his fedora showing his low fade and freshly lined up beard.

"Oh, I remember you. You used to be the homie." Jerome said to Denise as he sat down.

"Never that." Denise said, smacking her lips.

"I mean, you used to dress like a…" Jerome said.

"…I used to dress like what?" Denise said. "I can't just find sweats and boy short comfortable and safer…"

"I don't know about that but you thicker than racial tension in the south!" Jerome remarked.

"I was at the gym the other day and you know those lady body builders with muscular legs... they piss in the shower." Denise said ignoring Jerome.

"What?" My Tutor said, pausing eating a French fry.

"They go so hard on leg day that they can't bend to sit on the toilet, so they just piss in the shower..."

"That's disgusting..." My Tutor replied.

"I went on my second supervised repair call today." I boasted. "Every time I go into a facility I find that the employees aren't just misusing the equipment they are beating the hell out of it. Today, I walked into a facility and an employee was on the floor and they had the printer in a headlock!"

"I can't wait until hurricane season." Jerome said, sitting back down on the couch with a slice of cake on his plate.

"Why?" My tutor responded.

"Hurricane season means down tree issues, malfunctioning traffic signals, flooding, loss of power, downed power lines, boats in the road and all kinds of property to clean up. After it's over we roll up in our High-Water Vehicles and rebuild everything. Just the preparation for a hurricane cost millions. If hurricane season is bad I can make a year's salary in overtime in a month. State officials don't really trip because FEMA reimburses the cost." Jerome explained.

"Homes destroyed, cars washed away, insurance premiums go up and y'all profiting— they could reduce the power of hurricanes..." Anthony said.

"But why would they do that?" Jerome said. "They have to keep the economy moving while they expand laws and change the zoning as a first wave of gentrification. These things play a role in incentivizing minority arrests and police shootings. They force residents to move, and then the city purchases properties for pennies on the dollar."

"Sounds like imminent domain if you ask me." Anthony said.

"Don't say that phrase." I said. "Yes the area may be violent or have a crime issue and those things maybe artificial, but I'm not sure it's not some kind of big political plan... right... right..."

I handed My Tutor a drink. "None for me... thanks," she whispered politely.

"Political disregard for the well-being of all citizens is something we should all be concerned about." I said.

"People are callous and viscous in every group and at every level. They are big on holding everyone accountable, everyone except themselves. " Anthony said.

"A month before Hurricane Katrina, the average home price was $130,000. The next year the average home price was $35,000. I know your store sells out before a hurricane..." Jerome stated to Denise.

"That we do, that we do." Denise said.

"Where we see destruction and death, others see opportunity." Anthony said.

"It is about control and it doesn't matter if a hurricane is coming or they tell you, that you have to get vaccinated." William said.

"Never get one of those flumonivid shot, or take lexasemipro," Jerome interjected.

"Sometimes meaningless sex is amazing and sometimes meaningful sex sucks." Anthony said. This was similar to tossing a grenade into the room.

"If there is such a thing as mental disenchanted, then there must be sexual disenchanted." William interrupted.

"What?" Denise said.

"I'm sayin' that my 1st sexual experience was wack as hell; my 4th wasn't good either, I can still remember the wackness..." William said.

"They aren't all good, but you better say they are." Denise said laughing.

"We supposed to cum quick because the world is a dangerous place. You not supposed to judge a person on the 1st bust, maybe not even the 20th one." William said shaking his head. "It didn't help that I lost my virginity at 14 to an older ugly woman. The kind of person you don't want to be seen with in public."

"Y'all women don't want us enjoying sex more y'all do." Anthony said.

"There is some truth to that." Denise said.

"Too many bad sexual experiences might make you go the other way..." Anthony said.

"My gay friends do say 'no' less often to sex, so I can see that." Denise said.

"Bro, what kind of twisted sexual logic is that?" I said to Anthony.

"Yeah, what you mean...go the other way..." William said.

"Do you have something you want to tell us?" Jerome said.

"Naw, I'm just saying it's possible." Anthony responded. "Sometimes you got to bust quick or fake it with these ladies so it can be over with, your penis knows she's not for you."

"You n-words don't fake it…" Denise said, smiling.

"The hell we don't." I said. "In the moment when sex could happen, even though you want to turn her down or flat out reject her advances, you can't. Since birth we have seen the negative aspects of telling a woman… no. If you never get rejected, it's hard to deal with when it happens. This is why it seems like men are always horny and it's why sometime we have to fake it. I mean we are horny, but what you see isn't always what you think it is. And some women, the pretty ones will just lay there like they are doing you a favor, when you're the one sparing her feelings."

"I haven't had any complaints." Denise arrogantly said.

"Me neither…" My Tutor added.

"How would it benefit us to complain?" I said.

"If you complain you damn sure ain't getting anymore…" Denise said.

"Exactly, that's why we don't complain," I laughed.

"It does seem like some ladies are confused; we need to come back together like Missy Elliot, Pink and Mya…Moulin Rouge." My Tutor said.

"Those days are long gone." Denise said.

"Yo, look at this fine ass white girl gettin' at me." William stated passing his cell phone around the room. I went to her profile; it says she's a 9th Wave Feminist. She's hittin' me up with, I don't know why I'm messaging you."

"You know how that goes, it's overt in porn and subtle in everything else, look how they'll have either the over-sexualized or ball-less Black man character, who if he does have sex in space it will be with a white woman." Anthony said.

"White males create the love for black cock." Denise stated.

"By how they treat women…" Jerome said.

"No, by watching all these big sweaty black athletes on every big screen they have. Their young daughters see their father cheering like crazy while wearing some 20-year-old black guy's jersey." Denise said grinning.

"Your supervisor is a woman huh…You lucky…" Anthony said to Denise.

"Why?" Denise said.

"Because if your boss is a man and an asshole, you could flirt with him and he might be nicer. If your boss is a female, you're just screwed." Anthony said.

"Sounds sexist." My Tutor said looking in Anthony's direction.

"Is it sexist if it's just an observation?" Anthony said shrugging his shoulders. "Are women complaining that they're providing everything for a man and still not getting laid? Where are the men at that are complaining that women are just using them for sex?"

"Of course not, it's…" My Tutor responded.

"… ridicules… exactly, so a lot of stereotypes are just valid observations of our very real nature." Anthony responded.

"Denise would you like something to eat?" Jerome said softly.

"No thank you, I ate before I came." Denise replied.

"I can't wait until my repair tech school training is done." I said. "I am so over hearing customers complain that every time they come in here their order is messed up; if that's the case then you're the one making the mistake. A repair technician doesn't have to pretend customers are funny or that 'in the back' is some kind of magical Santa's Workshop."

"You are already working a low-wage job and motherfuckers come in to just make your life harder— no offense…" William said.

"None taken…" Denise said. "I have to deal with people who think they are smarter than everyone else because they downloaded coupons, customers who had bad parents and real dummies that think I'm behind the counter wearing a name tag because I got lost…"

"Recreational name tag wearing…" My Tutor giggled.

"Even with my name tag on I get called out of my name at least five times a day, lots of employees do. We don't post about it, go to the press or ask for apologizes." I said.

"Yeah, we've gone soft." Anthony stated.

"Every family holiday my uncles and aunts call me these little cute names they called me when I was a child. I keep telling them to stop doing it, but they continue to do so. They see me the way they always have. They are my elders; they helped raise me, so they deserve some grace… we all do." I said.

Divided Gender

What had begun as a no cost way of partying and had yielded uncomfortable, uncommon and unique discussion. Having multiple discussions going on at once was common. I was shocked at the frankness of these conversations. After about half a dozen heart to heart revelations, a smattering of philosophy and heated debates I realized that some people don't have safe places where they could really vent or express themselves.

Here, a person could be real. They had people they could talk to, people who would listen and people who would challenge their ideologies. People who would question them, demand answers and people who would hold them accountable if need be. We argued and disagreed and over time the gatherings helped us become aligned in approach, method and direction.

Various people would call for a gathering or they would ask me when the next one was. I realized this would only work if there was mutual respect. These were not paid influencer directed conversations. My place wasn't some social media site, so people weren't just saying things to seem edgy or to be popular.

Anthony handed out another round of drinks. William's music was underpinning each theme. Denise and My Tutor were giggling, but Jerome seemed distant. Jerome is tough but he's really sensitive. Not only did Jerome workout with me the most, he also taught all of us how to injure ourselves with skateboard and BMX tricks. Jerome has a big heart and he's genuinely generous if we needed ice, chips, donuts, food or equipment, Jerome was always down for a fetch-quest.

"You good?" I asked Jerome, who was sitting close to me.

"Between the courts, Sarah's behavior and just the world, sometimes I feel like giving up." Jerome said, sighing.

"We all have bad days." I offered.

"Not you." Jerome said.

"Man, I can't lie—I've had bad years..." I sighed. "We have all had times in our lives were we felt powerless to correct what's wrong. Times get tough for everyone and that's why we cypher, we share and we clear our minds. Sometimes you have to sit down, sometimes you have to listen, sometimes you have to build, but you always have to do the work."

"Without make up and alterations, these so-called 'bad bitches' are Anastasia and Drizella. Shantel, what do you think?" Denise said.

"I can't really speak on that... Nic, you said something about lying... You have to define, lie..." My Tutor asked.

"Not telling the truth..." Jerome said.

"If the lie seems true then it's protected speech." My Tutor said.

"It's not." I said.

"You can't get any righter than that." William said, pointing at me.

"Men don't have a lot of support with our issues. We can't make mistakes; we have no wiggle room. We can't see our children." Jerome said.

"It's not like we plan on becoming single moms…" My Tutor quietly said.

"It seems like some of y'all do." William said.

"They didn't become single moms by themselves." My Tutor responded.

"Some ladies aren't balanced that's why they have insomnia and migraines. A small percentage of people around the edges doing things that are considered not normal is within reason, but when the majority of people are doing not normal things and are being encouraged to do not normal things society is out of balance, it's warping." Anthony said.

"Contraceptives affect your hormones and make you gain weight." My Tutor said.

"So, does having a baby." Anthony said.

"When you're in high school you are exposed to so many things; you see and hear all of these things and you just want it all." Denise said. "You don't listen to anyone, you don't know anything and you're not really paying attention. I really wanted to be that girl that could be taken care of, driven around in expensive cars, taken out to nice restaurants, bought expensive meals and expensive bags.

"One day you're sitting in that expensive car with the panoramic sunroof and the heated seats and you realize just how unhappy you are. These material things were just a mask for something missing in your life or mind. It pains me to say this, but accidentally getting pregnant and having a child is easier than planning it. My daughter's father didn't get me pregnant. I had choices before, during and after. I knew when I was fertile, he didn't. I made a choice. I'm head of security for my vagina.

"It would be stupid as hell for me to complain about the choices I made. I was the one that chose to leave. For me now dating has a higher cost for me." Denise said.

"What do you mean?" My Tutor questioned.

"I have a child, so anyone who wants to date me has to take that into consideration."

"But you're beautiful... I feel like whether you have a child or not it shouldn't matter." My Tutor responded.

"So a person's choices and decisions shouldn't matter in a relationship?" Anthony said. "Having a child isn't just some random act; it's not just something that just happened... Like Denise said a lot of choices went into it."

"I'm just saying she's beautiful." My Tutor said.

"I would say that I'm pretty." Denise responded. "I believe that to be beautiful you have to have beauty on the inside, not just the outside."

"Right." I said. "I think we misuse that word. That being said... Denise, you are beautiful."

"Thank you." Denise offered. "And due to my looks of course men want to smash— no doubt, but long term is a different thought process. I am asking them to raise another man's child...off rip."

"We all have kids..." My Tutor said.

"... and a person can choose to deal with that or not." I said.

"I don't like that but it's fair." My Tutor said.

"Excuse me Shantel, but do you want something to eat?" Jerome asked.

"I have something already…"

"Do you need me to heat it up for you?"

"Ummm sure." My Tutor said giving Jerome her combo meal. Jerome trotted into the kitchen and put the meal in the microwave for 30 seconds and then brought it back to her and said, "Here you go, all nice and warm."

"I don't have any children and I don't date people who do." William said smiling.

"You're a real gentleman…" Denise sarcastically said while half turning to William.

"Hey, who doesn't like to see ladies poppin' de ass and shakin' de titties online, we love to see that but I'm not going to wife that. If she already got kids by another nigga, how is that fair to me? Somebody else can deal with that. That's not my kid! You ain't gon' have me at your Red Table talkin'. Find somebody else to star in your Cuckstables show. And she has to be in shape too…" William ranted.

"Here eat this because you've just become the villain." I said tossing William an apple.

"It's ok to have standards." Anthony said.

"I was in a relationship I shouldn't have been in. It's as simple as that." Denise said. "At first I did blame the world but it was on me."

"You can't just be dating women with children for sport, it's immoral." My Tutor said.

"You ain't gon' to have me buying all your kids McDonald's." William smugly said taking a bite of the apple.

"And what if they don't want to date a man because he's divorced or he has children…" My Tutor said.

"That's their prerogative." Anthony said. "William is out of pocket, but he's right."

"There's a lot of competition out there, some people just aren't up for it." Denise said. "It's easier to out-sexy a woman than to out-lose weight her. It is easier to rent an apartment or rent an expensive car than to actually put in the work to have muscles. People want what's the quickest."

"Ummmm Hmmm." My Tutor agreed.

"Life is easy but it's the harder thing you'll ever do. I mean in school I was chunky. I had braces and glasses. I was friend zoned so much it was like I was just one of the boys." Denise admitted.

"What?" My Tutor said.

"I was less like yes and more like no. I didn't always look like this."

"She sure didn't." William remarked. Denise shot him an icy glare and shook her head.

"I didn't lose weight because I wanted guys to like me. I wanted to like me. I didn't like feeling how I felt. I had to put in the work. I gained confidence, improved my social skills. I had to get out of my comfort zone, but it was for me." Denise said.

"You increased your vibration." I said.

"I needed to be balanced." She said reluctantly. "I don't really want to be a step…mom, but I'm probably going to have to be one. If y'all do date someone that has child, don't ask about how many people she's been with, you don't really want to know the answer, just know that mistakes were made."

"If you got one kid that's alright, but two, three, four, five by multiple dudes and you in your 20s…" Jerome said. "Hells naw! Look at all dem traps that didn't work."

"So, it's okay for you males to have babies all around town…" Denise countered.

"That's different." Anthony stated. "Because single motherhood is encouraged, even appreciated. They are having babies with dudes they don't even want. So on one side you have single mothers and on the other side you have women who want to be wives but don't want to be step moms. And in the middle you have decent men and women who had a child early, but they are already disqualified…It's a cold game."

"When you put it that way it seems like we are all working together to be unhappy and to keep children in single parent households." Denise responded.

"You don't have to look long before you see educators, articles and news segments that tell you the Black family doesn't include a man… tell me what other races are doing this?" Anthony stated.

"These things look like promotion because the family, whatever that maybe, that a single parent has created cannot be a mistake or an error. Add government and state programs that favor us to that and it became a catalyst for family instability. We ladies support each other even when we are wrong. Don't y'all do that?" Denise asked.

"Nope. We check each other constantly." I said. "If a dude wasn't raised right…he can't hang."

"Well, just believe me when I tell you that single motherhood is a gang." Denise said.

"Parents spend so much time demonizing each other; they forget about what's best for the child." I said.

"I'm too young to be a step anything, that's for old people with diminishing options." William said.

"Step dads and moms should get a lot of credit. They got a lot of bullshit to deal with from the start." Anthony said.

"Step parents are brave." I added.

"So now who wants credit for doing the bare minimum…" Denise smugly said.

"What's braver than going out into the wilderness or into battle with your private parts exposed and marrying someone with three children that aren't yours? That's the definition of bravery." Anthony said.

"Ant, you may be right… we have gone soft…" I said.

"I was out of the house at 16." Anthony said.

"I was out of the house at 19." I chimed in.

"Young teen clumsiness is now assault…" Jerome said.

"These teenagers should be scared of doing anything with a girl." Denise uttered.

"They need to be able to express themselves we all make errors. Always fearing that one bad date, one wrong move will hinder their whole lives is a like walking on egg shells." I said.

"See that's what I'm saying, how is this a better time period?" William said.

"I never say that this is a better time period, just a different one." Denise said.

"If it's different why does the age of consent still vary from state to state? Do youth mature differently based on the state border?" William asked.

"I never thought about why…" Denise said.

"Primarily it's a holdover from a different time period when life spans were shorter." Anthony said. "11 year old boys were working in the fields. Once a girl turned 12, she was considered mature enough to consent to sex and even get married; most of the people on the planet are the result of such relations. If society were really concerned about the development of its youth the age of consent would be 20 across the board, and they'd prohibit all sexual advertising.

"The other reason is that society just doesn't want young girls ran through by young boys. They want young women to be run through by men and it gives older ladies a shot at dudes their age. You don't need a report or an investigation to figure this out, you see they haven't changed the laws and there is no universally recognized age from this supposedly enlightened culture. This is done so they can be arbitrary with the circumstances and consequences."

"These kids just be sitting around the house actin' and talkin' like they know everything but they are really just scared. Not only do they not want to work, they don't want to contribute anything productive. They could just a little job hunting." Jerome said.

"Everything is just flipped. I remember my family being so poor that irregular clothes were for poor people, now irregular clothes are high fashion." Denise remarked.

"My dad was the breadwinner in our family; my two sisters and I were fairly happy. Now you need two or three incomes to live in the same neighborhood. If I didn't know any better I'd say that we have been deceived." William said.

"There's hope for you yet." I stated.

"Yeah, you D.C. Cab face fukka!" Jerome said to me.

"Oh, it's on. William do the damn thang." I said.

"Get him!" William said turning on an instrumental beat.

"Plant seeds a man's deeds is worth more, forget streams, I can't breathe, I stampede the church door." I rhymed. "Oh, hell, I'm doing well, check the optical. We come together like Voltron so either you're a bridge or an obstacle. Afraid to approach me in real life so you hide behind your keyboards. Detours, mental conditions and Vitamin D deficiency is your reward.

"When they say facts, I say fiction, knowin' allegations and rumors are just as bad as convictions. Stay willin' to take the stand in the court of public opinions. Diagnosed clinically, standing in lines for phones, shoes and Patti Labelle pies. If you've never seen the truth then it's hard to reject the lies. But I'm not a rapper. You ch-ch-ch-chia face fukkas!" I fired out as a reminder that I can get down with the best of them.

"That's fire." My Tutor said.

"Will, you have cleaned up since the last time I saw you." Denise said.

"I've always had style."

"But, your kneecaps are showing." Denise said and My Tutor giggled

"Ha..ha…ha…If I want to wear shoes with my ankles out, I wear my ankles out."

"But you showing more than ankles, you showin' yo calves." Jerome said.

"... Denise, I remember the beginning of senior year when you burned yourself with a flat iron... I bet you screamed like William Hanna in the Tom & Jerry show." William said belly laughing.

"What." I said shocked. My Tutor just looked around the silent room and covered her mouth.

"That burn looked like a big ass tattoo." William said still heartily laughing. "I don't how you burned a big ass 'Conair' logo into your forearm. I know that had to hurt…"

"It did." Denise said with a fake smile.

"The Conair Corporation should have sponsored your senior year." William continued. "You were trying to hide it. The school administrators thought your momma was Lynetta Gordon from the show Good Times. You got clowned until Homecoming."

"Thank you, that is in the top three of my worst high school moments. You know what I remember… I remember you not having any swag and always wearing those dumbass cargos. I remember you being broke all though high school…" Denise fired at William.

"Yeap." William acknowledged.

"I remember when you dropped the baton in the 4x400 meter relay finals? I remember when 'One-Punch' knocked the Sonic the Hedgehog rings out of you. He right crossed you to the PlayStation 2 startup screen. When I look at you I can still hear that sound. See, this is why you got curved in High School." Denise fired back at William.

"She's savage." Anthony said.

"What's up?" I asked William as I saw the life drain from his face.

"I mean, why I gotta be all that?" William said wiping the sweat from his forehead. "But, I can't deny the fact that it's true. Nic, how is having two incomes to be at the same middle-class level from 20 years ago a good deal?" William said changing the subject.

"It's not." I said. "People aren't unhappy because of crime rates or because of low wages. People are unhappy because we've all been lied to, and they don't see anyone really doing anything about it. That's what happens when you devalue half of society. Men are unheard, not allowed to have feelings, not allowed to have an opinion. Men have it hard...Generally speaking of course."

"Of course..." Denise said nodding her head in agreement.

"So many people see men as pathetic, narcissist, losers and predators." I said.

"Predators... yeah like that's somehow beneath human... Predator is the very definition of a human being." Anthony said.

"Right, women and men are predators...We are human, our eyes face forward... Why is saying predator so negative?" William added.

"Because when they use that word, it means man." I answered.

"Academics won't make any money saying this but women are just as if not more violent as men." Denise said. "A few years ago, this bitch with Queen Latifah, Set It Off braids took my clothes out of the dryer at the Laundromat. I dragged her up and down the vinyl floor, slapped her up against the washer... whew... I got her good. The police just asked us if we were ok to go home and that was it. I enjoyed it, but I didn't like how it made me look and I swore to never to be violent like that again. Honestly, women are scarier than men to me."

"I wish a...bitc... ummm. I wish a girl would take my clothes out of the dryer..." My Tutor said.

"Do you think there would be violence if it weren't for women?" Anthony asked Denise.

"What?" Denise said.

"Do you think there would be all this violence if it weren't for women?" Anthony said.

"You are really going to go there?" Denise incredulously said.

"How many dudes have lost their lives over bullshit some girl started?" Anthony said. "Best believe there's a lady or three benefiting from some guy's robbing, stabbing, killing, shooting, drug selling, embezzling or ponzi scheming."

"I never thought of the connection like that." Jerome curiously said.

"Are you really trying to say that the ills of the world are the fault of women?" Denise asked.

"What's good for the goose..." Anthony said. "Moms, wives and significant others accept drug and blood money knowing full well where it comes from and how it was gained."

"If ladies didn't allow it no one would be doing it." William stated.

"You need to shut the hell up!" Denise said scowling at William.

"Hey, we don't casually toss out terms like, if you have nothing to hide; if you haven't done anything wrong then... those terms designed to violate your rights and take away personhood. We are not a like-minded, thin-skinned group of people. We don't shut down discourse here. We don't move the goal post due to weak positions. We do not retreat to talking points. If we don't talk to each other we can't get to the truth. Is it fair to say that most negative interactions are due to relationships that we have with one another?"

"That's fair." My Tutor said.

"The media will actually have the truth, or they will find out the truth and still keep playing the narrative for clicks; they are just defaming, damaging reputations and moving on, this was not the intent of the 1st Amendment." I said. "I am not saying that we need cost-free speech, but we need an amendment that calls for the separation of media and state. Because having different opinions is one thing; having different facts is a dangerous public failure. And to answer your question… fair… would be the retraction being just as big as the headline and as long are the segments were."

Everyone in the room probably thought I interrupted the discussion to defend Denise but I didn't. About eight months ago, a friend of ours who works at a shooting range had us come down. They allowed us to shoot on the side for rifles with close and far targets and on the other side for handgun practice.

The loud bangs didn't bother Denise; the weight of the firearms didn't bother her. There were no awkward silences or forced small talk at the gun range. She scored higher than everyone, except for Anthony of course. Denise can hold her own.

"Males have plenty of privilege." Denise defiantly said.

"Dee, we all have privilege, whether its gender, height, beauty, intelligence— there isn't just a male privilege that trumps female privilege. We are different and we are supposed to acknowledge and celebrate those differences, because if we are being truthful, women get away with hell of a lot." I said.

"We do, but that's not on us." Denise said.

"Women will never know how it feels to have a defacto nationwide policy of not allowing fathers to see their children with very little recourse." Jerome said.

"Of course not and why would we care?" Denise said.

"Most mothers will never know the feeling of not being able to see their child because someone is playing games. How is that not abuse? Why do all of this if it's about the children and the family?" Anthony said.

"Because it's not about the children and it's not about family, it's about them." Denise started "People aren't going to have mercy on your heart. They won't understand what you have to go through. They don't want to have a conversation for understanding. They want to lecture you on why you are wrong. For the most part she will use any excuse, any reason to not take full responsibility. She'll use her hair, the child's disability, the child's confusion—it doesn't matter. Face it, a dog doesn't bring in as much money as a child does."

"The large and small terrors we inflict on each other in coercive, controlling, unhealthy relationships, can't be good for society." I said "You've got mistresses and cheated on wives get invited on morning talk shows and writing best-selling books. It doesn't happen the other way around. Look at all the gynocentric TV shows. Where are all the shows about men getting finessed, catfished, ruined and broken by mistreatment?

"Where are the exposés on mothers gaming and cheating the system? Where are the shows that reveal horrible mothers willfully raising demons? Anti-male groups dominate social media, unfettered. Where are the government programs for men's mental health?

"Our trauma starts before we can walk and gets magnified in the 8th grade when you don't get invited to the dance and you don't have any friends because you aren't attractive or you're socially awkward; that's when things get really bad. In high school, you know more people but you don't know how to date.

"College isn't any better but now you've learned how to drink and be angry about the hand you've been dealt, making you more antisocial.

You see other men go out on dates. You see ten women line up for the same guy and you're like damn something must be wrong, so you grab hold of an alpha or player narratives, because at least those things make you feel like you exist.

"When you get thirty, you realize that you haven't accomplished anything; all you have is a degree. You have a job but you aren't happy and you don't know why, because your clock is ticking every bit as much as a woman's clock is. And just when you're about to make a turn for the better you meet a cold-hearted woman that's just as fucked up as you are and she'll rip your heart out. Most guys grow up believing that they are worthless to society. This is backed up by women, who have no problem telling a guy that he's ugly and not worth her time.

"In a lot of ways mental and emotional abuse is worse than physical abuse, because it's not obvious so it goes on without being noticed. A woman can send him a text message and he'll be in jail or killing himself within an hour…that's power."

"If she doesn't get prosecuted or caught up for her nonsense, which she usually doesn't, all the drama she caused will be funny as hell until she's near 40 and single and that's probably when she'll realize that she ruined lives and made bad choices—it's usually too late by then." Anthony added.

"Men's sports magazines put up old ass overweight women." William said. "Women's magazines only highlight old ass overweight men if they are being arrested. Since society wants women to raise the children shouldn't her wisdom, discernment and judgment be of the utmost priority and not overlooked?"

"That would require everyone to come together and say, no more. There's just too much money being made on division for that to happen." Anthony said.

"Y'all goin' in over here." My Tutor said.

"Being a man is a lot of work, wait, being a man that's worth a damn is a lot of work." Denise said. "He listens to your gossip, he's helps pick out your outfits and hairstyles, he tells you that you look pretty in the morning, he's boosting your self esteem and he's watching the shows you want to watch.

"Why would he want somebody he has to constantly explain everything to? Who wants someone who is crying half the time? Who wants someone that always argues about what you are wearing, what you like to listen to and how you speak? Who wants to be with someone who talks bad about your car and a bunch of other things they really don't even give a shit about...They are just arguing to argue...who wants that?

"Men, have higher societal expectations. I've seen men get victimized with no sympathy. I mean, even if the father wants the baby the mother can still give it up for adoption."

"That doesn't seem fair." My Tutor said.

"You need all hands on deck when you're raising children so why cut off one of your hands?" Anthony asked.

"Society has told people that there aren't any real consequences to not having male energy around..." I said.

"Fathers are important; especially the good ones and being here helped me see that." Denise said. "It helped me see that the talks with friends and certain entertainment can make a person embrace the notion that women are under attack and that we the need to fight for survival... It makes us think everyone is a threat."

"Look at how these groups call themselves; Mother's against this, Mother's doing this, Mother's for this..." I said.

"And what's wrong with that?" My Tutor said.

"A nation's most powerful resource is its people and the structure of the people is the family." I said. "They are advocating for single motherhood. It's further proof that some are single mothers by choice. Women are choosing to get divorced, they are choosing not to get married and choosing to sleep unprotected with dudes they just ran into and know won't be around. Broken communities and broken families are easy to prey on. They'll claim they are doing this because males are not the target audience, it's just marketing. The truth is that to them, men don't exist."

"Come to think of I don't really see a lot of groups called; Parent's against this, Parent's for this… And you are saying that this is intentional…" Denise said.

"Yes," I said. "The smart ones get slick and call themselves, Families for something, we already know they mean just mothers. They'll just add a few fathers in so it seems like it's not full-on sexist."

"What happens when the child says, Thanks for the jacket but I rather have a family, or these shoes are cool but I'd rather have a father?" Jerome asked.

"It's hard enough being a teenager and then parents want to place their failed relationship baggage on them too." I said. "We need to take each other emotions and mental health into consideration more than we do. We can't evolve and grow as a society filled with broken people." I said.

"Right, it doesn't matter if your last name is Ledger, Williams, Bourdain, Schwarzenegger, Jackson, Tyson, West or Smith—our society will make light of your mental health issues until you die." Anthony added. "No man makes it out clean."

"I couldn't imagine always being suspected just because I exist." Denise said. "Some businesses won't hire men; some women won't purchase items from men. Men are always viewed with a heightened sense of security, and most of the times y'all aren't doing anything suspicious. I can see how men are not safe to express themselves emotionally.

"All people should be afforded grace. If officials just did their jobs regardless of special interest, most of America's nonsense would evaporate." I said.

"How are you traumatized because I exist?" Anthony said.

"It's not fair..." My Tutor said.

"See what yo people doing?" William said.

"My people..." Denise said.

"Yeah... your lady-kind." William replied. "They out here thinking men are emotionally stunted, but we just built different, we make it look easy."

"Things get deep when you really dismantle why you think what you think." Denise said sighing.

"It's sad." My Tutor said.

"Sad, is mourning the loss of a privilege you didn't even know you have." I said.

Triggered.

Everyone's cell phone made a loud ear piercing sound. Everyone pulled out their device and looked at it.

"That's the second Amber Alert today." Jerome said.

"Whenever an Amber Alert goes off on my phone, I just think that's the breakup of another family and another dead male." I said.

"You die cause you're being a dad that's really messed up." William said.

"These smart phones aren't smart enough to know if you're on a freeway or not." I said.

"They just want to disturb people…" Anthony said.

"Public attention is vital in missing person cases." My Tutor said.

"Black children go missing far more often than white kids but you wouldn't know that if you are watching the media." Jerome said.

"So you are saying there is a racial bias in finding missing children…" My Tutor said.

"Jerome is right… They act like rich families don't sodomize their children with toothbrushes." Anthony said. "And middle class suburban families don't have drug labs and slaves in their basement. No. White kids have no real reason to leave home— they must have been taken. Their little princesses had to be brainwashed to behave like this. It had to be foreign influence that made them want to leave America to join ISIS—it had to be."

"Everything isn't about race. Missing children isn't a white and black issue." My Tutor said.

"Right, it's an issue of caring and not caring. To them a black child's home life is so miserable running away from home is expected, they aren't missing—they just left. They are on the streets doing whatever kids from the hood do out there. Their parents are irresponsible; they sold the kid for drugs or rent money." Anthony said.

"That's fucked up." I said.

"Look at the media coverage, the alerts; the measures put in place… our children aren't the primary reason for it." Jerome said.

"They are the ones using music that we made popular. They are using our culture to market all of these products so you would think that as popular as black culture is that they'd be reporting on us all the time." Denise said.

"They do…when we killing, shaking our ass, or supporting them." Anthony stated. "Anything that has to be with us being human is a non-story… A caring parent—forget that… A stable, loving family— no way. They'll report on a pet goat before they give minorities that kind of shine."

"When our grandfathers and grandmothers were young they stood up for what was right!" I said. "They passed and struck down laws for moral reasons. They waged wars on poverty, not poor people. Those people sacrificed, cared about their neighbors, put their money where their mouths were, and they didn't beat their chest.

"They built great big things, constructed all of the grand projects around America, bridges, dams, tunnels, they drilled through mountains, they created highways and railways; they built the nation's infrastructure. They made ungodly technological advances, cured diseases and cultivated the world's greatest artists and the world's greatest economy. They reached for the stars and landed on the moon.

"They sought out intelligence; they didn't disparage it. They didn't identify themselves by who they voted for in the last election, and they didn't frighten so easy. This is why information is power because today, we have the best and brightest people from around the world, we have more money than ever, we have more technology and more people yet we can barely get a suspension bridge built that will hold people.

"Our people are our biggest resource and we aren't using them correctly. Now there is nothing but confusion. What occurs when categories change, definitions are altered and boundaries are removed...chaos."

"True dat." Anthony said.

"People are so confused it's just easier to go in the direction that makes them feel better." I said. "What I don't understand how you can have your dream job, your dream career, your dream goal, your dream home, your dream business, your dream family and everything you worked hard your whole life for and some random motherfuckers will do everything they can to destroy it... it doesn't make sense."

"We need laws for troublemakers." Denise offered.

"I'd vote for that." My Tutor said.

What I had gone through and my experiences caused me to hear everything and see everything. I saw that we as a people were not giving each other enough grace. We were not showing enough love to one another. I could see that everyone had beauty inside but I could also see that if you looked at a person long and deep enough you'll find something not to like. I prefer to look upon people with love, honesty and wonder and those that spent any time with me could sense that.

"What's good on the child front?" I said to Anthony. I asked him this because after his last statement he had a sad look on his face.

"Not much." Anthony responded. "Just shrapnel and mortar fire when I go to pick them up. I texted Melanie that I wanted to see my children and she went down to Family Court and the court said the text messages were domestic violence."

"You bullshittin'?" I said.

"Nope." Anthony responded dryly as he handed his phone to Denise.

"These text messages are not domestic violence." Denise said.

"They said it was, and that she was afraid." Anthony said.

"How is anyone responsible for the fear inside someone else?" Jerome said.

"She went in there and with a straight face and told them I was touching the children." Anthony said.

"You were gone for two tours of duty and they still believed that?" I said.

"They don't need to investigate, they don't need proof, they only needed the allegation. When I tell the court about her bad mothering, she just says I'm lying and they move on." Anthony said in a defeated way.

"So, she's under oath misremembering..." Denise said.

"I said lying..."

"Ok. So she's lying, keeping your children away from you and taking you through a lengthy legal process. You've been fighting for your children since the day I met you. Did the state give you free legal representation?" Denise asked.

"No. In the hearings she's an amnesiac, she doesn't remember how much money I have given her, she doesn't remember if I made any payments, she doesn't remember if I picked up the children. When they asked her if I paid the mortgage, she says I might have given her a couple dollars here and there. Mostly, she shakes her head, rolls her eyes, gnashes her teeth and says she's feels unsafe. She says she's incapable of working because she's taking care of the children."

"And they did nothing about her blocking your fatherly bond." Denise said.

"The attorney says I might get to keep the 30/70 custody I have."

"This is disgusting and it's more disgusting for the courts just to side with her like that." Denise said.

"Also, she just started raising my 4-year-old daughter as a boy."

"At 4-years-old..." My Tutor said shocked. "I'm going to pray for you."

"You agreed to that?" Denise said.

"I'm trying to stop her. That's while I filed for full custody, but the family court say she has that right."

"For real..." Jerome said.

"She's using drugs on your youngest..." I said.

"There has been no medical affirmation from my child. The only thing my daughter asked me for was a video game. My ex-wife just made the decision to give her puberty blockers…" Anthony said.

"Damn, I want to dislike women so much, but they get my dick hard." William said as his playlist shifted from Robert Palmer and Michael McDonald to Lauryn Hill.

"So you can't drink until you're 21. You can't vote or buy cigarettes until 18, but at 4 you can be hormonally blocked, that's deep." Jerome said.

"Children need to just be left the hell alone." Denise said.

"Do you know how it feels to be a Pokémon?" Anthony asked.

"Of course not…" Denise said.

"Then how do you know you want to be one?" Anthony said.

"I hear people saying things that really don't make sense like that." Denise said.

"After puberty blockers, then it's cross-sex hormones. Hormones have long-term and profound effects on body and mind." I said.

"She is inconsiderate of my time. She makes the children doctor appointments when it's my week. I have to take off work and take them to the doctor. When she takes the kids to the doctor she makes them bill the co-pays to me. I don't even know they went to the doctor until I get a bill in the mail with my name on it.

"I should have known when she started questioning everything and making me repeat myself multiple times. I should have known when where I put the remote control and how I folded the towels turned into an argument I should have realized what was happening." Anthony said sadly.

"Is she working?" Denise asked.

"She's a stay-at-home mom." Anthony responded.

"More like stay-at-home demon." I said.

"She probably needs a job." Anthony said.

"Sounds like her job is fucking with you…" William snidely said.

"Finally, he's adding to the conversation." Denise responded.

"Anthony, you are paying her money and she wakes up and actively prays that you lose your job and stub your toe. William said laughing "… couldn't be me."

"And she's patting herself on the back for doing it." Denise said.

"Sounds like mental and emotional abuse to me…" I said.

"There's a big difference between a stay-at-home mom and a wife who stays home with the kids." Denise said, looking at us as if we should know what that difference was.

"Ohhh, it sounds like her soul is broken!" My Tutor said.

"She doesn't have a soul." Anthony quickly replied.

"They got you niggas out here fighting all the battles and when you come home you get treated like Grey Worm from The Game of Thrones." William said.

"It was messed up how they did all the black people in that show." I said.

"But they got credit for trying..." My Tutor said.

"Fuck that." William said.

"Melanie wouldn't be doing these things if her son was a Cartwright; shout out to Ms. Sanaa Lathan." Denise offered.

"That was his best movie..." My Tutor exclaimed.

"I actually like Daddy's Little Girls," I said.

"I couldn't finish watching Precious," Denise hesitated in saying.

"Me either." My Tutor added.

"Diary of a Mad Black Woman was absolutely terrifying." Jerome countered. "Ole girl was just beating down a handicapped person and n-words were cheering..."

"Thematically we may have evolved beyond Unnamed Thug #3, but our minds haven't. There's a sizeable audience for n-words." Denise said. "Some of mainstream black content is trash but we have to support it or we might not get anymore." Denise said.

"Fuck dat." William responded. "It was terrible."

"Shhhh…" My Tutor urged.

Hey, kudos to Tyler Perry…" Anthony stated coming back into the living room with a full blender jar. He started refilling everyone's cup.

"Lupita is my favorite actress..." Denise said to My Tutor

"Why?" My Tutor responded

"Because her 110-pound ass was the only one strong enough to say no."

"Can't argue with that." My Tutor said. I see Latin women playing Black roles all the time. Lupita is biracial and she speaks Spanish, why doesn't she get Spanish-speaking roles?"

"You know why?" Anthony said.

"See you guys have to increase your odds of finding a suitable mate. Go to places where the odds are in your favor, like…" Denise said.

"…don't say websites because they just digital pimps. They be havin' expired profile pictures and are filled with double u's… the unhealed and unhinged." William said interrupting Denise.

"… I was gonna say, like farmer's market or church." Denise reassured us.

"Church…that's where the talented, pretty hoes go to rebrand." William sarcastically argued. "I think I speak for all of us by sayin', you got us fucked up if you think conditionally feminine, churched up, hoes, tired of getting dicked down and left is what we need. She's dated the whole metaverse now she wants to come to Jesus. And the pastor tells them they can lie, steal and hoe all their life, then donate some money, accept Christ and everything is cool. Talkin' about how they re-virginized, like its new ass, but it's the same old ass."

"Some of them church girls be doin' what you think they be doin'." Anthony remarked.

"Jesus walks with them…" My Tutor said.

"Broken, they may be. Hoeing… that's in the past." Denise said. "The older you are the more likely it is that you'll end up with someone who was run through anyway."

"You right there a lot of born-again virgins there. Sarah does go to church every Sunday." Jerome remarked.

"See, the Lord does move in mysterious ways." My Tutor said.

"These hoes ain't loyal, they be playin' games. A lot of daughters were born to be dropped off. They probably don't have any more oxytocin left." Jerome said smiling.

"People might need to do some hoeing to find themselves." Denise said, "Just because you're a certified hoe, doesn't mean you're a bad person. Some hoes are better people than non-hoes. If it weren't for hoeing and alcohol most of us wouldn't be here."

"I think the best place to meet people is at work." I said.

"If you have a loving involved father, why take him to court?" My Tutor said. It was apparent that she didn't like the conversation turning to religion.

"To facilitate the robberies," Anthony mocked.

"Melanie's hobbies include drama, rudeness and disrespectful behavior." Anthony said.

"You sayin' that like she just switched up on you, you Bob baker face fukka!" Jerome cracked.

"Maybe y'all were just too young." My Tutor added.

"Anthony you're dealing with someone who gains happiness from your struggles." Denise said. "She doesn't respect you. Look around; any man that has any kind of reach, who makes sense, has valid points or is making real progress without a woman being in the forefront, has to be put down like an animal that just tasted human blood for the first time.

"That's why corporations have men in dark suits flanked by women wearing whatever color they like. These businesses want to get in on any movement and out in front of any potential backlash. They want the money but they need it insulated. If one of our distinguished members isn't there to validate you, you're not really valid. The sisterhood will not allow it."

"One minute you think you're in a good relationship and the next thing you know you are with a Number Six Cylon. Denise, I don't mean to be dumping on women, but how do you make them stop trippin?" Jerome groaned, rubbing his forehead.

"Are you still hittin' it?" Denise probed.

"She's forcing me to hit it." Jerome answered.

"She can't force you to do it…" My Tutor remarked.

"The hell she can't!" All of the assembled men said in unison.

"As long as a thing is possible she'll be in your mind, that's the beauty of it. You men think with only one head." Denise said.

"Not all men." Anthony said. "There is a low radar cross section to these red flags, you never know what you are going to get."

"Naw, you can tell by her mannerisms, her bone structure, the way her eyebrows are arched that she's not ready to be taken seriously." William offered as he turned the music down.

"You can't tell all of that from just looking at a woman…" My Tutor said.

All of the guys looked at each other.

"Denise, do you want something to drink?" I asked.

"Do you have tea?" Denise asked.

"Sure do…" I responded and I quickly went into the kitchen. I came back with a cold glass of black tea with a few lemon slices in it.

"Thank you," Denise said before she took a sip.

"Denise, every time I make a suggestion or try to have a discussion with her, we end up arguing…" Jerome pleaded.

"Is she always watching The Man is Guilty shows or reality TV shows?" Denise questioned.

"Is that a problem?' Jerome asked.

"Sometimes, watching those shows creative treatment of reality changes the way a person views life. Her brain creates narratives, where you are the bad guy. You must be triumphed over in order for her to have her happily ever after. In order for her to be right, you have to be wrong, maybe dead wrong. No matter what she does don't cry about it; don't act out in fit a rage either... even though she's trying to make you react. We have all seen Sarah's body— when you are around her, don't look at it." Denise urged Jerome.

"Why not?"

"It's a trap." Denise exclaimed in a way that would make Admiral Ackbar proud. "… and she knows it. She's going to the gym and working out so you can keep on knowing it. All of that arguing is a trap. The next thing you know you'll be looking at her lips and breast."

"If I tell her no when she asks for the D, things only gets worse." Jerome complained.

"You have to be firm when you are dealing with her." I reassured him.

"There are some terrible people out there." Anthony said.

"I love my children, but even with joint custody it feels like I am borrowing my children. I just went through a bad episode with her."

Jerome said. "I had my children for the week and I gave my son his first haircut. When I dropped the kids off, Sarah went ballistic and called the police on me. She and her girlfriends were screaming and yelling that I had no right to cut his hair, that I wasn't authorized to cut his hair. Now mind you she and I had previously discussed cutting his hair because it was getting out of control."

"Wow…" My Tutor said.

"Hell isn't how people envision it; hell is a state of mind." Jerome said.

"That's hard to wrap your brain around." I said. "There's a good place, there's a bad place and there's a dumb place—we're in the dumb place."

"You in da stupid place." William interrupted me, laughing. "Pun intended…"

"That's not a pun dumbass!" Jerome said.

William looked at My Tutor who just shook her head.

"This guy." I said trying not to laugh.

"Ant, are you still giving your ex-wife the rhythm?" Denise asked.

"We are never, ever, ever, getting back together…" Anthony sang, enunciating each word.

The Fault is Yours

Denise went into the kitchen and put what was left of the cake into the refrigerator. She came back into the living room and motioned to William who lowered the music volume.

"Ok. I felt just as sorry for the guys who were in the club every day throwing all of their money in the air, as I did for the women who are on stage night after night believing they had no other choice. Usually my feminism won't allow me to speak negatively of other women but... y'all need honest professional help and what kind of friend would I be if I only cared about injustice when it is perpetrated on my kind? So I'm going to help y'all out.

"First off, Jerome, you married a devil, you have to own that. Anthony, did you ever think that Melanie chose you because you were going to the Navy? Don't people in the military have the highest divorce rate and the highest suicide rate?" Denise said.

"I dealt with all of her nonsense and she divorced me and you're saying all of this was some kind of plan..." Anthony seethed.

"Perhaps, divorce being a contingency in case you made it back alive and with all your faculties." Denise said. "You can best believe that she made preparations before she dropped the hammer on you. She was probably building a case against you from the start. She wouldn't have walked away from you if she thought you were still necessary.

"When you came home on leave I bet she didn't let you look through her phone."

"Ummm hmmm." Anthony cautiously said.

"And she didn't want to do anything with you saying that she was tired from the gym…"

"Yeah, she was always tired and sore from the gym…" Anthony replied.

"Right…" Denise laughed. "Leg day… when you weren't around every day is legs in the air day…" Denise said sipped her tea.

"More like third leg day…" My Tutor said laughing with Denise.

"I think I'm going to throw up…" Anthony stammered, holding his mouth and making retching noises.

"I told you that I was going to keep it real. Both of you are to blame for some of this; both of you should have married someone less attractive. What we are about to talk about will apply to everyone but Anthony you're going to need another session because, sir, you've got a full-fledged devil on your hands. I am sure that, Nic will ask us to help contribute to your legal fund."

"I don't mean to cut you off but he needs another session, I need help now." Jerome pleaded.

"Help you out like Venus and Serena losing to Naomi Osaka?" William said.

"William, stop playin', I need all the help I can get." Jerome cried out. "Every time she's wrong instead of admitting it, she just gets in a DeLorean with Michael J. Fox and goes back in time… 7 years ago you did this… When you were in elementary school you did that. I don't understand how I ever fell in love with her in the first place…"

"Titties…" William said.

"I loved that woman more than anything. I did everything I could, but now I see that she never fuckin' loved me!"

"There are a lot of people who have no idea how to really love another human being and they were raised by people who also didn't know how to love." I said. "A great philosopher once said love isn't true it's just something that we do…"

"That's profound…" My Tutor said.

"You know the Wheel of Fortune; well some women have a Wheel of Anger. They just spin the wheel and get angry about whatever it lands on." Denise said. "She's negative with you, she's spreading negative things about you to her friends and together they are cultivating negative thoughts about you. She's telling her family negative things and your children see and hear all negatives. Her co-workers hear all the negatives and she'll even put negative things out about you online.

"All of that negativity energy can cause negative things to occur…"

"Sounds like witchcraft…" William stated.

"This man is just paying attention." I said, pointing at William.

"If you are into Marvel then it's the Dark Arts…" William said.

"If you are in the good graces of one of our certified representatives you'll do well. If not, you'll go through countless court hearings, hire several lawyers, get drugged through the mud in magazines, in articles and in the public domain, lose jobs and money to finally be heard…and once all of that is settled, she'll try to reduce your visitation." Denise said.

"Why?" Jerome said rubbing his beard.

"Doing that will cause your financial support order to go to maximum." Denise said. Meanwhile she will tell everyone you don't want to see your child and that you're a deadbeat. The average man doesn't have the money, the resources or the guts to go through years of litigation to get their name and dignity back, so you need to make better choices.

"See when a man is good at something and they see other people completely incompetent at it, they make the mistake of thinking they're smarter than them. When they are simply better at doing those things than someone else is. It's not like we can't do those things, we just don't want to do them and y'all will, and that in itself requires a level of intelligence." Denise asserted.

"So it's a life skill…" I beamed.

"Oh, so acting dumb doesn't mean someone is dumb." William said.

"Conversely when a man acts dumb, he's dumb." Denise said. "A man's ability to produce is what makes them attractive and it's the same for women but you have to remember that we have been getting attention since they were little girls. We have more experience, more weapons, more tactics and more defenses than you will ever have."

"Men have trifling good-for-nothing abusive traps to…" I suggested.

"No doubt, but ours are better and last longer. One hit from you and you're an abuser. A hundred hits from me and I'm a victim. If I hit you first it's justified because I'm scared of you. In that regard men are simply at a disadvantage. Just because she dresses conservative and hasn't slept with a whole bunch of people doesn't make her marriage material. It's a novel concept, but maybe you guys should choose someone who has a good attitude and a right mind, but no...y'all want bad credit, no insurance havin', big ass earring wearin' Crazisha." Denise laughed.

"Dating someone you think is crazy is vastly different from dating someone who has been diagnosed as crazy." I said as Anthony gave me dap.

"Women date crazies and bums…" William said.

"Yeah, but they not ugly tho." Denise fired back.

"Trying to find someone sane to date is a whole lot harder than it sounds…" I countered.

"And it's going to get harder because now non-males and people that hate males are telling the youth how to be a male and teaching them what a male is… They are creating kinder, gentler victims and making being a coward fashionable…good luck with that. Meanwhile, they are poppin' bottles and smokin' hookah on government assistance. These broads out here fantasizing about yachts and can't even swim. You want to get flown out… Become a flight attendant..." Denise sternly said.

"Wait, aren't you getting flown out to Jamaica on a private jet in two weeks..." I said.

"I'm undecided on that…" Denise said.

"You gon' be on somebody's team…" Jerome said.

"I'm not a team player." Denise responded.

"Can you get on a private jet without suckin' dick?" William said smirking.

"I can, you might not be able to. Anyway, how did y'alls issues become about me." Denise said. "Back to you, Jerome… your ex knows when you are looking at her ass, she just plays it off. That kernel of possibility softens your interactions and makes you think about her in kind ways even when she's dragging you through the mud.

"There are young traps, old traps, business suit traps, nice looking traps, big booty traps, full figured traps but they are traps none the less. You got to watch out for these young thangs, emphasis on thang. There is a lot of desperation out there, some of y'all never get tired of getting trapped. The penis is a dreamer. Your mind sees things for what they are, but that thing operates off of what could be."

"Denise is speakin' facts." William commented.

"I can't agree with that, the penis is more like your personal hype man...always eggin' you on. Always ready to encourage you. *You is kind. You is smart. You is important.*" I said walking into my room.

"And Nic adds the sauce." William said.

"The bottom line is that men are easy."

"Shantel, do you need an extra pillow?" Jerome asked.

"I'm good." Shantel replied arraigning the pillow behind her.

"Why do things have to be this way?" I said, coming back into the living room.

"What way?" My Tutor asked.

"Not working together, always arguing, drama causing, violent, unappreciative and unreceptive. You want someone who identifies with your struggle, someone who has mutual respect for you."

"You know you can love someone and not have feelings for them." My Tutor said. "But it's best to keep that to yourself."

"You know, most of this nonsense is just western society. No experience can replace travel." Anthony said, referring to his international exploits.

"I was working 60 hours a week, trying to move up the ladder. She filed for divorce saying that I'm never home." Jerome said. "And I was taking care of her momma too."

"Man, bitches don't care about that shit." Denise dismissively said. "You did all of that and still had to settle for what was left over after her friends and her job…"

"You got the scraps." William interjected, "that's why I'm never getting married….ain't no way bruh."

"I'm giving you the psychology on this; use this awareness to your advantage. I'm only telling you all of these things because I have love for you. Now, in Sarah's mind you are not qualified to give advice or make suggestions to her. She'll take her friend's, a stranger's or an ex-boyfriend's advice over yours because in her mind she sees you as using her." Denise said.

"How am I using her?" Jerome wondered as he leaned closer to Denise.

"When you were married she gave you pussy, right?" Denise questioned.

"Gave…that's mutual." Jerome replied.

"If she was with her ideal man, she wouldn't have to be mutual on anything; she'd allow him to use her beauty, her skill or whatever she was good at for the benefit of both of them. Whenever she thinks about her ideal man, she sees you as unworthy of being inside of her…" Denise chided.

"The man of her dreams usually has money, two pumps and no personality tho." I said.

"So Jerome is being compared and contrasted to somebody she's never going to be with…" William declared.

"Sort of, if she speaks about how the guys who aren't with her are everything you are not. If she refers to them as kinder, gentler, more giving, knights in shining armor and to you as an empty, unoriginal, boring sac of monotony, you are in trouble. The funny thing is that she probably once referred to you as her knight in shining armor to her last dude. When she realizes the bullshit is wearing thin with you she'll contemplate going back to the guy before you; the same guy that she talked about like he was an unhinged foreign dictator.

"After your relationship gets to that point, everything is going to be an uphill battle. Everything you do is wrong. She's keeps B and C options warm with text messages and by telling you they are just friends. She won't make time for you because all she sees is that you're fucking up her happiness. These broads may as well be on a reality show…" Denise laughed.

"Why?" I said.

"Because being in a relationship is their biggest role." Denise said.

"Shouldn't the question be, why is an employer entitled to higher levels of respect than your companion?" I stated.

"No thanks." Denise said as Jerome passed the blunt around. "I stopped smoking."

"When did you stop smoking?" I asked.

"About nine months ago." Denise said.

"What happened?" I asked.

"I went out with this dude. He was a gentleman and when we went back to his place, he cooked for me. I got real faded and then his dick came out..."

"Sounds standard to me." William snapped.

"He ruined my high; my pussy dried all the way up." Denise said. "You get a better outcome if you walk instead of run."

"You can't get faded with everyone. There are a lot of bitch made dudes out there." I said.

"Indeed." Denise said softly. "Some women just aren't used to being sane for long periods of time; it feels wrong and accountability hurts them. See dudes have consequences for being out of bounds...we don't. Without rules and consequences they can't really work around others for too long without bullshit starting.

"You saw how those women behaved when they were charged for extra dipping sauce. A lot of women revel in the notion that they are above the law, not bound by normal standards of behavior. I've experienced the echo chamber of rage, hate, resentment, self-absorption, self-righteousness, victimhood and vengeance, it's deep."

"Capitalism is really cracking the whip, especially on women. They got you paying a premium to be piled up on top of each other. Competition, high pressure, noise, following orders... we were built for that type of work. Capitalism got women out here working as hard as us... When you go from 50k a year to 100k a year, your lifestyle doesn't change that much. These developers aren't building for you."

"I mean there isn't a lot of real world value in ass shaking." Denise said. "People just don't work as hard as they used to, whether it's technology or whatever... sweat will mess up your hair, you might break a nail. They all want to do something in the beauty industry.

They just want to wake up wash their face, brush their teeth and get paid for doing so… Labor has a threshold." Denise said.

"Fuck that, how are you traumatized from what happened to someone else?" Anthony retorted.

"Adopting trauma…It's called empathy." My Tutor responded.

"If empathy stops you from living your life, then it's too much empathy." Anthony responded. "See y'all just can't be honest with each other."

"We are honest with each other…" My Tutor said.

"Not really…" Denise sighed. "If we were there wouldn't be this many Internet models with all of these people in the comment sections telling them how brave or beautiful they are."

"Some of them are beautiful…" My Tutor stated.

"Some of us were raised by side-chicks and hoes, so reshaping reality is just what we do, at first we don't always know these are fantasies or waking dreams." Denise said crunching ice in her mouth. "We love our fiction. We have been known to recruit other women into our reality. If you have to beg for affection and they are being secretive, randomly going to the gym, get out of the relationship." Denise said.

"Relationships are supposed to provide balance, growth and structure and guys need that just as much as ladies do." I said. "The wrong situation can really mess up your life, just like the right situation can really move you forward. We cannot be 100% God and 100% man without having a great counterpart." I said.

"Jerome, yo girl is like Kanye, she'll do whatever it takes to get a rise out of you and then she's gonna to keep doing it, she's da terminator, she won't stop." William said.

"Things are tough all around." Jerome said.

"At least you have money…" William said to Jerome.

"Naw. I make money. I don't have it." Jerome countered. "Between the apartment, the children, counselors and the lawyer… not much is left."

"Motherhood, sisterhood, singledom and alternative lifestyles members often fight like Lannisters, Tyrells, Targaryens, Wildlings and White Walkers." Denise said. "They have different names and locations but they're the same people. At the end of the day money, property, fame, being a good person or being talented won't insulate you from us.

"Honestly, children spend more wake time at school with teachers, coaches, caregivers, in after school programs and looking at video screens than they do with their parents, especially single mothers. On the weekends the dad has the child at least 18 hours of wake time. I have never met a single mother, we always have help. She'll be over here acting like she climbed the mountain all by herself, but she was carried to the top. Half the time women don't care about spending money."

"Why?" I asked.

"Because they are spending the city's money, the government's money, the university's money, the significant other's money, the patron's money, they're not spending their money. That's why they appear generous. If they like you they'll buy you things, they'll give you money, and they'll bring you marijuana, alcohol or something like that. Jerome at first you didn't recognize me but I've seen you around and you're a good man but when I first met Sarah, by just her attitude, I knew you were in trouble. She's not going to change, you have to find it within yourself to cut your losses and move on."

"Won't the Lord do it?" My Tutor said.

"You married her and then you let a few off in her, that's like being sentenced to life…" William said. "The long walk…"

"Sarah knows she fucked up by leaving you." Denise said. "If she can't get someone obviously better than you, she'll stay single. If she is messing with someone they'll only come around under the cover of night. Taking you to court serves multiple purposes. It keeps her on your mind and it slows down your recovery.

"It doesn't matter if it's the ten pounds you needed to lose, an I.R.S. garnishment or a vacation not taken, men just don't how close they are to tasting another dude on his woman. Decent men are easy prey."

"For a large portion of my life I disliked my father. I'm only now realizing that my mother's hatred for him rubbed off on me. So, I can see why some dads aren't with the mothers." I said.

"I've seen that." William said.

"For a user, the problem will always be someone else's fault." I said.

"The reason why you can't tell the woman you're with is a hoe, is because she acts just like you momma." Denise said.

"Shots fired." My Tutor stated.

"Awww damn." William sneered.

"If you don't love him or want to be with him, why not just leave?" Jerome lamented.

"How would leaving now benefit them?" Denise responded. "Users need to be dealt with harshly. Kick their asses out, put them on blast. If you don't call them out you enable them to use others. A user will drain money, protection, energy, a place to stay, emotion; they'll drain blood from you if you let them… That's probably why men die early."

"They damn vampires…" William said. "No reflection, shape shifters, straight Dracula status."

"They are worse than vampires because they operate in the light of day. They don't know how to stop using people; they don't know how they started. Their minds are more cut up than Edward Sissorhands' girlfriend's face on prom night." Denise joked.

"That's messed up?" Jerome said.

"Sis, you are so beautiful" My Tutor whispered to Denise. "Your purse is everything and I really like your nails."

"Thank you …" Denise replied stepping closer so she could get an up-close look at the purse.

"I got it at the regular price store."

"The regular price store…" She said puzzled

"Everybody calls them outlets. You're in school and you're tutoring Nic…right?" Denise asked.

"Yes. I'm getting a Bachelor's." My Tutor answered.

"That's what's up." Denise said. "When my daughter gets older, I'm going back to school."

"I know you get harassed a lot." My Tutor said.

"Not really, most of the time what people call harassment is just a way of saying; I'm not attracted to you why are you trying to talk to me." Denise answered. "People don't really approach me or repeatedly bother me. If someone doesn't pick up the cues that I'm not interested, I just tell them I'm not interested. I haven't had to call anyone ugly.

"You know the other day I went to the doctor and there were two dudes with full beard in the waiting room."

"What's wrong with that?" My Tutor said.

"It was the gynecologist and they had on hoop earrings." Denise said.

"Oh... So you like guys that play video games." My Tutor asked Denise.

"I do now." Denise replied.

"Why?"

"Nic showed me how everyone plays video games and that the negatively attached to guys that play video games is part of a larger anti-male narrative. We are all playing video games, while we are looking down on someone else for playing video games."

"We don't all play video games..." My Tutor said.

"The order food video game, the picture video game, the social media video game, the browse for things video game, the writing messages video game, the video watching video game..." Denise responded.

I stopped mid-drink and pointed at Denise and added, "However, there is a limit to any distraction when your life isn't on track."

"With all the power women have, why are so many of you sisters attracted to jerks and assholes?" Anthony said.

"We aren't attracted to jerks and assholes." Denise began. "It just so happens that jerks and assholes have what some of my sister's desire, security, money, confidence... This Ken Doll just happens to be an asshole. Sometimes you attract what's inside of you. Life changes when you realize the thing you are best at involves lying on your back. Sooner or later people like that end up in situations they can't fuck or suck their way out of.

"And it's always what someone else did as the reason they are doing what they are doing. They are the main ones that be trying to get you to go to church with them. Those soulless heifers won't go by themselves because they are afraid. Still, I see people gladly do nasty things for a whole lot less than a movie role."

"Okay." My Tutor replied.

"You don't want to go through the struggle with him and you think a child wants to go through the struggle with you." William stated.

"I'm paying child support, but every few months she asks for more. Every time I see her, her hair and nails are done and she has new clothes and shoes." Jerome stated.

"This shit is making me mad." Anthony frowned.

"Maybe there is a reason she isn't she working…" My Tutor said.

"She's not working because she picked the right father." Denise said.

"When I call her on her bullshit, she says it was both our fault." Jerome said.

"Because it's your fault." Denise scolded Jerome. "You could do everything right, you could be treat her like a queen but if she's over the relationship she'll talk about it like it's mistreatment. When you're not the person she turns to, when your voice isn't the one she wants to hear, it's over. If your woman is talking to or messaging someone else, she's being unfaithful."

"I'm way too drunk to be talkin' like this." Anthony sang.

"I'm way too high to be trippin' like this." Jerome followed.

"I'm way too young to be livin' like this…" William joined in.

"Ask me why we do it? I'ma put it like this… God damnit… We luv it." I sang.

"We luv it, We luv it… We luv it, We luv it" We sang in unison expressively swaying our hands. William's music accompanied us as we finished singing.

"Did I miss something?" My Tutor said looking surprised.

"They're just being guys," Denise smiled nonchalantly waving her hand.

"We don't want to join the military but we put the needs of the family ahead of our own. We do those things because of a greater purpose." Anthony said once the song ended.

"So he's breaking his back working to provide and it's his fault that you're lonely? It's his fault that you are cheating on him? It's his fault that you have to spend all the money to be happy?" I said.

"If she'll challenges your character in any way, she's ready to ruin your life and the children's lives all because she isn't happy today. Putting your happiness ahead of the family is selfish but you should have known what kind of woman you were dealing with, so yeah it's your fault." Denise said. "That goes for side pieces too; don't give them the full D."

"Why not?" My Tutor inquired.

"See, I know what time it is and unlike them I'm not going to be hoe running my way through life to become a grandma gone wild, like half of these broads. They engage in vaginal mismanagement and are now Vitamin D deficient." Denise responded. "Give it to them and watch them lose what little minds they have left.."

"Usually the wrecking ball is outside the house, but there are people inside their own house wrecking it and blaming it on someone else. Most men are cuckolds." I stated.

"See, just like men can spot simps and shady dudes, just like we ladies can spot sister home wreckers." Denise said.

"After we had our first child, we were in the hospital and I was holding my son and Sarah smiled at me and said, 'You can DNA test him if you want to, just know if it comes back that he's yours, our relationship is over'. I should have known then." Jerome said rubbing his forehead again.

"You should have known before then." Denise maintained.

"And there it is ...all of the blame is on the man! The system is sick" Anthony said upset. "You got 30 year old woman pretending to be high school student because she 'felt that was safer time' and the authorities are just trying to get her some help.

"A woman runs a red light at 130 mph, kills six people, men, women and children and the media is posting articles about her depression, layers of grief and pragmatic relationships. They are doing segments on how she was bipolar, had a mental collapse, lost consciousness and now has amnesia. But she was a nurse for 20 years; they didn't even extrapolate the damage she could have done during that time. This is how they have frame the conversation.

"Yet with all of that, society won't admit that we just aren't equal?"

"I mean have male reporters been in women's locker rooms... just pretty reporters huh..." Denise replied. "I agree with you. As a society we don't want to discuss it out in the open. I don't want to have to deal with the things men have to deal with any more than men want to deal with the things women have to deal with. Everything that's been going on is a tacit social admission that we are not equal, the way women get away with things, how courts favor us, how we can exhibit psychosis with little push back.

"I constantly hear people talking about the lies and delusion… "

"That's not an admission and admission would be saying it and having open discussions about it so it can be corrected." Anthony said.

"Isn't that what we're doing here? Isn't that why we have these honest conversations to plant the seeds of change? I'm not running. We are not running on this side."

"Yes, but it needs to be out in the open."

"Wait…wait…wait… you can't say the affirmative and follow it with a 'but'. Why do you need to add the but?"

"I understand that, but." Anthony said.

"See…you did it again, you are basically saying that I am right, however you refuse to accept it... stop saying it."

"Don't look at me… she got on that one." I said to Anthony.

Having Everything Revealed

"I have to ask…Why be in a relationship, if you are just going to use a person?" I asserted.

"Some people don't know how to do anything else." Denise shared.

"So the bank accounts, the marriage, the children, the whole relationship is one big lie. Meanwhile she's looking for proof that you don't love her...what the hell?" Jerome sighed.

"We serve you at our leisure." Denise said. "We are not out here putting on makeup, perfume, tummy tighteners and wearing clothes tighter than clothes have even been worn before for nothing. We do it for the attention and the opportunities they garner."

"Sarah was on birth control. I saw her take birth control pills every day. I found out later that she had switched out the birth control pills for iron tablets. She didn't want to wait another two years; she wanted us to have a baby now and how is that my fault?" Jerome stated.

"…Because you didn't recognize her mood and behavior changes, you didn't do more, and because you didn't see the end." Denise said. "There were signs you should have seen and precautions that you should've taken, that's all your fault. Long story short; if your wife doesn't respect you, it's your fault. If a woman stays with someone she doesn't love or respect due to money or security, soon as those kids are out of school, she's out as well. She'll leave when all the juice has been squeezed out or someone better looking is giving her attention..."

"Better looking..." William mocked.

"I know it's hard to believe that someone might be better looking than you... If she thinks she's already with an ugly person, she's not going to cheat with an uglier person. If a man cheats on one of us, the Women's Union will make him out to be the worst person that ever lived but if we cheat there is always a justification for it....right." Denise said.

"It's not anyone's place to judge." My Tutor said.

"You were cheating—tell the truth." Denise asked Jerome.

"Nope. I wasn't and Black Men don't cheat." Jerome said.

"The hell you say." Denise said smirking.

"How we going to cheat when we don't commit..." Jerome smiled.

"I see what you did there." Denise said.

"People are human." I said. "I don't cheat...and I won't assist you in cheating either. Cheating may temporarily bring peace to your mind and body, it won't bring peace to your house and that's where you need peace the most. If you really think about it, there's must be something about dating and cheating because all the greats have done it; actors, entertainers, singers.

"But after they get exposed or so-called caught and limited to one relationship, the winning slows down or just stops and their performances just aren't same. Whatever they were doing that powered the celebrated activity is now missing. There's something in the cheating and drug use that added to their competitiveness and fueled their passion, something that made them better."

"You right, they are forever taking a thrill out of shit." William said.

"When Serena was dating all these dudes she was number one in the world, then she got married and started losing." I said.

"Right...right..." Anthony agreed.

"Tiger had like 18 relationships at the same time and he was number one in the world, by far. When monogamy was forced on him, he couldn't win anymore." I finished.

"Most Black men get *Order 66'd* or *Snow Bunnied.*" William explained.

"Snow Bunnied..." My Tutor sneered.

"Yeah, Black Women in important positions get set up too." William said turning down the music.

"So what you sayin'." Denise asked me.

"I'm just sayin' that somehow their vices seem to be intertwined with their talent." I responded.

"So what do you suggest?" My Tutor asked.

"If they aren't harming anyone, leave them alone, let them use the drugs, let them be with whoever they want to be with."

"And what if they are cheating?" My Tutor asked.

"That's between their partner and them, we shouldn't care and either way, it shouldn't be news. All the public is going to do is try to turn it into a scandal because they don't understand that the sometimes it's love but it's always a business arraignment." I said as I got up to refill my cup.

"When it's your birthday, or its Mother's Day, y'all take the whole weekend, but Father's Day is like an hour." Jerome grumbled.

"Aren't Black Women the most attacked?" William asked.

"No, the president and outspoken celebrities are the most attacked, Black Women are only the most attacked if you count Black Women attacking Black Women." Denise said.

"But every week there is a show on proclaiming the virtues of women, talking about how women rock." William replied.

"Don't hate." My Tutor smiled.

"Men rock just as hard." William responded.

"What about fathers, who teach you to skate, ride a bike and who encourage you when you try to give up? Fatherless homes are at the root of most of America's issues. The extreme of having nothing and having everything is still a lack, a lack of balance." I said.

"Follow the money." Anthony said. "More money is spent in broken homes, fewer gatekeepers means more control is gained. They say they can't afford to take care of the child but won't give the children to their fathers because motherhood defines people and it cuts off society's profit. Look at Nic. He is always with Nichole. Her grades are good and she's well adjusted. She is engaged, plays sports and is in school activities. I have never seen her or any of the children that come over here get into trouble. He's not the only father doing that... he doesn't get any programs, benefits, money; he doesn't even get a tax credit and if he makes one mistake it's all over."

"Women always want credit for the thought, the intent, not the action or result." Jerome said.

"It's the thought that counts, but only our thoughts." Denise replied.

"Not when it comes to paying your bills." I said taking a sip from my cup.

"When it comes to ladies is always *I can't believe it*. When it comes to men it's always *of course he did it*. All women do is get praised for basic shit." William offered.

"Hey, we have good intentions…" My Tutor said.

"You can't deposit intentions." Jerome said.

"See this is why I try stay away from nonsense, but there's only so much jerking off a person can do." William said.

"So you just violatin' yourself…" Denise said giving William the side eye.

"Your Doctor Lanoin's ass needs some discipline," Jerome said to William.

"Will is out here treating his body like an amusement park…" I laughed.

"I got season passes." William said laughing. "Is surrogacy human trafficking?" William randomly asked.

"Ummm…" My Tutor uttered looking at William.

"It's hard to be with someone who's worth a damn, when you're not worth a damn." Denise said. "If she is taking pictures of her ass for the Internet and she got a man, she's most likely for the streets. Getting ahead is why we make you feel guilty for even suggesting going 50/50 on bills. That's why most of us are in debt when we are single. We really want those men that got their money quick. The ones that think are playas, because the money came to them to quick for them to develop the discipline to manage it."

"So we just supposed to put money y'alls pockets?" William stated.

"Think of it as contributing to the cause." Denise replied.

"I bet most school loan debt belongs to women." Anthony said.

"I'm sure it does and it's not because of the wage gap or whatever political narrative being tossed out." Denise said.

"Then why is it?" I asked.

"Because we don't want to pay it back." Denise responded. "We never intended to pay it back. We always intended to get someone else to pay it back, friends, lovers, husbands, family, or the government. She'll tell everyone that she's paying it back, but really— y'all paying it back. It takes money to raise a kid but not the kind of money they saying that it takes. They don't know what moderation or budgeting is and they don't care."

"So you're on government programs, you have your hooks into several people, you're not paying for dates, you getting a support check or two coming in and you still don't want to pay your bills?" Jerome said.

"You have to be single to be on most government programs. So, don't knock the hustle, a lot of people spend a lot of their lives having or getting someone else to do for them, they never learned to do for themselves."

"Hold their ass accountable..." Anthony chimed in.

"Society doesn't want to see women laying in the gutter even if it's a gutter of her own making. Y'all have a lot to learn..." Denise responded.

"Example..." I said.

"Usually we won't ask for the meat but all that tossing and turning in bed will get your ass up so you can put us back to sleep."

"So insomnia means you're horny..." William said.

"Hormones and biorhythms are no joke." Denise said. "Everyone has a frequency. Just be careful because if you open your heart she'll break it. If you open your home she'll tear it down and don't tell these women all of your hopes and dreams."

"Tell me more…" Jerome said to Denise.

"Most relationships have hidden clauses that are triggered when once a break up occurs." Denise said laughing. "Such as the, you shall have the full power and authority to hit it until something better comes along clause, or the I might show up at your job trippin' clause."

"They sure do." My Tutor said

"What about the, you might just pop-up at my house without any negative consequences clause?" William said.

"I hate that one." I responded.

"Or the, you have to be the personal camera man clause." Anthony said.

"Right," Denise said shaking her head.

"Who is taking those candid photos of you?" Anthony said laughing.

"And the standard, now that we aren't together I'm going to the gym and dress fine as hell clause." Jerome said.

"The, I still expect gifts on my birthday and Christmas clause." Denise said laughing.

"Good one…" I said.

"I know…" Denise said. "One thing is for sure; love without respect is disaster."

"They make movies, we make black movies. They make music here we come with black music. They make sitcoms but wait here are the black sitcoms... the culture isn't even owned by us bro." William said gulping down the rest of his drink.

"Very few things are. Just know that the people you admire are often not admirable. The people you dismiss are often heroic." I said.

"Nic, you showed me that a person is bigger than their mistakes." Jerome said.

"The first time came over here, at that barbecue. I heard that aerospace guy talking about how the nation was spending all of this money to colonizing other planets and I was silently enraged. I thought how could we spend all of that money and time on that but IVF is ineffective. He said they had found life in frozen microbes on some planet, but on this planet we can't decide what life is. Some discussions have profoundly affected me. There have been some moments that stay with you. I have found myself here a few times." Denise added.

"Nic does cast a wide net." Anthony acknowledged as he handed out more rum runners.

"What we do is bigger than one or two people." I stated. "There are people who want to be free but no one is saying this is how you get that. There are people who want to stop the hurt and pain, but no one is saying this is how you do that. There are people who want to be aware, but no one is saying this is how you do that.

"Here we collectively talk about how to do and get those things. We help with each other's vehicles, painting apartments, clearing yards but more than that we give out information, we help hurricane proof homes, we give out food and we clean up neighborhoods and beaches.

But before any of that, we all had to take a step back to work on the individual."

"Why?" My Tutor asked.

"Because you save yourself by doing so and that's the process. Nobody is perfect and negative forces will use any imperfection to mute the message. You must build a better you to build better families to have better communities."

"Nic, I've never seen anyone do so much with so little, and they don't have no award for that..." William added.

"I appreciate all of you." I began. "We've just started; we must stick together because there forces are ready to tear us apart. Somehow within the last 20 to 30 years joy was lost. There are people out there who will see a couple or someone happy and it will actually make them upset. They'll want to dig into their lives trying to make them unhappy, simply because they have a hole inside of themselves that they cannot fill. They think organizations, causes will save them from themselves and sometimes it does other times it doesn't."

"It's a sad state of affairs because people are actively profiting off this loss of joy." Anthony said.

"The loss of joy." My Tutor said, biting her lip.

"I won't allow anyone to take my joy." I said.

"...Ooohhh no..." Denise said in a surprised way.

"There is a crisis at the border." My Tutor offered.

"Which scenario is more likely: That a nation that occupied two other nations, while maintaining 800 worldwide bases, engaging in several proxy wars and half a dozen covert regime change operations in South America, Africa and Asia simultaneously, is having an issue with its own border or that somehow these border issues serve the United States' imperialistic purposes?

"Today's word boys and girls is cahoots. All these government agencies and the media are in cahoots. They are in it together... covering for each other. These politicians, open border protesters and advocates are really with the cartels and sex traffickers..." Anthony said.

"So we owe a debt of gratitude to the government for helping solve the problems they created. I think that we are all being tested..." I said.

"Did y'all hear about that tragic shooting?" My Tutor said.

"There is a tragedy every hour..." Anthony maintained.

"But this one was on the news..." My Tutor said.

"News reports just tell us how far gone society is, like what number circle of hell we are in." William said.

"What are you saying about America? America is not violent..." Denise said.

"The hell you say." William said. "If it's a 3-day weekend, they shoot each other up for 3 days."

"All of these special interest groups are unhappy and they all are killing people. We have sonic, infrared, x-rays, guns, intelligence, morals, rights, body guards, educations, security systems, medication, laws, rules and regulations, cameras, the justice system, technology, freedom of religion, social media, senate hearings and sharp sticks and somehow we choose deceit and lies and more often than we should." I said.

"That's depressingly sad." My Tutor said.

"Even sadder is how the emotions get played by politicians." I said. "One side yells that we need harsher punishment and more law enforcement. The other side screams we need more social programs and more funding, either way it's a win-win with no real solution. You are right America is not violent, Americans are.

"People all over the world love America they just hate Americans. We tout American virtue but allow companies to hire Chinese slave labor. Politicians shouldn't be able to introduce or pass laws that are unconstitutional but we the people allow it.

"All that's needed to make Americans think every situation requires some grand gesture or violence is to take an easy solution and complicate it and the next thing you know we have system we can't correct or extract ourselves from so most people just throw up their hands and say. They can vote different, they can choose different, but We The People have consistently chosen violence." I finished.

"I think that in America the ABCs must be taught differently; A is for assault, B is for binary and C is for contraception, but violence that's our trademark." Jerome said.

"If you talk to some people long enough you can talk them into doing anything and believe me the people in power have mind control down to a science."Anthony said straightening his dog tags. "There are no intelligence failures. The people of this nation own half of the firearms in the world, and this causes us look at life differently. Now every tragedy is an opportunity for politicians and an advertisement for corporations.

"They usually start off by saying ban this or that, the media covers the bodies on the ground, speeches are made, sells go up, money pours in to organizations, poll numbers increase, industries get bids and in six months with just enough fanfare to last until the election they pass quarter measures."

"I had this gig, coordinating a middle school dance and let me tell you, these children are dumber and more violent than we ever were." William scoffed.

"You've only been out of school four years; school was pretty rough for all of us." I said.

"Don't hate because you niggas watched the live broadcasts and I watched the reruns." William responded.

"I expect chaos from a corroded society; most of these shooters don't have fathers." I said.

"I know that men take care of babies, they raise children better than some mothers do." Denise said.

"I think we are average," I suggested. "The circumstances and your partner's mentality play a big role in how a child is or not cared for, but if men were given all the same resources and a legitimate chance to raise the children the world would see a difference in how children develop. It may not be the way you would have done it but it will be done."

"It's all fun and games until the child is a wild teenager and the father is powerless due to your years of bullshit..." Jerome said.

"That hurts society." William said. "They don't want minority children to have fathers..."

"Oh the Great and Powerful Theys," Anthony interjected. "Absence of fathers... there is an excuse for everything."

"Well if Americans are really honest, virtuous examples then why do we need a constitution?" I said. "Why do we need a piece of paper telling us how to treat and respect one another? Why do we need a piece of paper telling us not to enslave one another? Aren't people still getting shot over mayo and stabbed over chicken sandwiches? Is your car is still being hit by uninsured drivers? Is your pension fund is still being raided? Is your identity is still being stolen? Are innocent people are still being incarcerated? If America and its citizens were true to these ideals we wouldn't need 99 different bathrooms we would just need one. So what is that paper really doing?

"I hear all that so just imagine what would happen without that paper…" Anthony responded.

"Decent human beings shouldn't need it…" I said. "You can raise your child right. You can want the best for them. All your child does is play video games and do silly social media challenges but it only takes one well-financed, thinking they are special, armed, off their meds child to alter dozens of lives."

"Right they weren't special before the nonsense, but now because of the nonsense you are popular and have followers that praise your strength and courage. They constantly tell you how brave you are." Jerome offered.

"The attention is why the nonsense was done in the first place." Anthony said. "You have no idea how many baristas, burger flippers and stay-at-home children think they are Casey Fuckin' Ryback!

"These children live in a world of exceptions, and everyone has to change for them. They want to be validated for doing nothing. And when they don't get it, they want to destroy everyone. All it takes is for the wrong person to get elected, a comedian to offend someone or for them not to be invited to the dance and they might feel slighted enough to harm people. You don't see people just randomly shooting up CEOs, board meetings or retreats?" Anthony explained.

"Nope." I said.

"Some people have been programmed to shoot up public places." Anthony continued. "Places where people who don't earn a lot of money go; places where they know no one is actually going do anything. Places where cameras have a good view of all the hoping and praying. When you turn around there will be people out here carrying signs and yelling that the police aren't doing their job, that are getting paid to protect us and that they should be trained to deal with this—So for $53,000 they're supposed to run into a hail of bullets to save us from monsters you've raised?

"That's how a person who believes they are saving lives with donated money thinks. It's easy to criticize someone who is the thick of things from behind a mic, a desk or a keyboard. It's easy to talk all of that shit about the police until you need them. When someone is bleeding out, screaming because they are on fire or bullets are whizzing by— what is the average citizen doing? Real soul searching is something that a 22-week training course can't provide.

"Most people just repeat things that play into established narratives to blame the police, the politicians, the gun manufacturers and mental health for tragedies, instead of the teacher that left a door unlocked. Corporations love the violence, the chaos, because it's all profit. Though various ways they encourage the mentally ill; they promote candidates that will keep grow the nonsense. And the thing is that corporations and politicians can't be directly tied to any grand plan of mayhem, but there is a certain capitalistic energy that guides weak minds to cause these events to happen..."

"Voting is a right but you still have to register to do it. They love guns but not when a Black male has one. We need to look at gun rights..." My Tutor said.

"See, what you did... People just skip right over all the bad laws, injustice and wrong things that need attention in their city and state and they go straight to, let's change the Constitution. That's just a political tactic that triggers inaction. That's why government leaders work with loud mouth activist that they can control with the media." Anthony finished.

"A society isn't bad because there is no good there," I offered. "A society is bad because the good there can't help it. Paradise was nice when we stole it. Now all of these unhappy people are being wound up to despise poor and disenfranchised groups."

"So, if every shooting is an advertisement..." William said puzzled. "So how do we stop these ads?"

"Take the advertisement components out of them." Anthony said.

"Look how we all laughed and moved on from what William said awhile ago." I stated.

"Wait... wait...what..." Anthony said. "You right...William could have been a father at 14 and it was a grown ass woman that assaulted him... nobody cared..."

"Man, I got lucky." William said. "That shit is more common than what is reported. A saw a report of a 30 year old woman who had a baby with a 13 year old boy and the authorities didn't do anything to her."

"This is a lot to absorb." My Tutor said looking at the story on her cell phone.

"Of course not, for her the womb was a get out of jail free card and that's exactly what we've been discussing." Anthony said. "Watch the courts make him pay child support..."

"I don't think so..." My Tutor said.

"He can't even work, what are they going to do garnish is lemonade stand money..." I said.

"They'll just wait until he's in his twenties and then they'll hit him with a back child support and a current support order. They get crafty like that down there, see the state will ask for your cooperation but they don't need it and the child is just a walking receipt." Anthony explained.

"So he has to pay for her crime?" Jerome said.

"I mean is it a crime? If these things were crimes wouldn't the authorities be obligated to do something about them? Just watch…" Anthony said.

"This is really fucked up!" Denise said. "This young man's life will never be the same; this woman is out here ruining lives with really no consequences. It's not right, it's immoral and sick but this is what we've allowed society to become. Every day I see people look the other way."

"People only care about children when they can be used for profit and gain." I said. "Sometimes I don't blame William for being bitter or lashing out… This one sidedness hurts all of us."

"What was going on with her?" My Tutor said.

"It shouldn't matter and that's the point." I said. "We are not talking about an adult who can fight back, was inebriated or should have known better we are talking about a child. This leads into the teaching situation teaching…"

"What teaching situation?" My Tutor asked.

"And these teachers aren't teaching children how to math right anyway." William said.

"Hey, teachers do a lot of work." My Tutor uttered from the corner of the couch. "Teachers do the work parents don't want to do and they deal with children that parents can't deal with. Educators are the backbone of our nation; we are overworked, underappreciated and underpaid..."

"I wouldn't call $60,000 a year underpaid and teachers have a union." Jerome said.

"Well, that's what the union tells me. I feel like we are underpaid..." My Tutor said.

"Don't let facts get in the way of what you want to believe." Jerome said.

"Emotions are the same as facts." Denise added. "$60,000 is more than any of us are making."

"What a group talks the most about going on strike, the teachers union and it's because they know they can threaten your child and you can't do anything about it." I said.

"Why does Sex Education need to be taught in the 3rd grade?" Anthony said.

"Science..." My Tutor said.

"What if you'd child isn't ready for that..." Anthony said.

"According to the school district, they better get ready." William quipped.

"A lot of people had their mental and emotional growth stunted in high school which is why they wanted to teach in the first place." Anthony said.

"He is kinda right." I said.

"We have all seen it." William responded.

"Why do you think a majority of young women are in that field, it's not just because they love kids." Denise stated.

"Sexual interactions and adult relationships are hard and confusing for adults who never matured beyond 15 years old."Anthony stared. "Going the teaching route is a way to get back to a simpler, happier time for them. In middle school everything was new and exciting, now they are married with a child or two. In high school they were popular, they could relate and people listened to and respected them. At home they have to talk about budgets, pretend to be interested in someone's day and try not to burn meals.

"These children aren't fully developed and are dealing with the politics of recess and now they have to navigate the deviant mental settings of these twenty something instructors. Everybody around these teachers is at least ten years younger than them and that's only creepy if you're a male. A teacher can be many things, drunk with power, an indoctrinator or they diddling these kids.

"Because of gender society acts like she's helping them with their homework. You think teachers are wearing sexy, tight fitting outfits and low-cut blouses as a part of their everyday wardrobe? Come on now. They want the attention. If these ladies get caught touching a child or two all they'll get is a slap on the wrist, they might lose their teaching license. But, teaching was their side job anyway..."

"Oh... then there is that." My Tutor said.

"Ummm, I kind of wanted to get with a couple of my teachers." Jerome said.

"I tried to make headlines with a few of mine..." Denise slyly said.

"It's not really molestation when it happens to boys." My Tutor said.

"The hell it's not!" I said.

"I mean, it's not looked at as serious." My Tutor said, backtracking

"Don't you think that's a problem?" Anthony said.

"On what grounds do we deny justice?" I said. "Abuse can alter one's thinking and the thoughts of most Americans have been altered! How can one not be abused when America's very tenets are abuse? What have we become, what kind of society have we created that allows the issues of half the population to be discarded?" I said.

"Here, anything could be considered abuse." Denise noted.

"I'm sorry; I can't be abused unless I allow it." My Tutor asserted.

"Boys are abused daily and sweeping things like that under the rug is why society will always have problems." Jerome said.

"When you're married your craziness is contained within your family. When you're single everyone has to deal with your shit." Denise said. "Being married or being a mother puts people into a different category and gives people excuses for certain behaviors. It provides cover for personality and mental health issues."

"I agree. It's probably linked to the constant messaging to children and that has produced adults with mental conditions that they don't really have." I said.

"Why do you mean?" My Tutor asked.

"I mean all the nonsense that people are doing and saying; they aren't doing and saying those things when they are with their mother and father, so is it really mental health…" I replied.

"A lot of them are adults with the social skills of a sophomore or junior in high school. They play politics just like in high school. They get into relationships and even have children because it stabilizes them and keeps them from imploding." Anthony fumed.

"It's not just the teachers." I said. "A lot of parents are guilty too. They're raising monsters that destroy anything they come in contact with. The parents can't wait to unleash them on the world."

"Right..." My Tutor said.

"It seems to me that no matter what, you'll have a relationship with your father whether you realize it or not. It doesn't matter if that person is your actual father or someone you've put in the place of them. It'll be a hard sell but I think parents should get 10% to 20% of whatever the child gets sentenced to." I suggested.

"So the parents get 2 years, if the child gets 20?" My Tutor said.

"That would put accountability back into child raising real quick." Denise said. "That actually sounds reasonable, so why do you think it's going to be a hard sell?"

"Because children can't vote, parents do. They got the student/teacher union but it is really just a teacher's union." I stated.

"True dat." William said.

"Parents aren't going to vote to put themselves in jail, they'll only vote to put your kids in jail; besides the majority of these parents are single moms, who will just blame the fathers for not being around. It'll just become a whole circular reasoning clusterfuck, thus... hard sell." I said.

"You have to be like a politician and sneak parts of it in on them when they are too busy to see it coming." Anthony said.

"So you don't want people voting on any ballot measure that's unconstitutional, you want W-4's to be able to designate what public services their taxes go towards, mandatory non-racial, non-political adulting classes in high school and for teachers to be at least 50 years old." My Tutor beamed.

"We have to try something different." I said.

"Hmmm... It's nice that someone who doesn't have to is thinking about solving problems." My Tutor said.

"I'm not into politics but when you expand it out, I feel like to some extent the sisters are being used because there is an anti-male sentiment, but there is definitely an embedded anti-Black male movement focused on discrediting and destroying the reputations of any high-profile Black man that goes against the grain. To me it seems like this is done so that certain political factions can maintain in control of Black politics." Denise said.

"Oh okay." My Tutor said.

"Do you see white mothers and fathers being dragged on television shows and sports shows?" I said.

"Nope." Jerome said.

"Exactly my point." I said.

"I'm sayin' those white kids were showing their ass at the school event I put together. They jumped a kid because they thought he was throwing up gang signs, the kid was deaf."

"Wow..." Denise said.

"... and you can't pepper spray or taze them..." William laughed.

"Why?" Denise said.

"Because white kids get pepper sprayed at home, by the time they're grown and impeding you in public, pepper spray is like a breath mint to them." William said.

"I have seen a few of them taze and pepper spray themselves…" My Tutor said, shrugging. "They are fighting, pouring glue in the printers and repeatedly putting hand sanitizer in the teacher's coffee."

"I was like, these Generation Brittle kids are wilding. I wanted to grab one of them but the ancestors said, don't do it." William said.

"The people are out of alignment." Anthony stated.

"Alignment with what?"

"Aren't the Magic playing tonight?" Denise asked.

William promptly turned the TV on and the basketball game played in the background.

"My pet peeve is people who make complicated passwords, like they are in the witness protection program or something." My Tutor said.

"Don't nobody wanna to steal your information and you don't have any money." Jerome laughed.

"Yeah, they act like you'll have to do multivariable calculus to steal their information." Denise said.

"They making passwords they know they not gon' remember." William added.

"They compound that by having the nerve to try and make a crazy ass complicated password that they're not going to remember while you're sitting there tryin' to help them." I said.

"Right." My Tutor laughed.

"But see it goes to show you how much they value their privacy and time, but they don't value yours." I stated.

"Man." Anthony said.

"I do think men need more societal protections," I announced.

"It's not like y'all are giving out gift bags and signed baseballs when she leaves in the middle of the night, depending on how we feel, we are liable to say anything. When a dude get trapped like that it's because his mother didn't love him. If she loved him she would have taught him about love, emotions and how to stay away from minus sign people." Denise responded.

"Maybe she didn't teach them that because she didn't know either." My Tutor uttered.

"The ass shaking hustle is real." Denise admitted. "Becoming a mother made me realized that all the shit talking, ass shaking, sucking and drama causin' I did, didn't amount to anything. I realized that my organizing, cooking and cleaning skills were bullshit too and I was salty about it."

"Men have to go through all this extra nonsense and all y'all have to do is lay there…" Jerome sneered.

"Wait a minute… I put in work for who I want to put in work for, but there is a culture of laziness. I shouldn't call it laziness; some people don't know what they are doing and are so self-conscious so they just lay there. It is impressive, but you have to be able to do more than unhook a bra with one hand to get with this. I find things so much better with a good give and take." Denise said.

"She's just laying there; she not even burning any calories." Jerome laughed.

"They can't handle the top. You can really put in a lot of good work from the top." Anthony grinned.

"Most of them act like it's enough just being present and she won't tell you when she nuts." Jerome said.

"See, y'all just can't face the fact that y'all married active sluts." Denise hissed. "I know y'all think not, but there will always be someone with a bigger dick and longer cash."

"Blasphemy!" William coughed into his hand.

"You have nothing to say and yet you won't shut up." Denise said to William. "Honestly, sometimes genuine love fills the void treachery otherwise would have. If they didn't have a child, someone that is their own, they probably would have killed themselves. A relationship can save someone from themselves." Denise continued.

"This doesn't sound nothing like oppression…" Anthony said.

"It's infuriating me." Jerome roared.

"We all have privileges and hardships due to height, skin tone and social gender." Denise said.

"Y'all act like y'all not getting in clubs for free." Anthony said. "Like y'all not getting the benefit of a doubt. Isn't a black woman a double minority when it comes to hiring? Can she have a bad attitude, be out of shape and still get the job, the votes or the role? I am woman hear me roar routinely gets thunderous applause. You don't have to cheer, you don't even have to clap, if I say, I'm a man or demonstrate what they feel are masculine traits, how does it diminish you? What is it inside of a person that makes them work for my downfall? What is it that instantly turns me into a villain?

"Women have thousands of platforms for their issues. They qualify programs and positions that some are unqualified for. They can cry, be emotional and get sympathy. They can commit crimes and not go to jail, they can live a good life with no money… that's easy mode."

"A man can walk into a bar and have his pick of any woman he wants, but he has to be the ruler of the free world. A woman has the exact same power over men but the only thing she has to do is her hair." Denise said.

"If male grievances are being overlooked and disregarded who's really oppressed?" I asked.

"I'm sorry, but as far as American culture is concerned, we haven't been oppressed for a long time." Denise said laughing. "If you are going to give us something, we're going to take it."

"There is no such thing as fairness or equality." I said.

"Isn't that what they call it toxic or mansplaining..." William mockingly said as his Vbzy Kartel, The Ohio Players and Justin Bieber vibe began.

"They call it that, but they are just abusing language, they think it is impregnable wisdom but it's really an unsuccessful copy of virtue. Instead of tackling real problems, they just master a set of propositions to put themselves on the winning side. A winning side that is full of people with unearned virtue, instructing others on how to be virtuous.

"We do not derive pleasure from draining people of theirs. We are not finding minor faults in people. We do not claim to uplift voices but only the ones we agree with. They want to make definitions as broad as possible so opposing sides can argue about every word. We don't use buzz words to confuse or to make others feel less than around here." I responded as I organized my bookshelf.

"Don't you hate making sense?" William said.

"It's a curse." I responded. "There are men out here with no money, and no clue and they're still trying to find a way to get it done. When things go wrong, I'm probably on a short list of people call first...that's a lot of pressure. Yes, some of us are driving around, paying bills and living their lives but they aren't men they're just dudes. They've never had to face any real hardships, the things that build character. Even the men they idolize as alpha men aren't men. They just used the Internet to skip a lot of personal growth."

"If you have power, you are going to use it, period. As you know, women fail up, men not so much." Denise said.

"Tyranny knows no gender." I offered.

"People just can't see the damage they are doing to society." Anthony said.

"There are more Not Sees now than ever…" I said.

"Not Sees…" My Tutor said.

"Yeah… Not Sees."

"I see what you did there" Anthony said, saluting me. "I read somewhere that those tech billionaires are so rich that they lose money if they take a shower or have sex." Anthony said.

"Fuck being rich!" William responded.

"Ant, would you go after a woman that has a man?" I asked.

"What! We created the carburetor, we built suspension bridges, you see the lions in the cages at the zoo…we did that. We put restroom outside the house, we change the borders of countries, we put strawberries in vanilla ice cream…that's our shit. The Van Belts didn't deter us, so why would her having a man deter me. She can still keep her boyfriend." Anthony said.

"Denise do you want something to drink?" Jerome asked.

"Ummm…" Denise replied.

"Nic, what you got in the kitchen to drink?" Jerome asked.

"What? You, Nobody Beats the Wiz face fukka, why you keep offering people my shit?"

"Hey, don't blame me because you weren't raised right." Jerome replied getting up to go into the kitchen.

"Sit your Mr. Belvedere ass down." I said before going into the kitchen and bringing Denise a glass of ice water.

"Pass the blunt." William said.

"You always want to puff on it and it ain't never got enough on it." Anthony said hesitating to pass the blunt to him.

A Woman With Skills

My pastime had become watching people. There were many people who had nothing holding them back, nothing preventing, no one blocking them but they refuse to take advantage of opportunities... I just couldn't understand the lack of motivation, the lack of effort. I was the personification of Bon Jovi's "Livin' On a Prayer" I was limited, but my friends didn't treat me as such.

I had to sink or swim on my own merits. All of us were going to need more than values based on opinion, this is why we used statistics, philosophies, multiple points of views, research and different thought patterns. We operated not from theory, not from talking points; we operated out of real-world application.

Getting hit with various unfiltered perspectives produced different emotions. We all learned something even from people we didn't agree with. These conversations and discussions helped us gain clarity of thought, helped us navigate through this world and society. Everyone got along and we were beginning to evolve. People always come back to the gatherings maybe not immediately but they came back.

"Most people just don't have a good hygiene they think they do but they don't." Denise said.

"That's a big pet peeve of mine." My Tutor said in agreement. We all just looked around the room at each other.

"I don't like women I don't know violating my space, but these moms take the cake. They really out here thinking they are marriage counselors, hair dressers, seamstresses. The mothers I really dislike are the ones who think they can cook, but she's really just holding her family hostage with her subpar chefery. She's just fuckin' up her children's stomach worse than Takis and Flamin' hot Cheetos..." Denise said laughing.

"Social Media's Mother of the Year is out here ruining taste buds." Jerome added. "The kids have to grow up smelling burnt breakfast."

"She's out there bragging about her cooking in front of her husband and he's afraid too say anything..." Anthony joked.

"I mean what else can they do? If they go out all the time they'll go broke. The children were raised with garbo cooking, so they don't know any better either." Denise snickered.

"Every time she's goes into the kitchen everyone in the family gets nervous." I said laughing. "The family is living under a communist regime."

"She bought all those TV gadgets and utensils, she really thinks she's in there burnin'..." Denise laughed; even My Tutor started laughing. "That's the reason older kids beg to stay over their friends house. You don't see other family members asking her to cook..." Denise said.

"But you still love her with her flaws." Jerome said.

"But she won't love you with yours..." Denise countered. "Taking a box meal and chopping up some onions and tomatoes, isn't your signature dish, honey." Denise said laughing. "If the husband has had enough and tries to cook something, she'll be in the kitchen trying to supervise him. Telling him what to add and how long to cook it."

"Why?" I said.

"Because she doesn't want whatever he's going to make to be better than what she can whip up and she wants him to be so annoyed that he won't try to prepare anything else. She doesn't take out the trash,

153

she doesn't clean the kitchen and she doesn't have skills that translate to learning or growing in a relationship or benefitting the family. So don't take cooking away from her…don't do that." Denise said.

"Bro, she said the kid's stomach be fucked up from their mother's cooking." William said.

"She's right tho…mine was." Anthony said.

"My mom had one dish, one… that I'd go back for and it's a dessert." Denise said with a laugh. "Your woman cooks maybe twice a week but she tells everyone that she's breaking her back cooking for y'all every day. Y'all know that estrogen, in general, makes us remember things and specially people in a filing sort of way… that being said…All these bitches be lying!" Denise said, pausing to look around the room.

"I mean we don't all lie…"My Tutor said.

"I like your hair, your jacket your jacket is cute, your baby is beautiful— all lies and for no reason really." Denise said.

"There is a reason." My Tutor offered.

"What is it?" Denise asked.

"Practice…" William commented.

"That's our way of saying that we are looking at you, so here's a compliment...whether or not there are pure lies is open for interpretations." My Tutor said.

"They sound like lies to me…" Jerome offered.

"These bitches be calling other bitches whores and home wreckers when most of the time the name calling hoe is wrecking her own home. Take the man out of the mix and a lot of these people would be bankrupt, on prescription drugs and selling ass. She half-washes the dishes, which is why she needs a dishwasher. She won't even sweep up around the house – well, that's probably not true. She sweeps, she just doesn't put what she sweeps into the dustpan or if she's really high class she has a Swiffer." Denise said.

"I thought you were finished..." I said laughing.

"Nope..." Denise said. "I'm still putting y'all up on game." My Tutor continued to laugh.

"Stop…my side is hurting..." Anthony said holding his side.

"At least we know it's not from her cooking." I said.

"If you are going out with a woman and she has no skills, I mean zero...that's a thankless project. You are basically raising another child— just don't take cooking away from her... let her have that." Denise said.

"At least she tried..." My Tutor said laughing.

"Did she tho?" Denise teased. "When you get home she'll let you know how hard washing clothes all day was, bitch the washing machine washes the clothes you just put them in and walked away."

"She turned a few buttons and waited for 35 minutes." William said mockingly. "Now she's tired."

"Now my side is hurting...y'all need to stop..." Jerome said laughed.

"Don't forget she has to dry the clothes too..." I said.

"How long does that take, an hour... bitch, learn how to multitask." Denise said. "When the clothes are dry it's time for some wine after a hard day's work. And don't let him wash the clothes; she'll say he's not doing it right. He put the detergent in before he put the clothes in or he put it on the wrong setting."

"Again to discourage him and magnify her importance." Jerome said.

"Gold Star for you, you're catching on." Denise responded. "She's passing how to disrespect yo ass down to the kids." My Tutor giggled.

"Damn!" Anthony roared.

"A woman with skills beats a woman with thrills every time," Denise asserted. "Some people really do need a curfew and hard fast rules or there will be chaos. And people like that really can't be alone. They have their hooks in people. They do just enough so you think you are in a partnership, just enough for you to believe they are working their ass off. They are just bidding their time. They just in store after store shopping because they don't want to go home to their husband and kids all the while their family believes she's providing a valuable service."

"And you?" I asked.

"What about me?" Denise responded winking at My Tutor. "I'm a legit 7-course meal. I can cook, bake and a lot of other things. I constantly get offers from guys that want to be broke and miserable just to smell this."

"Well..." I said.

"It's hard for me to pretend. You can have good qualities, you can have money but you still need to be able to communicate. We all use sex to cope but I can't be with someone I don't want to be with. I can't do it for money, comfort, security, a place to stay, status or whatever. Those are the main reasons people are together and the main reason they are miserable."

"Can I use your charger?" My Tutor quietly asked. I went over and fumbled around trying to plug my charger into her phone.

"I'm sayin' don't ask Nic about technology, he's been rockin' the same cell phone for 5 years." William said mockingly.

"So... it works." I responded, finally getting her phone plugged in.

"That it does." William conceded.

"Every device you buy and wear is tied to something unethical or immoral, so how do you decide what to be outraged about?" I fired back. "I can't get my head around purchasing things that I don't understand or control. Why would I want a watch, phone, car or doorbell telling on me?

"You want me to a spokesperson that doesn't use the products I am pitching. You want me to tout prototypes that will never see the light of day. You want me to join the free marketing program of Crypto and A.I. companies to broaden their reach and goose their stock. You want me be one of those content creators whose only creations are commenting on the works of others...

"Maybe you want me to start a podcast, but then I would have to go to the dentist, buy some new clothes, get a haircut, put on lotion, get a brand microphone, video camera and editing software and lighting. Then I could sit behind a desk or have interesting books in the visual frame; invite on diverse voices that repeat the same refrains about people, groups and entertainment.

"And to spice it up I'll invite others podcasters on and have drinks, smoke, use vulgar language while deeply discussing ignorant takes about things that really matter. Maybe I could play video games, do some exercises, comment on the works of others or make weird noises. And I could profit from it by making shows that take advantage of the young, the weak, the angry, the confused and hopeless masses, by feeding into their psychosis. That's some real groundbreaking work right there.

"It's funny but that's where the youth are getting advice. These are the hot takes we've all heard before but this time in a different package. The nature of having to make content every week, every day to earn a living by repeating things we've already heard is rarely insightful or helpful."

"If the microphone is a character on your show, it's just entertainment." Anthony laughed.

"Some of them do act like they are breaking down research papers on those shows." Denise said.

"You can't make love to a podcast." Jerome said. "Woke poetry won't make you a meal. You can't hold hands with a video game console."

"Nic just got a computer last year..." William said laughing. "You're no slave to fashion or trends." William said.

"Why would I want to be manipulated by the unreal or pay top dollar to wear a name on my ass?"

"Nic, be havin' these kids out here like they in Nas' 'I Can' video. You be havin' children outside playing chess, exercising, jogging, doing gymnastics, math and getting their haircut... you Major Payne-in' these kids." William said laughing

"I wish my father took an interest in me like that." Denise said.

"I still don't get why pre-ordering something that's digital is a thing?" William asked.

"You don't have a digital money scheme unless people on the Internet support it." I said.

"After all the years of denying people positions, roles and magazine covers, now companies announce that they are letting one or two dark hued people in— they call it diversity but didn't we have a world war because a group of people were discriminating and selecting people based on race?" I said.

"That's not why we went to war but that is the narrative." Anthony said.

"Why are we celebrating this?" I questioned.

"I don't know." My Tutor said.

"I think that kind of behavior comes from not having anything else." Denise said. "We don't have a powerbase. They built the pop music genre off the backs of Black entertainers from days past and we just accepted it. They took the melodic contours of Black musicians from bygone days and just reinterpreted those works in different ways. It bothers me to no end that Black people have to sing and dance better than everybody else and they have to take off their clothes to even get a piece of the fame and money that these half singing, half dancing stars get."

"It bothers all of us..." I said. "The sad thing is that there is better music behind us than before us. I mean how did we not only lose the word woke, but have the word weaponized against us?" I said.

"I don't even know playa." William said.

"We failed to gatekeep on that one." Anthony responded.

"That's not to say there isn't an anti-black woman movement because there is." I said.

"Coming over here has made me examine things more." Denise said.

"What do you mean?" My Tutor asked.

"White women have been having plastic surgery for a century, but when Black Women regularly started getting these surgeries they became self hatred…" Denise said.

"Okay." My Tutor said.

"People raised by single mothers are the main ones blasting songs that talk about how damaged they are—how ironic." Jerome said.

"Minorities have real issues they aren't singing about rainbows and being afraid to tell somebody that we like them, we singin' about fuckin'." William said.

"If we do sing about rain it's, Can You Stand The Rain or Umbrella Ella-ella,ayy." I said.

"…or making it rain." Denise joined in.

"If the police aren't going to shoot, mistreat or harm their cousin." Anthony said. "They aren't going to shoot, mistreat or harm people in the same group as their cousin, not even if they ran up in the capital, wearing a Viking helmet and fur vest, ya feel me."

"Anthony, this is the best rum runner I've have ever had." I said.

"I second that, do you have some more?" William asked.

Anthony went into the kitchen and returned with a pitcher to filled empty cups.

"Here is what y'all need to keep in mind." Denise said. "Her relationship status doesn't matter… I'd say the majority of the time a woman stirs up a conversation with you it is because she wants something to happen, even if that something is only in her mind."

"I can't believe you're over here explaining your rationale for being irrational." I abruptly said.

"It's not about your money, your car, your clothes or your job it's just her playing with power. Some of y'all are just poor safe crackers." Denise smiled.

"Men are constantly told there is something wrong with them. They are never told that it's okay to be nervous. It's okay to make mistakes. It's okay not to know what to say and they should not be vilified for those things. Some guys simply just don't want to get used and abused. Sex and relationships are important, but being celibate for a time can be therapeutic…" I said.

"A lot of these prizes, not really prizes." William uttered. 'they should have got on that last train."

"They out here reading books on how to meet their Abusemate." Anthony said fist bumping William.

"Whoa." My Tutor said.

"There are a whole lot of guys that have went out on a few date or have gotten married and they think they have figured out women. And people follow them believing that they've cracked the code. No matter your issue there will always be someone that will capitalize from selling game under the guise that they are helping the disaffected masses… those guys just got lucky." Denise laughed.

"Why do ladies call someone controlling whenever they don't want to do something?" Jerome said.

"Why doesn't she want us to put a condom on?" William asked.

"I advocate for free contraceptives, can I get free condoms, lube and spermicidal gel..." Anthony said.

"I hear ya. Society doesn't want us to have babies; society doesn't want to hear about our monthly visitor; society wants us sane, so society needs to make it easier for us to do the things it doesn't want.

Y'all need to talk with your state representatives." Denise fired out while crunching ice in her mouth.

"Why are they getting rid of words with 'man' in them, but keeping bad man, evil man, fisherman and manicure?" Anthony asked Denise.

"Hey, some word and phrases needs to go like, Master Bedroom has ties to slavery..." William said.

"Whoa... don't start that. It's not even true. It's just another lie." I said starring at him.

"You know what you have to do; you've been called out..." Anthony said.

"Research it..." William said somberly.

"We'll wait..." I said. "Anthony, to the blender..."

Anthony blended another batch of drink and refilled cups as William scoured the Internet for information.

"You right... it's not true." William finally said.

"See... how easy that was..." I said.

"Yeah. Ant, thanks for the refill... Why do y'all ladies want the guy that all the other ladies want, but get mad when that guy explores his options?" William said trying to get the heat off of him.

"Why does a man become more accountable when he smokes or drinks but a woman becomes less accountable when doing the same?" Jerome asked.

"William, I have to give it to you, your music vibe is damn good." Denise said ignoring Jerome's question. "This was more fun than my last three dates. When I get home I'm going to burn some sage." Denise said.

"You leaving?" I said, watching Denise.

Denise slowly stood up and straightened her blazer. She picked up her purse and said, "I'm not doing anything just for pleasure. We can be whatever you wanna call it."

I got up and opened the door, "The least I could do is walk you to your car." I said.

"What's the most?" Denise softly said as she walked by me; everyone stared in silence and I walked her to her car.

If you've been to Orlando, Miami or Disney World, you're over it after the second or third time. We did cartwheels, flips, flew drones, had water balloon fights and philosophy discussions in my yard, when I wasn't hosting my Nichole's ever-growing skateboard crew.

The friends went on road trips to trips to Key West, Tampa and a few times we hit up Las Vegas and we had bonfires on the beach. Of course there were also times when we partied so hard that the next day we moved around like a broken video game character stuck between worlds.

Every day at work I listen to people speak about their petty, mundane problems and how unfair life was for them. I was the living embodiment of life not being fair. On top of that two weeks ago I sprained my knee. I couldn't bend my leg. It was swollen and it hurt like hell. I still had to drop my daughter off at school. I still had to drag my ass to class and my boss still made me work. Actually, he said if I didn't come in to work, I wouldn't have a job.

I often had to do back breaking work to make ends almost meet. I did these things just to make sure my bucket of a car functioned well enough to get my daughter to and from school. These employers were going to grinded me up and when I was no longer useful... I'd be tossed away. My knee being sprained allowed me to explore other employment options.

My on-the-job training had started and soon I would be a Medical Repair technician. I would get more money. I would a wear a tie every day. I had just started college and I could see a promising future ahead. I felt like a phoenix rising from the ashes.

The police stopped me at least once a week whether I fit the description or not. I spent at least an hour a week on the side of a road as the officers took their time checking my information. The police would see my uniform and nametag and ask, "Where are you coming from?" From these encounters I learned how to hide my normal assholism. Once my car broke down I had to ride my bike seven miles to work and you guessed it, the police stopped me.

"Where did you hide the bombs?" the officer asked after calling for back up.

"What's to blow up around here?" I responded.

After 10 minutes of sitting on the curb the officer asked me to open my jacket and I did. After I opened my jacket and they saw my semi sweaty suit, tie and medical badge and they immediately sent me on my way.

Sometimes my sisters would come by my apartment to hear some our tamer discussions. Sometimes I allowed them to see some of these interactions. Sometimes my apartment would be packed with as many as fifteen people.

When My Tutor was at my house she did her school work, read child development and psychology books. She laughed and occasionally commented, she never complained. Her eyes widened whenever a colorful drink filled a glass. She always turned down cocktail offers and she didn't smoke. She saw all of this and she never complained about it. The fourth week of tutoring she waived her tutoring fee, but kept ordering supersized meal combos.

One evening, My Tutor and I were at my house going over my midterm review. My Tutor stopped and put her notes down and said, "I don't really remember this part."

"What part?" I asked.

"All of this..." She repeated while making circular motions with her hands.

All of that was what I needed to understand, the drinking and smoking sure as hell weren't going to help me understand it. I had given her over $100 and bought sixteen McDonald's supersized combos and I was still getting a D. I poured myself a drink and thought 'Did I expect her to take a dumbass like me to the Promise Land of passing grades?' I swallowed the liquid, shook the ice cubes around in my glass. I could feel the cobwebs reforming.

Somewhere between pouring the drink and finishing the drink I realized that My Tutor would no longer be of help. I ran the numbers in my head, tuition—two grand, algebra book— $500. As I sat on the floor, I wondered would I have been more or less thoughtful, appreciative, happier, or productive if terrible things had not happened to me all those years ago? Happiness is found in work, in education, in awards but it is also found inside of oneself.

As I watched people, I learned that people aren't as complicated as they nade themselves out to be. I learned that I had more passion for others than I did myself. Before I could get too deep into doubting myself there was a knock at my door and my friends and I did what I always do and I dropped My Ex-Tutor off in the morning.

Sent ta Mental

There are certain people that simply can't function without dysfunction. They have to repeat themselves; they have to cause drama; they have to be involved in some kind of nonsense; they have to lie; they have to cause chaos. They use public platforms to lob unfounded accusations, to charge people that haven't been charged publicly, to call things that aren't crimes... crimes.

In the midst of the nonsense were The Gatherings; they put life and decisions in context and kept me focused, kept me sane... They kept all of us sane. I was working, I was going to school, but for the most part society had turned its back on me.

My algebra class is 4:30 in the morning. The thing is that if you really want something you'll get up and go jogging at 6 in the morning, you'll take that break of dawn class, you won't complain when you could have, you'll put in the work, you'll make a plan—one dribble, one shot, one play at a time. I had to keep going, and I had to do so with my head held high. For me every day is a battle, some days I win, sometimes I lose, I might even get knocked down, but I can't break. I have to keep pushing forward.

A week later after my tutoring experiment failed I had another gathering at my house. People from around Florida were scheduled to be at my apartment. They drove past homes with big yards that people paid top dollar for and don't even use, except to decorate for holidays. Anthony arrived at 6 pm, which was a little early for my gathering.

"I received medals for the people I've saved, and nightmares for those I didn't. Am I not supposed to be upset? I don't ask forgiveness from my choices, just understanding." Anthony said.

"Sometimes there are no easy answers." I quietly said to Anthony.

"Two tours and a year in Venezuela to fight for flag and country and I gotta deal all this VA's bullshit paperwork." Anthony lamented.

"They have those help groups…" I said to him as I continued to tidy up my apartment.

"I've been to those meetings. All they do is say things like, 'My depression is getting worse' and 'My PTSD is acting up'. At those meetings they talk of depression and trauma like it's an old friend. I don't feel like being around that type of energy, it rubs off on a person." Anthony said.

"Are all of those meetings like that?"

"Mostly, some people need that type of help but then they start hugging. I'm not depressed enough to be hugging random people. The only thing that bothers me is the way family court works. Melanie went down there saying that I'm crazy, when she's the one who aborted our third child when I was overseas; she literally wrote that in a post script, like an afterthought. Do they have a group for that? You know she didn't even pick me up from the airport when my tour was over?

"She said she'd moved on. She said my military salary was inadequate. The salary and our vows weren't enough to keep my wife from being built for the streets run through and run over so many times, ain't no curves left. The court gave her 33% of my paycheck and I have limits on when I can see my children." Anthony confided. "This is not what I fought and almost died for, is it?"

"Does she have an unstable living condition?" I asked.

"No. I pay for that."

"Does she have a documented history of illicit drug use?"

"It seems like it." He said.

"Does she have diagnosed mental health issues?"

"I think so."

"She has that right..." I said.

"And what rights do I have?" Anthony said.

"It seems that we have rights in the collective general sense; not always in the individual sense." I sadly responded.

Anthony was oddly reflective about his shortcomings. He spoke openly about dealing with family court and his ex-wife, his voice quivering at times. He didn't regret having his children, only his choice in the mother. The perfect life he thought he'd have was now an evaporated shadow in his mind.

"You're going to get through this; it's going to take time." I said.

William arrived with his wireless speaker repeatedly blaring Muhammad Ali's famous words, "The Champ is here!" He cut off his music and greeted us and then he put his backpack on the floor.

"I had to put a dude down the other day." Anthony said. "He thought I wouldn't get out of my work truck and make him exercise, the odds weren't in his favor. I also met a nonbinary Pokémon."

"So there is no such thing as too far…" I said.

"I think that's what they are aiming for..." Anthony responded. "When I was an EOD, I saved lives in the harshest environments. I disarmed improvised explosive devices, neutralized chemical threats and rendered nuclear material safe on the ground and in the water. And yesterday I had to deal with the judge believing every lie my ex-wife says about me. The judge reduced my visitation to 25/75. Not being in my children's lives is not worth my two Joint Service Commendation Medals and Bronze Star."

"EOD, I thought you worked with the outside apartment people." William said sitting down.

"What?"

"The homeless."

"I work with the unsheltered..."

"Unsheltered, that sure sounds like homeless." William said. "Why is it that if one of the unhoused hurts someone they get sympathy? If I hurt someone I go to jail and lose my job. Why give someone living in the gutter money, when the people working in stores and behind counters have legit and obvious need for funds?"

I didn't really have a good answer for him.

"Unhoused or unsheltered persons live on the streets, some push shopping carts or live in tents, cars or abandoned buildings. I help them get assistance like healthcare or transitional housing." Anthony said.

"How's that going?" I said.

"It's a losing battle; I'm seeing more and more children on the streets." Anthony said as he finished his cocktail creations. He handed William and me a glass. "People die living outside."

"So what's the problem?" William asked as Anthony sat down on the couch.

"I'm trying to get these department heads to give a damn. They have huge caseloads and expanding waistlines. People are just a file number to them. I'm trying to get them to understand that fixing the state's unsheltered issues can't be done with sleeping bags, tents, blankets and politics. Department heads are far too entrenched to understand the unhoused need to be classified." Anthony said.

"There are classifications?" I asked.

"Yes. Some struggle with rent prices, abuse issues, debt and low paying jobs, some just need a little extra help and the rest they can do themselves. There are those who are in need of therapy or they are addicted. Some people just stopped by the homeless encampments for the drugs and ended up staying.

"Some of them can't be housed with others because they may pose a danger. Incentivizes are pointless because some of them believe working, paying taxes and going to school is for fools. They are against the social order. They don't want to be slaves to society. Some believe that they have evolved beyond the four walls of a home. At times, I can see why some of them have had it with systems; I can see how a person would opt out of that."

"All I know is that poverty sucks when you want more." I said.

"So they aren't just crazy?" William asked.

"There is surviving and there is living. Some people just have competing ideals of liberty. Maybe mental illness presents itself differently due to age or being hormonal. Perhaps, midlife crises maybe tied to mental illness." I interjected. I said this because I had learned just as much from the poor as I had learned from the well off.

The majority of the world's population came from poor people. I look down on no one; everyone's experience is valid to me." I said.

"I mean psychopaths…" William said correcting himself.

"You can't be called a psychopath unless you commit a crime." Anthony continued. "To answer your questions, no, not all of them are psychopaths but the administrators tend to lump them into one group or put them in facilities that are no better than large scale half-way houses. My bosses constantly create situations that I have to de-fuckafy. I do what I can, but the half brains above me are Autobots one day and Decepticons the next, they won't listen to reason.

"You know bureaucracy is like a child the more you feed it bigger it gets and it just keeps growing so you have to keep feeding it. These issues are why we have bureaucracies so they want to keep the issues."

"Solution…" I questioned.

"Nic's ass is over here trying to put people out of work by fixing problems." William stated.

"Within a populace of disintegrated minds and depravity, we need more humane outcomes. We need outcomes that lead to getting resources, training and medication attention to those who need it. Not just moving them around or locking them up, there are fire crews, woodworking and brush clearing programs, Everglades' conservation crews and vocational schools. And for those that can't or won't do those things we need to personalize their recovery, personalize their reinsertion back into society…otherwise they'll just be moving them from one hell to another." Anthony said.

"I hear you making an argument, but the majority of those programs are in the northern part of the state…" I countered.

"That's why it's going to take a lot of psychologists and a lot of policing."

"And some law changing... There is no way you forcibly move people, hospitalize and medicate them without violating their rights." I said.

"What else can you do when there isn't enough housing and not enough space…" William said.

"We are told that there isn't enough housing and there isn't enough space, but a lot of land in America is not developed or lived on. Only like 5% of the land in American is urban."

"Really..." I said.

"Damn!" William said.

"Yes, the housing market, real estate, capitalism, zoning and politics cast a huge mind fog. It has people wrongly believing America is crowded. We have the space; we don't have the will. Businesses and nonprofits make a lot of money from this situation. They are lucrative contracts to feed, house and advocate for the unhoused to be awarded. That's why I say we are too far gone for piecemeal measures. If we want to really change things, we will have to have to violate some rights and make people upset, and hopefully it'll just be temporary." Anthony offered.

"But that would make your solution just like the solutions of those we fight against. They will say that the end results justify the violations of the one thing we hold sacred, our rights." I said.

"When in Rome." Anthony said. "Either life moves you or removes you."

"Let me guess, men will be the prime ones getting their rights violated, right…" William said.

"That's the only way the public will buy it. What I am talking about can't be executed from the bottom. It cost the state about $25,000 to house an inmate and it cost the state about $32,000 per homeless person, so the money is there."

"$32,000 a year!" William said, looking up from his Earth, Wind and Fire playlist.

This statement from Anthony made me choke on my pink lemonade cocktail. I knew that Florida was spending about $9,000 per student but this was new information for me to absorb. Florida has about 100,000 inmates and spends 2.5 billion dollars a year to house them.

"How many homeless are there?"

"Florida has about 27,000 unsheltered persons." Anthony answered.

"What!" I said clearing my throat. "That's about a billion of dollars."

"That's like; three people per unhoused person, one officer per inmate and the children have 1/20th of a school teacher." William said. "That's a hell of a racket."

"Just imagine how many people, how many teams, how many offices, how many departments, how many systems, how many organizations, how many heads of organizations and how much money is spent dealing with problems we could take care if we just pulled together instead of pulling apart?

"These are self-sustaining industries. It's not just housing; it's hospitalizations, emergency room fees, clothing, feeding, providing various services for almost 30,000 people. You have to pay for the department, the facilities, the administrators, the offices and ground level coordinators like me. If you want something done, it's going to cost the public." Anthony said.

"So, as a nation we basically take a societal problem, add politics, money and incompetence to it and build an industry that will always require more of the same." I said.

"When that virus first hit people wanted the simplicity of the single shot vaccination." Anthony said over the noise of the blender. "People ran around with a sticker on their clothing or they'd arrogantly say 'I got the single shot'. We use the single shot one on the unhoused population, because we don't know if they are going to come back. We can at least ensure one vaccination."

"Did they fill out paperwork to get the shot; did they know why they needed to get the shot?" I said, watching Anthony blend in the kitchen.

"Some of them don't even know where they are." Anthony responded. Our tagline is that, 'Housing should be stable, accessible, safe, healthy, energy efficient and above all affordable'. A mission statement this broad virtually ensures that there will never be enough housing. Look at a zoning map; look at the single-family zones. I am dealing with people that have PTSD, depression, mania, ADHD, schizoaffective disorder and bad luck and my reports are being ignored."

"People aren't living their values because they have concerns." I countered.

"Concerns…concern that once someone is lifted up they won't need your platforms anymore?" Anthony said as he handed me a strawberry vodka infused smoothie. "When you have all the power will you build affordable housing, are you going to distribute resources equally? Nope. When you have all the power you get really good at making signs and showing up at marches.

"Limbic capitalism does have us selecting the brightly colored, glistening, arousing, morally questionable, calculated chaos." I said. "Nuanced bullshit is still bullshit and it seems that some people in leadership positions are card carrying members of the bullshit-a-lots. We have sitting members of Congress not showing and saying what they are going to do about inequity, injustice or strengthening the nation...no... Instead they're posting derogatory memes and disparaging judges on our tax dollars. It doesn't seem very congressional to me.

"These industries and the variations in education is why I believe people don't actually share the same concepts of even the most basic things. They think they are hearing and talking about the same things that they come from a common foundation, but they aren't That's why there is so much disagreement."

"What do you think, Anthony?" William said.

"I mean, corporations want people to eat unhealthy, they need for there to be a drug crisis and they need unstable family structures and confusion because it brings more profit and more control. This stuff isn't hidden anymore, but they just won't come out and say that they need racist, they need sexist, they need assholes and they need violence for content, for views and for ratings... so of course they want those things to exist and grow.

"If it ain't Black and White, it's Men and Women, it's Muslims, it's Hispanics, it's Yellow Peril, and it's the words you use. It could be the god you worship... all the way down to what school you attended and where you were born. These industries, these systems are not playing, capitalism has all of us right where it wants us and it's not letting go.

"We are dealing with systems that thrive from exploitation and the most irredeemable people seem to also be the most philanthropic. For every $1 a business gives to charity, tax payers pay .75 of the donation because of tax rules. 5% is the minimum amount of donated money that has to actually go to whom the charity is for; the rest can go to the foundation or organizations, who often invest in the very companies or situations that caused the need for the charity in the first place." Anthony said.

"Using private property to alleviate the evils that result from the institution of private property is immoral." I said. "The priority of capitalism is growing the economy, not serving the people."

"Some of it is political, some of it is capitalism, and all of it is bullshit. From what I have experienced, most agencies form because people suck at their job and they'll continue to suck at it no matter who is in charge." Anthony countered.

"What do you mean?" I inquired as I tasted the smoothie.

"Most of the things that go wrong, do so on the executive side. How many funded and staffed organizations have been created within the last century to prevent war, famine, poverty?"

"There have been a lot of them…" William said.

"Have they prevented the things they were created to stop?"

"No." William replied.

"I remember protesting in the streets, for weeks, in the cold." I said. "As I look around, I can't help but ask, didn't we already fight this?"

"Well it was profitable, so it's back reformulated." William said.

"They are out here complainin' about how it's racist to not be allowed to be racist." I said.

"No one pays their taxes to be treated unequally and unfairly." Anthony said, pouring another smoothie. "Look how the government uses social media to police speech and launder propaganda. Harassment, hate speech, bullying...all they have to do is censor a little bit every day, until all people know is censorship. I just don't know how we got to a place where we have allowed social media to be the realm of censorship and shadow banning."

"On some level, everyone is a hypocrite." I stated, drinking the rest of my smoothie. "Look at the people that always talk about second chances, God breaking chains and shaking prison walls and that's the main group trying to put bodies in prison."

"Justice isn't guaranteed; that's why I doubt— my doubt, because sometimes the bad guy is you." Anthony said. "It's easy to identify the evil outside. We do that so anything we do to bring about justice is justifiable. There are many leaders who history remembers for doing terrible things, when they only did what their people cheered for the most. What I can tell you is that any movement that leads to corporate gains is an industry scam. Enlightened human beings have done terrible things in the name of progress."

"Is that how you got those medals?" William asked.

"That's classified. I could tell you but then I'd have to kill you." Anthony said as he sat down. I've seen Anthony neutralize many civilians so I wasn't certain if he was joking or not.

HUMBLE.

Sometimes the homegirl brings her homegirls over and the gathering's becomes a whole thing. When a friend brings over someone they are dating, you already know they want to impress them. Sometimes as a group we would go to a club, drive up the coast or to other parties. I could only go on a third of these adventures due to my full time dadness.

William usually had his hands on my surround sound system all night; his mode is unique and imaginative. William started to play DMX's "Where My Dogs At?" as Jerome arrived. Before he could sit down Kyle Miller arrived, dropped off by his fiancée, with two children in tow. Jerome and Kyle fist bumped everyone and Anthony handed out smoothies. Kyle's red hair was crew cut, spiked in the front with a short beard. He was 5'5" and stocky, with green eyes. He is a stay-at-home dad. Kyle is Caucasian, Jessica; his fiancée is a black woman.

"People with weak personality settings shouldn't take mind altering drugs. It will expose the weakness in your personality, don't take LSD." Jerome said as he rolled a strawberry flavored blunt.

"Put a video game in while I fire it up." Jerome told Kyle as he eyed my video game setup.

"Last time we played, you whined about how you kept pressing the A button, but your kart wouldn't go." Kyle remarked

"I've been practicing. I'm not losing this time."

"I ain't gon' lose to no cripple!" Kyle stated.

"I'm not a cripple, it's a limp," Jerome replied as Kyle handed him a video game controller.

Kyle always brings his own, well-kept video game controllers and each one had a name. He doesn't allow anyone to touch his controllers, not even his kids. I can't blame him, I don't like people putting their grimy hands and crusty fingers all over my controllers either, but I'm the host so my controllers aren't the cleanest.

Jessica is an office manager; they both have a child from a previous relationship and they have a two year old girl together. Whenever Kyle was allowed to get away from the house, he would come over to my house. Jessica only came over to pick him up or drop him off.

I had brain games, board games, sports, Family Feud, fighting games, driving game and adventure games, multiplayer games were more conducive to our party atmosphere. A few of my friends could have been professional video game players but that would have turned gaming into a job instead of a way for them to vent. These games didn't always start over at next gathering, you might just show up and you are already down a lot. Although every gathering is different someone always embellishes records and scores.

Somehow within these walls competition was fostered, even the petty kind. We were all good, but some of my friends were specialist. You are going to have a tough time beating Anthony in any game that deals with the military or is strategy based. Kyle is unstoppable in fighting games. Denise likes to complete adventure games, she also likes to headshot people with no reaction on her face. Everyone that regularly came to my apartment talked shit, simply because they are good at it.

The new generation wakes up every day loud, well-funded, geared up and like most things in society... soulless. I can't really blame them; their parents ruined the world's sense of discovery and destroyed the wonders of the world. New gamers believe that if you aren't studying frame data and sour spots that you are inferior. Egaming be damned we had gaming sessions so intense it would make these sponsored egamers soil their pants. Jerome had a fake gold championship belt made that could be won or lost.

These youngsters won't acknowledge that it was our 'old school', non-micro transaction, unmodded tricks that led them to pick up a video game controller in the first place. When these young gamers trot into my apartment talkin' shit, it's not going to end well. Were my friends and I wrong to delight in the youthful screams of disbelief as these youngsters lost a variety of games to me and my friends? Nope.

Sometimes my friends would wager money on these video game matches. If someone picked up a video game controller they battled as if their pride was at stake. Occasionally the losses were so horrifically bad that the loser wouldn't show their face for months. We don't quit, we had to be beaten, but even the losses made us better players. Besides, fathers don't have the luxury of quitting. If you were over my house often enough you might just leave you controller here. You might walk into my house but you might limp out. It's like Beyond Thunderdome— two men enter, one man leaves.

"He's not even looking at the screen!" Jerome said, marveling as Kyle stared at him while beating him in the game.

"He's over here doing rapid jabs, and I'm punishing him... every time." Kyle laughed.

"I told you not to pick up the controller, it's above me now." I chuckled.

Michael Smith picked up Brandon Lewis and they arrived at my apartment about 8 pm. They were still in their work clothes.

"I was wondering when the Wonder Twins were going to show up." William exclaimed as they entered.

Brandon came in looked around and starts smacking his lips.

"This guy is already salivating." Jerome said.

Would you say that Cab Calloway is the father of Hip Hop?" William asked Brandon at the door.

"I would." Brandon responded.

"Then you may enter." William said moving out of his path.

"How's Nichole?" Brandon asked me.

"…Getting big. Sit wherever you like." I said as I moved my weights into the corner.

"How old is she now?"

"6."

"How are your kids Jerome?" Brandon asked.

"My son is doing well, but my 7 year old daughter has a special ability to disrupt. She walks into classrooms and disrupts others. I pray spanking comes back…" Jerome said, raising his hands to the sky like he was someone's old aunt."

"Whoa…I'd be terrified everyday if I had a daughter." Brandon admitted.

Brandon was single and about 5'9", a little shorter than I was. His hair was buzz cut and lined up. He was fit and he liked to go to the gym. He spoke in a slow authoritative manner, his skin complexion was similar to mine. I no longer had a tutor, so I figured having more intelligence around would rub off on me in time for my finals.

Last year Brandon was a professor at the University of Florida in the Entomology and Nematology Department, now he's in the Biological Science Division at Fort Pierce. He works with insects but he has a running, shrieking fear of insects. He always tries to educate us on insects and other creatures. He says that the way we harvest food is damaging the planet's ecosystems and that 50% of insect species are declining, and a third are endangered. First the insects go, then us, he said.

"You look taller than usual, are those new shoes…" Jerome said, accosting Michael as he entered into my apartment.

"These are cognac leather shoes I just got them, they stylish, right?" Michael said trying to pass Jerome.

"Nah man, this is the tallest you've ever been. You almost looked me in the eye when you came in." Jerome said again, blocking Michael's path.

"Why are you making a big deal about my shoes, I came to chill…" Michael said.

"What does Marcellus Wallace look like?" Jerome said, drawing Michael closer.

"Nah man, don't start that." Michael said.

"There's a heel inside of them, right…" Jerome quietly said into Michael's ear.

"Man, come on, let's just vibe…" Michael said his eyes pleading with Jerome to end the conversation. Jerome looked Michael up and down and moved out of his way.

"Y'all ova there actin' real niggerish right now." William said.

"How's the project going?" I asked Michael when he sat down.

"We are doing some amazing things." Michael responded.

Michael was book smart. He had a number of degrees and a government security clearance. He always wore his hair short and he usually wore suits, even to the gatherings. He stood out that way. Michael's skin was probably the darkest of all of us. He was also the shortest at 5'4". He spoke quickly and sharply. He had been married a little over a year. He worked for NASA on the Mars Project based on Merritt Island. He randomly says things like chicken strips or various sandwiches.

"Vaginas come standard." William said randomly.

"Word…" Brandon dryly said his eyes bulging.

"Why you gotta say hurtful things?" Anthony said to William.

"Because…" William responded.

"I avoid women who wear symptoms rings, have shaved heads, armpit hair and the ones that look like 90s drag queens. I don't tolerate manly women, so I be skippin'." Brandon said sitting down.

"Skippin'…" William responded.

"Yeah, skippin' to younger women…" Brandon said.

"This guy comes in talking about masculine vagina." Anthony said shaking his head.

"What does it mean to be in love?" Kyle said, momentarily looking up from the video game.

"You in the wrong apartment for that kind of question." Jerome said.

"Is your personal happiness more important than the freedom and well being of others?" I asked those assembled in the room.

"No." Brandon said as he scanned my apartment. "When you don't have any values and principles, you have to oppose anyone who does."

"Why you still coming over here?" Jerome randomly asked Michael.

"I come over here because I can't talk about relationship issues, police shootings and political things at work; those Blacks are more concerned with the killings going on in Sudan and Ethiopia." Michael said. "I come here so I don't have to spend my free time discussing wave function. Now, who's going to hand me a drink?"

"Damn that… Jerome, why are you here?" Anthony questioned.

"I'm just here so I won't get fined." Jerome responded.

"Nic I know you got some nut milk in your refrigerator…" William said smirking as he got up. William went into the kitchen and came back with a drink for Michael. "No nut milk."

"You niggad make more money than all of us put together and you come over here empty-handed." Jerome stated to Michael and Brandon. "Hell, even Kyle brought Absolut."

"Empty handed…we brought our brains. Ya whack a mole faced peasant." Brandon said. "I ain't like you; you the type to bring over food and then eat it all up…"

"He right, you not supposed to be the first one to touch it…" William said.

"There still be some left." Jerome said defending his actions. "Y'all know I have a high metabolism."

"… Brandon, go ahead…" Michael said smiling. Brandon reached into his coat and started passing out Cohiba Esplendido. "Nic you know we wouldn't do you like that, unlike some people. I know Jerome didn't bring anything." Michael said sarcastically.

"Michael, I thought yo black ass was too good to come ova here?" Jerome said.

"I see you're still as rude as ever, you're uncouth." Michael remarked.

"Let's go outside and fight in the grass." Jerome quipped at Michael.

"I'm good." Michael said picking up the drink William brought him.

"Why you want to fight him outside? You silver back gorilla face looking fukka." Brandon said.

"Because…" Jerome smiled.

"You two always fighting like cats, and cats. Don't let the suit fool you, he grew up in this hood." I said, smelling a cigar.

"Yeap, you don't get that kind of swag unless you're from North Miami." Anthony said.

"This ain't Sanford. This ain't the hood no mo. It's middle class now." Jerome said.

"And this is straight from the government's marijuana fields in Mississippi." Michael said, tossing a medium sized bag to Jerome. "What ya know about rolling down in the deep…"

"Now you're talkin' my language…now you're talkin' my language…" Jerome said, smelling the contents of the bag.

"I thought that the government growing marijuana was a myth." William said.

"That's what you get for thinking." Michael smugly said.

Anthony went back into the kitchen to make more smoothies.

"We're not staying too long. I have plans at the strip club." Brandon said.

"Strip club... You should feel guilty...ashamed..." I replied

"I do.... after all the twerking, clapping and throwing it back..." Brandon smiled.

"It's sad that I can't even go on social media any more. It's an outrage exchange. It's an emotional stock market." Michael said loosening up his tie.

"Reporters won't ask the right questions, even if they have the videos and receipts. The media is talking about how Florida schools are banning books... All school boards ban books, it's called a curriculum." William said.

"Outrage equals engagement for social media." I said. "The masters use psycho politics, emotional blackmail and collective fits of anger to move the masses. Outrage is a resource, a currency that has given rise to outrage entrepreneurs. Culture evolves faster than biology, but that's not what is occurring so it has to be a socially sponsored mental illness, a social contagion that causes unwell people to believe that everyone should just satisfy and validate how they feel, they don't even care that there are individuals on the other side of their outrage.

"The same people that claim to be marginalized turn around and marginalize others. People have found utility and commerce in outrage and as a result social media has made unreasonable human reactions into acceptable things. The math breaks down like this: 60% of people are followers, 25% of people are slightly aware, 10% are gatekeepers, 4% have true leadership qualities and less than 1% runs everything. We are just dots in a network of other dots, afraid of our own insignificance all of us waiting on someone else to correct things— held prisoner by thought."

"Irrational impulses are easily manipulated…" William said.

"Word…" Brandon said without looking up.

"No matter who it hurts, or if it's true?" Anthony said.

"It's true to them," I responded. "Ideologies give the disenchanted a home."

"Hey, some people are just messed up." Jerome said, gesturing to Anthony for another smoothie.

"JJ take it easy on those smoothies they sneak up on you." Anthony said, handing him another smoothie.

"You know yousa lightweight. You know how you get, throwing up on people." I said.

"I want this drink, and another one." Jerome said grinning as he quickly downed the smoothie. "I got da drink in me goin' back-to-back."

"How can people not be messed up?" I said refocusing the discussion "People have to deal with so many screwed up things at once that you have to take medication to desensitize yourself. A million people accessible at the touch of a button, you just have to type it in and it's there. We weren't meant to see thousands of people in a day; the brain can't process all of that information in a meaningful way, so it simplifies things and starts putting people into a box. Pornography drove the development of the Internet and the Internet became like pornography, all the pleasure without responsibility."

"The world has always been in a state of transition. Only now those that promote chaos are blurring grand narratives to benefit new platforms. People used to lead others to social change, now algorithms do." Brandon said.

"Manipulating people is easy, look how they got all those people to go to that fake island party. It's just easier to point the finger where the least sympathy will be…" Michael said.

"That's because everyone is damaged with past traumas, stress or mental health issues. It's hard to communicate with people who have trauma." Brandon said.

"Doesn't trauma affect the ability to connect to past lessons in a useful way?" I said.

"Trauma is psychological material that can't be used." Michael said, finishing his drink and gesturing for another. "Some people are able to reshape traumatic events as opportunity."

"Y'all trippin', our ancestors had trauma and look what they created… These people just need to get over it… it already happened… move on." Anthony countered.

"You never know anything could be the last straw that makes a person lash out, so we have to be understanding." Michael said.

"If the same doesn't apply to men being abused how could it be real?" Anthony responded.

"So bullying isn't real…" Michael questioned.

"Bullying is real; America does it to other nations all the time. The problem is the time, money and effort spent on campaigns and laws to tell you not to do it or that it's wrong are disingenuous when we are the main bullies on the planet." Anthony stated.

"Do you ever lose?" Jerome said to Kyle.

"He tasks me, and I shall have him!" Kyle stated with a grin.

"He was born with video game controllers for hands." I remarked.

"I knew I shouldn't have played him." Jerome said, waving his hand in a request for another smoothie.

"You didn't know enough to stop." Kyle laughed.

"All my life I had to fight short people." Jerome said dramatically, looking at Michael. "Short people really do have that complex… Seth Green, Sylvester Stallone, Stalin, Napoleon, Bono, moms…"

"Too funny…" William said laughing.

"My wife, Joan has it where it counts, the mind, the hips and thighs. I'm trying to have smart children. Every study shows that women with fat hips and thighs have the most intelligent children." Michael stated proudly.

"Is that so, then why are curvy women the targeted the most and their children the most killed." Jerome said.

"I can't deny that some of this is engineered. I wonder if we are intentionally being made dumb." Michael said.

"Naw you ain't getting off that easy, Omega-3, fatty acids in the hips and thighs is not the same as being fat." William said as he started making unsuccessful air hugs. "For some people there are extra layers of protection."

"There you go…" I said.

"No, this ain't a fat joke you got to think bigger." William said grinning.

"I see what you're doing." I said shaking my head.

"This is a two-fold argument." William said again making air hug motions.

"I rebuke you." I said.

"Hey Nic, some shots you just can't block." Anthony said laughing at my futility.

"I mean enjoy your life but they be enjoying it too much." William said. "Not conventionally attractive people would be happier if they dated each other…"

"Not conventionally attractive people…" Jerome said.

"…ugly people." William said. "Hey don't get mad at me it's a new day, ugly people don't have to stay ugly. When you know that your child is going to be facially challenged you have to make sure they know to add, subtract, multiply and divide. They better be smart, have a skill, speak properly and be able to type fast cause they gon' need to put in some work… 9 to 5 status and some women just don't want to put in the work."

"Which women?" Brandon asked.

"The ugly ones..." William stated as we all started laughing. "Face it, some women shouldn't get anything easy in life, some women should have to change tires, pay for dinner, pay for furniture movers and some women shouldn't have doors open for them..."

"Oh man, you gon' burn in hell for dat." I said laughing. I immediately went into the kitchen and grabbed a bag of apples. I handed the bag to William.

"William goin' full Kang the Conqueror," Brandon laughed.

"Sir, your application to join the niggaverse has been accepted." Anthony laughed patting William on the back.

"Things are going downhill because we keep allowing nonsense to happen and not saying or doing anything about it." William said. "Nic, you of all people should be up on this. You all about the kids, right. So think about how many children have shitty lives or are depressed because their parents are fat or don't take care of themselves. Everyone is too afraid to say anything.

"No one bats and eye when women straight up call men ugly, fat, skinny, creepy, unattractive, monsters, gremlins or incels but if I say some women are so messed up that they have to settle for a career or single motherhood because no one wants to start a family with them, or if I say there goes a woman with hooves or look at those fatletes… People come out of the woodwork to attack me.

"And somehow I'm a whole ass marvel villain— the sheer fuckin' hubris. We have all heard women say things like 'Nic has too many muscles, Brandon is too nasty, Michael is too short, Anthony is too experienced, Jerome is too divorced, Kyle is too ginger and I'm too young and that's okay to say… I'm not being an asshole, I'm saying' that you're being an asshole by trying to make me look like an asshole…asshole. I didn't even say when you are pushing maximum density you gotta share people….it is what it is."

"Well… you have a point." I said taking back some of the apples and brushing imaginary dirt off of his shoulders.

"Man, this herb got my brain firin' in ways I can't even understand. I mean…if it takes away from my spins I hope it takes away from my sins." William said taking a bite of an apple. "These apples are good."

The conversations and laughter soothed my frustrations with my classes. When the pressure is on you can't really see it on my face or in my behavior, but I'm no robot. I often experienced a wide range of emotions at the same time, you just couldn't tell. I wasn't doing well in school; I was beginning to think that maybe I was just not smart enough for college, that I didn't deserve any more than what I already had. I wouldn't allow those around me to give up, so I couldn't either.

The Walking Dead

Most of us grew up together, but when it came to our tastes in what we found attractive there was only minimal overlap in our preferences. Anthony and I were international, in regards to dating and I didn't discriminate. Now every now and then for entertainment purposes we would have our girlfriends hook up a friend with their friend, and of course we would praise them before hand. You could bring a date to my house, but the vibe doesn't always lend itself to being boo'd up. When there are multiple couples it works, but if you are the only couple and you are trying to party it usually doesn't go well.

When someone brings their significant other to the gathering, the other dudes present feel like they have to marginalize their talents and gifts. You can't be dancing all up in the videos. You can't piss in the middle of the water, only near the porcelain. If someone did bring their date over they'll be fighting over what she's wearing and what he's saying in less than hour.

The drama castrates the vocabulary, causes different actions and quells the inebriated singing. Sometimes simply their presence can throw a person off their game, I have been thrown off many a night. It is hilarious when a friend is playing a video game underneath their girlfriend' disapproving glare. Often, you can just see and feel the passion and the energy leaving a person's video game ferocity.

They can't block, they can't shoot, they can't drive straight, they just play right, it's silently comical and it will be exploited. You're about to have a long night of getting your ass beat by those who didn't bring a distraction with them, it's probably best to not play. So not bringing them was an unwritten rule simply for the sake of competition.

There are some discussions you might not want them to hear. The conversations and interactions between friends can often be intense. Here people could express different views and viewpoints and some people just aren't used to that. It's hard to enjoy yourself when someone keeps asking you questions. For purely selfish reasons I wanted their girlfriends to come by and I always invited them back. You don't want to carry new insecurities and new fights home.

Arguing via text message during the gathering isn't as bad, but it's not good either. It usually leads to early departures. Things get really interesting when someone's ex-girlfriend randomly shows up at the gathering.

"Michael, if the gas tax pays for roads and road repair, how do we pay for the roads if we go electric?" William asked Michael

"Once electric vehicles stop becoming statue symbols and a way of flexin', every household, every facility and every business that uses electricity will get taxed... its genius." Michael responded.

"And what's up with climate change or that virus... with all of their research and funding, you'd think they'd be able to identify the high-risk groups while leaving lower risk groups to just live out their lives?" Anthony began. "That was probably their first conclusions, but thousands of scientists agreed that this other way was the best course of action and the media killed any opposing narratives and of course that was the more profitable direction."

"Well...won't the science self-correct?" William said.

"Nope. They don't really know how much it will cost, they don't know how much global temperature will lower or how many lives will be saved." Anthony said. "Brandon…Michael, say I am wrong…"

"You're not wrong." Michael said. "Research, statistics and stats are fraught with inaccuracies, bias and other conclusions that make them holy unusable, but often we use them just to back up whatever angle we need. The science is agreed upon, it's not settled. They can't even reproduce the studies they published. P-value is only valid for a single measure; once you start adding variables you increase the likelihood for false positives. The data doesn't speak for itself. Scientists are human beings too; they have incentives, want popularity, money, notoriety. They know that if the finding isn't novel or produces an unexpected result, publications won't pick it up."

"You know they are launching missiles and dropping bombs again…" Kyle said randomly.

"And the USA is probably all in." I said.

"Why not?" Michael said.

"Why for?" I responded.

"Often nations have legitimate grips with one another, these issues can usually be solved fairly easily; these conflicts are not designed to be short. Sometimes the US promotes conflicts, so peace can't be achieved. More often than not conflicts seem to always suit our purposes. That's why when someone mentions peace or mediation they get digitally flogged." Anthony said, handing Jerome another smoothie.

"They always have money for wars but no money to feed the poor." William said.

"We ignore our cities that don't have clean drinking water." I began. "We ignored genocide in Rwanda and Bosnia. No matter what the stated goal is it's not protecting the people. Gangs have overtaken Haiti and somewhere a UN started pandemic is raging. Where was American concern when a third of Pakistan was underwater? What have we done about the crimes committed by UN peacekeepers? Aren't we still doing business with China even though Uyghurs are in concentration camps? Aren't we still funding nations that are openly racist?

"And the thing is that both political parties engage in this wardom and at different times for different reasons, so you can vote one party out but the military machine doesn't stop."

"So we need better messaging..." Michael offered.

"Man, these people know they are voting for war."Anthony firmly stated.

"Ant, other nations wage war all the time." Michael replied.

"Yeah, usually with their neighbors..." Anthony bristled. "Think about it...what's behind where America intervenes and where it doesn't? No one can give any believable moral accounting to how the money and missiles are dispersed. Is the richest country in the world intervening to saving lives and to increase in the quality of life or is it a strategic military intervention for territory, resources and control? Why does one nation deserve assistance while another doesn't?"

"I disagree with that. We are a world power, we are trying to be fair." Michael said.

"We realized long ago that dominating the entire world might bring about peace but peace isn't economically good." Anthony said. "You have to understand that no government gives money or weapons without wanting something—we call that diplomacy. Which is why they don't refer to the two or three world wars that occurred after World War II... world wars."

"So you are saying that we are on like World War V..." Michael questioned Anthony.

"At least... If you believe that the US can be hit by a missile from another nation, then you've been brainwashed. Once you realize this is nowhere near true you'll start examining all the other odd things that stem from why this fear is pushed. They saw how fear motivated citizens in WWI and WWII. If United States citizens knew the United States really couldn't be beat or attacked it would be harder to utilize fear to move the public.

"Citizens need to believe that we can lose and that somehow there are holes in our defenses and somehow we're not prepared... that's how money and goods flow. We have even helped build up some of our 'enemies' so that later they can be a threat. All they had to do was make sure that the US mainland couldn't be attacked, which they did half a century ago. Now they maintain healthy fears just to get things done abroad."

"Things like what?" Michael asked.

"Things like moving chess pieces, obtaining mineral rights, money laundering."

"We are aiding them..." Michael stated.

"Yeah... aiding who?" Anthony said.

"Sounds like a conspiracy theory bro." Michael said.

"I didn't say that. I'm just saying these things are odd." Anthony said.

"You're saying all of this like they are bonefide conspiracies; when it might just be that people just don't know themselves all that well." Michael added.

"Okay, look at what they are doing……." Anthony said. "Just like holidays have given rise to lesser holidays. Religion has given rise to lesser religions. Some of these people seem to be having a religion experience. Mofos just can't be honest with themselves and accept who and what they are. Hard looks in the mirror can bring about mental instability… that's why people create self-definitions."

"They are well meaning, but delusional." Michael said.

"Are they…"

"Like I said, people just don't know themselves and actions speak louder than words..." Michael said. Michael said.

"Isn't speaking an action..." William said.

"Well yeah." Michael answered dryly.

"Even if that explains some of the hypocrisy..." Anthony stated. "If they don't know themselves why are they in charge of other life forms? Why are they in charge of pensions? Why are they in charge of the government? In the middle of a news reports, like clockwork, they will bring someone on that will say this leader, dictator or person is evil. And everyone who questions the direction we are headed in gets a drum beat of people yelling that they are genocide apologist, debating in bad faith or somehow subhuman.

"And to make sure the people stay in the interventionist mood, the media, again like clockwork, floats stories of children being killed and heinous crimes being perpetuated against women. The profiteers are the ones that screamed about violence against this group not being acceptable; they are not saying violence against anyone is unacceptable. Their platform is that violence is acceptable as long as it's not being perpetrated against the group they make money from.

"There is too much money in these industries to stop and to ask ourselves: Why help these children but not these? Why save these women but not these women? Why does the global cop only police certain neighborhoods?" Anthony finished.

"Asking those questions is like intersecting right from wrong. We must protect the political global order…" Michael said.

"Must we… The selective outrage is deafening." I stated.

"You can't allow a nation by force to change the boundaries of another nation." Brandon added.

"We allowed it in Yugoslavia; borders do change and most of the time it's because they were poorly drawn borders that failed to accommodate the ethnic tensions and allegiances of the region in the first place." I responded.

"We have coalitions of nations standing with us." Michael stated.

"The coalition gets bigger and easier to manage when you are funding it and dropping 50 bombs a day. The United States is spending more than half of every dollar on the military, we have capabilities that no one else has. We aren't worried about any kind of invasion." Anthony responded.

"The claim is that there are dictators and "bad actors" all over the world, but it's the United States that locks up people at a higher rate than any other nation." I added.

"Why is that huh?" William asked.

"But we are spreading democracy to make the world safer." Michael quickly answered.

"… at missile point." I said.

"Democratic countries don't use weapons of mass destruction, they don't invade their neighbors and they don't harbor terrorists." Michael said.

"What the record doesn't show is exactly which nation are assisting and funding these "bad actors" you referred to. These democratic governments will weaponize legitimate humanitarian crisis so they can create more humanitarian crisis that profit their interests. These democracies have every weapon known to man but for some reason almost every human catastrophe around the world can be attributed to democracies." I said.

"If we are giving money and weapons of course we are dictating terms... our aid comes with strings attached." Michael said.

"A lot of things about war appeals to those that don't go to war and it appeals even more to those who profit from war." Anthony said. "Our weapon's effectiveness in these conflicts is a warning to other nations but more than that, they are advertisements. There's a market for war. You can't have battlefield conditions without a battlefield. So there will always be a need to create a vague ubiquitous enemy of unknown capabilities to pit the people against.

"The goal is never peace and ending war isn't the primary policy. There are various reasons to promote war. And once it's all done, we can talk about the other threats and how our supplies are depleted or need updating, which of course means more money. You don't find it odd that every time something is invented or discovered people find ways to harm people or profit from it. It's amazing how peacekeepers are always quite violent. The United State's biggest worldwide exports are war, American culture and mental health issues." Anthony stated.

"We aren't the ones cutting throats with machetes." Michael stated.

"No, we're the ones killing with remote control drones." Anthony fired back.

"The less fortunate get a lot of charity." William said.

"That's what you think. Charity is partial restitution for the ills of society. Charity is a little band-aid on the most gruesome wounds of capitalistic alignment." I said.

"A year ago, Anthony pointed out how within a year there were 2 wars between 4 different nations, mass protests in 10 countries that saw hundreds of thousands of people in the streets being burned, shot, killed and getting arrested. A handful of Prime Ministers stepped down, got removed or were embroiled in scandals. And whole countries of nurses, doctors, teachers and transportation workers on month long strikes! And all of this was occurring at almost the same time and every time we turned on an American news channel they were doing stories on a politician they didn't like or a celebrity eating dinner at a restaurant—that's when I realized that these people have to be working together." Kyle stated.

"Anthony, break that down further..." Brandon requested.

"When have you ever seen Americans come to a country and solved the drought problem, or come a country and there was no more famine, or they came to this country and everybody became educated... It's always... America came to this country and upheaval followed. Americans have chosen war; charity is just a way in.

"We partner with and protect nations that don't give their citizens the right to free speech. On multiple fronts we incite conflicts and violence then spin the blow back to our advantage. When a dignitary visits a nation in person it not just a photo op or to engage in illicit sex, it is to also offer deals that can't have a paper trail. Did you even notice how after a few visits a nation will increase their military budget or makes some reforms. A statesperson visits a country and a new semiconductor chip plant gets built in Arizona. These people have rooms of people thinking shit up. There is always a plan further off than you can see. They are basically moving around resources..."

"What kind of resources?" Michael said.

"The women... Yes, they are testing new military equipment to sell and tactics to use with distance and deniability. Yes, they are exploring the capabilities of other nations. They'll throw in talk about relief packages and humanitarian aid and that's how they sell the narrative on the surface, but it simply boils down to access to women you don't already have access to..." Anthony responded.

"No way..." William said.

"So whenever there is a conflict all of the women and children can leave the country; all the men have to stay and get blown to bits..." Anthony responded.

"Word." Brandon said.

"Hmmm. Poor schools and low wages are the best ads for military recruitment." I said.

"That's how they got me." Anthony said.

"People call any activity that they don't understand crazy." Brandon said. "Imagine having enough money where you honestly don't give a fuck. You say and doing things that the average person can't comprehend and that's why they see it as crazy. Imagine being rich enough to buy a social media platform, rich enough to do pitch meetings while playing video games, rich enough to actually change the world. Imagine having enough money to actually really be free."

"There isn't enough money because there is no free. You can only attain freedom in moments." I said.

"This all sounds terrible. I see why they can't be honest about any of this." Kyle said.

"People don't have to follow corporatist, influencers and political parties. People have free will." I said.

"That may be but programming exists, and programmers need jobs." Michael said. "I thought all of that conspiracy talk was bullshit until Ye remixed what Malcolm X said and corporations called a Code Red on him... I was shocked to see all of these people... all of them backing up the corporations... I was like wow. Talk about a powerlessness."

"Right." Anthony said.

"It's a choice." I said.

"That does explain a lot." Kyle said.

"Wait...Kyle you can't comment on this, you're not even half black." Jerome said.

"What does being Black have to do with this subject, he's human." I said.

"It's open season on white males. It's hard to get a job, no one wants to talk to you and I am being told that everything that's wrong in society is somehow my fault. We are being treated like we are subhuman..." Kyle growled. "I'm out here every day just like you."

"Are we supposed to feel bad for you because the loons have turned you into a Black Man..." Jerome growled back.

"Look, watching them attack white males, mostly unwarranted, is humorous but it trickles down to all males; on its face it's wrong." I said.

"All white people are racist… no offense." Jerome stated to Kyle.

"All white people are racist. What does that even mean?" Brandon remarked.

"I mean that… all white people are racist. I know how the white mind operates." Jerome said.

"Jerome your tab is closed…" Anthony sighed as he stopped the blender.

"Bruh… come on…and I'm only half offended." William said as he cut off the music.

"No… I agree with him." Kyle said. "When people retreat into their self reinforced tribal bubbles that don't challenge ideas or expand minds…that's the real problem… tribalism is no joke."

"The love and hope coupled with the back flips and cartwheels black people do to give out social passes to non-black people that have offend simply because we like them, is disgusting. I can see why slavery went on for so long." I said to those assembled. "Blindly allowing others to use our bodies, our minds and appropriate our culture…just to be accepted. It's not like we protect our own.

"And don't be like oh, they just don't understand. The hell they don't. The one thing Black people know is how powerless they are. Instead of doing something about the tearing down of people in public, they just pile on so it seems like they aren't also a threat too. They don't want to be targeted. They won't even align themselves with you for fear of wilting underneath the white gaze.

"Black people talk down on each other every day, killing each other and they are the 1st to throw dirt on you and they'll kick you when you're down. Black people have a 100% conviction rate against one another. And don't make a movie, a business or products for them most of them won't support it. They think that being quiet, less visible or silently tolerant will engender them more. They are the main ones starting shit and be the first person to run on you. They won't celebrate you on your way up, but they will damn sure celebrate on your way down!"

"The people have chosen powerlessness." Brandon said.

"That's why I love Nic, he keeps it real." Anthony said.

"We were taught wrong but that's not the problem. The problem is that most people just lack courage." I said. "Aren't all people racist?"

"Studies say we all harbor biases…" Michael said.

"So you want the whole world to overcome their in-group biases because someone stared at you today longer than normal." I stated. "Who doesn't want to love the group they're from; especially your family. Asking people not to have racial bias is not a smart solution. Every group has a tendency to demonize anyone who is in the out-group. These race hustlers are the vilest people on the planet but still there are divisions to exploit and profit from. It's okay to be white. Kyle, you don't have to explain…"

"Nic, it's okay, the nation has never fully had this racial conversation." Kyle said standing up. "Honestly, y'all have let white people off too easy. I had to stop listening to most of them, you have to watch what they are doing and some of them do conspire and do think as colonizers.

"As a people we aren't always mindful of how we have and are treating people. We are frightened to have that conversation because a lot of white people have anti-minority positions, but for some reason there is a real undercurrent of anti-black sentiment. It borders on obsession, it's like who hurt you. Not one of these groups have harmed us, besides hurting our feelings but the sheer power and size of our group has real world repercussions and can harms others.

"We will recall you, block your access and we will skirt laws until they don't matter anymore. We utilize the system to our benefit and we will grind the gears to a halt, even if it makes the lives of those around us miserable. That's why a lot of people who have no business agreeing with us or validating us do so... they want some of that power.

"If we set the table, if we set the agenda the outcome will always benefit us—always. I mean it's not even low-key; we are always having white celebrations. A white woman is pregnant... she's on the front cover. A white women is doing this...bring her in for an unchallenged news segment. A white woman looks better than average... make her the beauty standard. That's how we remain in the dominate position we have to put out a lot of derivative, subpar, unnecessary fair and then we reinforce those things by giving it votes, awards and sequels."

"So, Jerome, what do you propose people do?" I said. "Do we not love anyone specially or do we love everybody the same— it sounds absurd when you say it out loud. Here we call out the nonsense, but no group is immune from doing nonsense. I mean no one is actually black and no one is actually white. This was all constructed for division and it works. Is white racism why you can't get the job you wanted? Is it why you couldn't get in the school you wanted to go to? Is it making you not love yourself? Is it why got divorced?"

"No." Jerome said.

"So then it's not significant enough to affect your everyday life." I responded. "It's not enough to make you stop being the best you can be. If it was something that was holding you back that would be different but there are dozens of other things holding your ass back and you're focused on this one. When you are obsessed over something like this it leans into the 'us versus them' narrative which can make a person feel like they have a sense of purpose as if they are part of something, but in here, this place, we are part of something; we are friends.

"Groups don't censor themselves. Traitors get punished more than enemies—so real opposition stays quiet. People identify with big ideologies to make themselves feel better. Groupthink will not allow you to be the best you can be. You can't live an excellent wholesome life with distorted views, you just can't."

"Word." Brandon said, sipping his drink.

"I don't take my presence in any of these conversations lightly." Kyle said. "My daughter is Black so all of these things affect her, me and my wife. A big reason why Jessica's baby daddy has a problem with me is because I am white. He wasn't even going to try to get to know me, and I understand that which is why we didn't go tune him up that day."

"Kyle, I was wrong for that." Jerome admitted. He nodded his head and fist bumped Kyle. He sat back down and opened the bag of marijuana with a smile. He rolled up a blunt, lit it, and passed it to Kyle.

"Oh, this is good." Brandon said, pointing to his cup.

"Now, white women, there is no one scarier..." Kyle said hunching his shoulders "They talk mad disrespectful to white men when no one is watching... We have to pass laws just to protect them because they are always somewhere they aren't supposed to be, normalizing things they are supposed to be ashamed of like, trying to destigmatize gonorrhea and showering twice a week."

"That's nasty." William said.

"They are really out here saying they are oppressed... I mean are people marching the street because the police are randomly killing white women?" Kyle offered.

"Nope." Anthony said.

"We are cooking with gas now…" William said.

"They are chaining themselves to basketball support beams, pretending to be other races, protesting naked, not understanding, making up accusations, yelling into cameras and cutting off penises." Brandon said.

"They glue themselves to basketball courts, slut parading, accidentally murdering people, moving into black neighborhoods, fake crying and throwing hot soup in people's face…" Jerome said.

"Wanting you to snort cocaine off their stomach, altering children, throwing paint on people, yelling racial slurs, rage crying, pathologizing natural behavior and sexing everyone in the police department." Michael said.

"So y'all have seen them?" Kyle said.

"Who hasn't?" William said smirking.

"Their breaches of public decorum are the madness of privilege. White women like to talk about fighting for black rights but they don't know a black person and won't hire one. They are using our plight and putting their white face on it, drunk with their own significance." I said.

"Who you tellin'," Anthony said. "They are talking about how they hate white males when they're the only ones that can create a white male. They hate their father, their brothers and their sons and on top of that they also hate your father, your brothers and your sons…"

"…And rules…" I added.

"They have the fewest things to complain about and they complain the most." Kyle pleaded. They rant and rave, call you manbaby, talk sarcastically about you being fragile or threatened."

"It's psychotic…" I said.

"And everyone wants them, everyone is talking about them, everyone is attacking them, everyone is chasing them…Kyle, white dudes are the main reason they think like that…" William said.

"We have to or they'll turn on us!" Kyle stated. "Look how fast they go from pushing women to the forefront to claiming that having a virtual assistant is training people to think of women as servants."

"Right." Anthony agreed.

"White women are menaces." Kyle stated. "They're never happy, professional agitators… Look how many chances someone like SoHo Karen got and it only empowered her behavior. Feminism is terrorism here and imperialism abroad."

"They behave like their protests are worse than when folks were being beaten, tear gassed and had dogs released on them during the Civil Rights Movement... oh no this right here is much worse." I mockingly said. "Every protest they have is a Tiananmen Square moment. When the Xanax ain't working, volunteer tourism is next."

"White liberals are the most terrifying creatures on the planet." Brandon said. "Instead of looking at their deviance, bias and reasoning they would rather examine yours. They include minorities on the platform, as long they follow their script."

"They've been tamed…" Jerome offered

"Pretty much…"Anthony said

"It's not your race though, it's what you represent, and they have to protect those brands." Brandon said. "If you happen to catch their unfairness, they'll try to appease you and they'll want to give your group a specifically branded spotlight."

"These groups wouldn't need a spotlight if everything was above board." Anthony stated.

"Why would a platform support something that would destroy it?" I said. "You wouldn't have to apologize all the time if you owned the platform. These are their platforms, their systems and they weren't built for you. This shadow racism only changes if that change can be monetized. The truth hurts the stock price, it doesn't get you invited to university campuses and it doesn't sell. It kills me when they run a movie franchise into the damn ground or when they are all out of ideas and then they give it to black people... like we are supposed to be thankful."

"Y'all droppin' bars." William said.

"Liberals engage in the soft bigotry of low expectations and pandering, they even use innuendo that you can't quite call racism— It's not quite the n-word. Because soon as they say nigga. Everyone will know and we'll be like..." I said pointing at William

"Gotcha bitch!" William quickly said.

"They can't wish brown eggs were white out in the open. They have gotten smarter with their racism." I continued. "They're not making the world a better place; they are making it a place where it's easier to insult and belittle others. They really want to say, 'You're just a Black person, so you don't know any better.' But they won't say it because their mask will be off."

"They aren't racist enough to not have their food cooked by black hands or services not rendered with Hispanic fingers or products not made with Asian sweat. They aren't feminist enough to not have anything built by a man's hand. They just need an audience for their shenanigans." Anthony stated

"I'm glad you said it." Kyle said.

"They will specifically say they want to help families and to support victims of domestic violence." Anthony said. "Everyone knows full well that they mean… women. Men are not easily allowed into shelters nor do they get services. They never say they want to stop violence. They want women to stop getting hit but they don't want women to stop hitting. It's a whole sick industry."

"An industry… then why are they colliding with each other?" William asked.

"I think a lot of these groups are really working together to cause controversies, merely making people think they enemies. They attack one another for headlines and fundraising." I offered.

"To me, the worst part about being white is that you don't have to learn anything if you don't want to that's why most of us can't tell if we are racist or not." Kyle said.

"The world likes to see us run and jump, but not love or express ourselves." I said. "If you really think about it you understand that most crime is perpetrated by non-gang members, you realize that the square root of people in a given disciple produces half the results, you can see those in power have allowed the creation of new capitalistic games just so more people feel like they are included and winning. We need to realize that we are only lucky because those that came before us made good decisions." I said.

"B - B - Bars…" William said fist bumping everyone.

"That's why the value of these businesses and sports teams keep going up because minorities are making more money." Anthony stated. "They price the real wealth out of range so a so-called minorities can't be sole owner. They need to monitor and watch you, so you got to be a minority owner.

"Everything will be settled on the basis of figures, yet everything isn't about money; fitness gives you more options than money does. While money has a lot to do with respect, some guys who pay to keep the lights on still can't get respect or pussy…" I said.

"I know dats right." Anthony said giving me dap.

"There will always be somebody with longer, bigger or more so the things you do together when you aren't under the covers matters. People hide bad heath and less desirable genes with surgery and medication and that's a bigger problem than you know." I said. "I believe in love and being in love. But cultural variation is so minuscule, that we are hardwired to be attracted to those genetically dissimilar regardless of race. There is a genetic hierarchy, which is the main reason some people want destroy standards."

"Being attracted to pheromones and scents is subconscious." Brandon offered.

"But having preferences makes people feel bad." Michael said.

"Even if it's genetic…" Jerome said.

"But it makes people feel bad." Michael said.

"It's not all height and muscles, your health and earnings are socially relevant." I said.

"See Nic, you too smart to be in the stockroom. A lot of guys are delusional, they won't work on themselves, they won't stay fit, they don't earn money, they don't know how to talk to people but somehow the world has slighted them in the dating arena... well, your share goes to me." Brandon said going into my kitchen.

"Let me ask everyone a question: If right now extraterrestrials came to this planet and asked to meet our best Earth representative who would we agree to send?" I said.

"Hmmmm…" Anthony said.

"What about....naw." Brandon said from the kitchen.

"How about... nope." Michael said.

"What do you think Nic?" William said.

"I think those aliens will be enslaving and colonizing us while we're still debating who to send." I said.

"You know this is really sad." Kyle said.

"Everyday..." I responded as I took a sip from my cup.

"This conversation took two blunts and it needs another blunt." William said lighting another blunt.

"The free time provided by relative peace has allowed this bullshit to take hold. I ain't Thanos but half of these motherfuckers need to go." Anthony said.

"They can't see that they're sick." Jerome said.

"That's okay I can see it for them." I said.

"Naw y'all wrong... They real ass zombies, open your eyes," William said waving his arms. "They be milling around at dey job, with dey kids or doing whatever, but soon as they hear a noise they run over there. When they see a light they run over there. Zombies only come together when targeting someone...tar-get-ing someone. They don't have to know why.

"And when the zombies are wrong, or they attack the wrong person they don't apologize they just move on to the next person... Zombies don't get tired of being fooled. Zombies don't stand up and say, we're not going to take this trickery anymore; no they just walk right into the fire and the ones that don't just keep on zombieing"

"Maybe there's a little bit of zombie in us all." I said.

"Look how they just move the baseline for morality and once you have no morals or beliefs, your brain can be emptied and corporations can put inside what they want." William continued. "They celebrate sickness. They won't even know the person, never heard of the person and with no context they will go out of their way to trash them. If someone says something they don't like they want you to lose your job and burn in hell... Dats zombie behavior right there!"

"Are these kinds of people worse than racist?" Michael asked.

"Hells yeah." Anthony said. "Indoctrination compromises the ability to reason. Remember I was in the military with some of the most vile, sick in the head, violent, misguided and tyrannical motherfuckers on the planet, but there was respect there. You can say fuck you, but you do it respectfully..."

"Many people just need therapy..." Michael said.

"Man, zombies can't go to therapy! No matter how many of them there are, no matter how much they consume they cannot be satisfied. It ain't just drugs turning them into zombies either. You look at them and they seem similar to you so you think they can be reasoned or negotiated with, but they can't. Zombies aren't objective.

"Things don't have to make sense to them, dey zombies. They don't wanna be understood... Why do I have to do all the thinking? Do you know how much thinking needs to be thought? I gotta do all the thinkin' for 1, 2, 3, 4, 5, 6 people and myself." William said counting those in the room.

"I don't know about zombies but there are many people, who instead of getting articles written about them, featured on covers, sponsorship deals and speaking engagements should be getting placed on 72-hour holds." Jerome said.

"Stop playing that 'hold my purse' music..." Anthony said to William. William started playing some Ampiano groves.

"Enough of this causal moralizing, you Bob Lazer face fukkas! Michael, this herb is bomb..." William said coughing.

"I know, try this one, its 4 ounces of that good-good." Michael said passing around another blunt.

"Why don't these young shirtless artists give Bobby Brown any credit?" William said.

"We all lacked perspective when we were young." I said.

"And...there are different kinds of zombies. Anyone can be a zombie and you can be a zombie about anything!" William cryptically said. "They use improper terms and words that are nothing more than grunts and moans that other zombies recognize. They don't need to kill a person physically, they killin' them mentally. All you have to do is stop thinking and that how you die. When you stop thinking you... are... dead. People that are alive are a problem to zombies.

"A zombie will even attack different zombies because zombies can't share common ground for long. Zombies need to be triggered. If you trigger one, others join in. Zombies don't even know dey zombies, dats what makes them so dangerous."

"Hmmm, many people are governed by outside forces." Michael said analyzing William's statement. "Would a lack of consciousness correlate to a mind-body dualism of some sort? It is really sad how people disregard one another. I pity them."

"You need to stop analyzing 'em, you need to stay away from 'em. Stop trying to save 'em, dey don't wanna be saved. This isn't the film Warm Bodies... love ain't gonna going to change 'em. If I didn't know any better I think some people like being zombies." William responded. William may be the youngest but occasionally he says something profound.

The Quiet Part Loud

I realized a spent a lot of time and energy defending those who wouldn't do the same for me. I didn't have time to be on the Internet arguing with avatars and Internet personalities. My friends chose to be here, they chose to listen, they chose to engage, they chose to act and they chose to share and to me that meant something.

The solution to the negative aspects of capitalism cannot be more capitalism. Whenever the remedy for negating the effects of adverse societal influence or the solution to close achievement gaps in urban schools is more capitalistic exploits such as the center for this, the platform for this, the non-profits for that, there are people planning to profit from societies woes, people who may have had a hand in the causation of such woes.

The road ahead of me is going to be hard; pushing further could be fraught with perils. There were many people in the business of politics that caused inertia, which caused those in government to not focus on ideas and problems and they chose to focus on an easier targets. People that know systems appear smart, intelligent and competent. This is how politicians become career politicians and make millions of dollars off of things that require simple solutions, so being on the wrong side of political power is dangerous.

It seemed to me that most people and organizations only care about oppression and injustice if you fit a narrative. Some organizations do good work but at some point they start doing things contrary to their mission statements that is why I can work with you but I can't work for you. I wasn't exactly a core constituent. I wasn't exactly photo-op material and if anything negative happened in the community, I would be body count. No sympathy or concern would come my way, or the way of those that looked like me.

The interesting thing was that once I received enough information from professionals and participants inside and outside of the problem, corrected for bias and mistruths, the answers found me whether I liked it or not. Then question became, do the answers leave this apartment, do they go beyond those assembled. In order to take this further, in order to be taken seriously we could not collectively be seen not as an entertainer, athlete or the culture. We would have to be seen as something that had nothing to do with being Black, Hispanic or Asian. We would have to present visible obvious minorities in a way that those around them had no other choice but to accept their expertise and ideas.

Things that mattered to me didn't matter to most people. I saw things others did not. My experiences led me here. Our experiences had led us here. It wasn't hard getting businesses to donate paint or plants trees. The trick is to agree with those in power and when the time is right expand the comment or offer a different perspective. The right idea has to come at the right time, from the right person. It's going to take more than getting people jobs, stopping children from being abused and foiling suicides...a lot more.

"Last time I saw you, you were doing something with ions..." William asked Michael.

"The ion drives... That project is complete. Now we are optimizing ST suits." Michael answered.

"What are ST suits?" Kyle said.

"Surface Tension suits," Michael pulled out his smart phone. "You see these images of Olympic swimmers just before the water's surface tension is broken, that thin film covering their face is the kind of spacesuit we are creating. We are literally drifting to the edge."

"How long before what you are doing is weaponized?" Jerome said.

"Ummm…Brandon and I work with the military, so…" Michael said.

"We come up with the tools; we don't have control over how those tools are used. However, I'm not one of those people that thinks Earth's problems can be solved by terraforming Mars and sending a thousand people to it. Logic and common sense dictates that if we have the ability, the time, the money and technology to terraform another planet and to transport and supply a thousand people living on another planet, we have the ability to avert or mitigate whatever disaster that may befall the Earth. That being said, the job pays well." Michael stated.

"Did you know that in the Amazon Basin butterflies sip turtle tears for sodium? This is also why they eat dirt and fecal matter. Last month I came across a new kind of larvae, Y'all want to see it?" Brandon said, pulling out his smart phone.

A collective 'no' came from those in the room.

"There you go; you Beast Master face fukka…" Jerome said, lighting up another blunt.

"That's right beast…listen to me. You Harpy-Eagle face fukka." Brandon said.

"You just misgendering people…" William said.

"Harpy eagle is not a gender…" Brandon responded as he went into the bathroom.

"Not yet…" William said laughing.

"See what I had to deal with on the drive here... 2 and ½ hours of how Burmese Pythons are rampantly slithering through the Everglades, killing endangered species." Michael stated as he sipped from his cup.

"Soon to be 5 hours..." Brandon responded, coming back into the living room.

"Absentee father and single mother are just terms used to trigger people. The majority of the people who cause mass death are fatherless. The majority of the violence in the streets comes from those raised by single mothers, but they elevate women and cast dispersions on males at the same time." Anthony stated, bringing out more smoothies for everyone.

"Let me introduce you to Mable." Kyle said plugging in a silver controller that had a bright red kiss mark on it.

"Kyle, I'm ah show you that you can't beat everyone, give Leonidas a controller." Brandon said, adjusting his position to the TV. Kyle handed him a video game controller.

"I don't want you to tap out...I want you to go to sleep. I must break you." Kyle said as he and Brandon started battling in a fighting game.

"When you don't allow male energy in your home, a child will seek that energy outside the home. Studies show children raised by one parent are more likely to become psychotic..." Anthony said.

"I read the studies you're talking about and basically they were about children who grew up with a mentally ill parent that became psychotic..." I countered.

"Yeah, well in general why do you think there is only one parent in the household? As a society, we have to stop just co-signing the bullshit. Study after study shows that women hit first and mothers can be criminally immature. What is being done about it?" Anthony said.

There was fury of button presses followed by a loud commotion as Brandon dropped his controller to the floor.

"Losernidas has been defeated. Who's next?" Kyle announced, holding up his silver controller.

Amidst the laughter, Brandon was visibly frustrated, so I decided to pile on. "I told you, you not gon' beat him." I said.

"He's in yo house. Why you letting him kick ass like this in yo house? You challenge him..." Brandon cried out as he wandering into the kitchen.

"Challenge him... I need my hands for work." I said. "Kyle doesn't win all the time. Sometimes I beat him. Sometime Anthony beats him, so he does lose. When Kyle loses really bad he packs up his controllers and leaves."

"It wasn't long ago that I was beating Kyle like he stole something." Anthony proudly chimed in.

"Oh, he remembers," I said laughing. "Kyle called Jessica to come get him."

"I only did that once." Kyle said defensively.

"But you did it." I said.

"You probably cried in the car..." Anthony taunted.

"Everyone has an off night." Kyle said.

"... or two." Anthony smirked.

"What time you gotta go home?" William said.

"Hey…whoa…I don't like the way you asked that, like I have to check in or something... for your information... I don't." Kyle responded.

"People are the problem that cannot be solved." Brandon said returning to his spot on the couch in time for Anthony to pass him the blunt.

"As fear rises people's faith in each other erodes." Michael said.

"There are people who put babies in bags, set fire to them, drown them, bury them, stab and shoot people and it's as if there are no laws to stop them." Anthony said.

"There are laws." I said.

"Then why are they getting away with it." Anthony chided.

"Every time justice is distorted or someone is let off the hook because of race, gender, money or agenda, it hurts society as a whole." I said.

"It makes those of us who are social witnesses have less faith in the systems. It makes the youth grow up with an accountability gap. You are going through the same cycle over and over, but it's everyone else's fault." Brandon said, ignoring his repeatedly vibrating smart phone.

"The main problem is that children are being raised with this one-sided mentality." I said. "There are large segments of society that gets offended at the slightest thing. Everyone is too sensitive to hear the truth, so they ignore it and what's left is a society that refuses to acknowledge to the truth."

"Damn, that's deep." Anthony said as he finishing blending another round of drinks.

"If you can't handle the truth when you're single there's no way you can handle it when you're in a relationship." Kyle said, taking the blunt from Michael. "I remember being in the 8th grade listening to lunch room stories about dudes getting their dick sucked in the locker room. I was like, hold up... You getting your dick sucked, on school property.

"I must have things twisted because I'm coming to school to learn. And just like that, it was pussy over Pokémon, because now the pressure is on. All I hear about now is the numbers game. I didn't realize how hard it was going to be chasing women versus collecting Pokémon cards, and those cards go up in value. The next thing you know you're grown and serially sexually active and not successfully managing it all.

"You're alone not because of choice, but because your sex game and mentality aren't suitable for a stable relationship. One day you'll be sick, your stomach is hurting and your dog will be loudly licking its asshole— that's when reality hits you. That sick feeling I had in my gut was called rock bottom.

"That's the day you realize that you weren't enough, that you've been maintaining years of relationships with people that you can't even hold a basic conversation with. You had sex, you went out on dates, but usually they call you and it's already nine or ten at night. She comes over, y'all drink, smoke, put on some bullshit movie neither of you are interested in, have sex, go to sleep and in the morning you kick her out, there is no time to talk, because you haven't made any.

"Now that you can't move because of the pain in your stomach, you are sitting there thinking, she gives me her body and I don't even talk to her. Now, that I'm sick this is the first time we just sat and talked because she cared enough to bring me some chicken soup. What made that moment sadder was that before me she had some real P.O.W. stories, so to her my bullshit was a breath of fresh air.

"She looked me straight in my eyes and said, 'I appreciate you because you don't hit me.' She gave me credit for not beating on her. I mean do you say to that. No one else wanted to spend the rest of their life with me and she did, all I had to do was act right." Kyle finished.

"If that story doesn't make you cry a little inside you don't have a soul." I said. "Hopefully we won't all have to go through all of that before we figure things out. A lot of people talk but they never mention the role they played in their dysfunctional relationships. They never talk about how they contributed to the situation. They don't know how to fix themselves and they won't seek help. They never talk about the steps they took to healing or about going to therapy. The way they tell it; somebody randomly picked them and just started abusing them."

"That's why I try to stay away from abused people. They try to cancel you when you tell the truth. On the real, people don't become a public figure just because you are on social media or because the media turns you into a public figure?" Brandon stated.

"The rules allow the media to treat everyone like a public figure so anyone can be attacked." I said. "Pointing out the flaws of others makes certain people feel better about their own flaws. Look how quick the media is to investigate and report the cornucopia of felonious activities throughout Florida, yet they are silent on the white-collar types which are the majority of committed crimes in Florida."

"That's deep." Brandon said.

"They will have your own people come after you." I said. "That's why only select few minoritie are allowed to rise to various levels of prominence this is how control is maintained. It doesn't matter if the culture war is over Christmas, your children, gas stoves hamburgers, green M&M's or coffee cups, it all becomes a distraction so the battle of ideas can be won.

"Democracy demands that power is diversely and widely shared, it does not play favorites, and it does not enact vengeance using government agencies. That's the opposite of democracy. As long as corporations are allowed to engage in tax free political power there will be no good billionaires. Politicians are renaming schools, canceling people and virtue signaling to avoid talking about their inept record and to us it seems like progress is being made.

"Corporations and special interest groups control establishments and institutions, but they are The People's establishments and The People's institutions. It's our oil; it's not Mobile's or Exxon's oil. People just don't seem to be able to think beyond what a talking head on a screen is telling them.

"I see ordinary everyday citizens being criminalized, punished and restricted for just having an opinion. They are called radical or problematic simply because they don't agree with the mob. Politicians have millions of followers, are they utilizing their reach to mobilize people. No, each post is a quip, slander or echo chamber fodder for job security. I see that people don't have good, affordable health care, half the country can't afford a $500 dollar emergency room visit, 80% of workers live pay check to paycheck, the average American has $5,000 in their saving account, 50% of wage earners earn less than $30,000 a year and it's not because a lack of resources or solutions, it's because our government is corrupt."

"The Internet's influence is overstated, yet too much to be healthy." Michael said.

"That's one of the reasons we are in a collective creative downturn in terms of art and creativity." Anthony said. "The other reason is that all of the great talented actors, directors, performers and entertainers have been accused and taken out of circulation, all that's left is the mediocrity who make up for the absence of talent by focusing on identity."

"Their identity is their talent." Kyle stated.

"Naw, that's because entertainers aren't getting paid like they used to." I said.

"Sheiit... they gettin' big bucks." William said.

"They get attention and money but that isn't why they started doing it..." Anthony said. "The main reason people become an athlete or a celebrity is to get sex. You can clearly see people are not putting out the best work or efforts, because some of the joy has been removed. Athletes and celebrities are having problems because they slept with a lot of groupies. Soon as they're not acting, performing or pulling in the money they used to, the negatives stories about them start to come out.

"And when the celebrity gets older and is no longer seen as a trophy, someone's feelings about their time together may have changed, they might say, oh they touched me inappropriately. They don't even have to be a groupie, it could be someone you gave a chance that turned around and stabbed you in the back because their star didn't shine as bright. I see why some of these people are private; they don't want to deal with that.

"Just having the power of accusation can make a person feel better about their life choices. That's why athletes keep on playing until they are broken down and celebrities spend what they can and try everything just to stay attractive and working. Hell, they might even win but lose their soul, their family, their morals, their integrity and their community in the process."

"To them those are just words... All that matters is the brand. The brand isn't real; it's an illusion, it's PR, its marketing, it's mind control and that covers up a lot. Deezam... You see... you see I can drop dopeness too... I don't even know why I'm on dis track!" William stated.

"We all think our moms are saints but most of us wouldn't even be here if it wasn't for hoeing and drugs." Brandon said. "Nobody's story to their child about how they came to be, begins with I was a hoe."

"If we are really canceling our grandparents and parents then we are canceling our very existence..." Jerome said blowing out smoke. "To me it seems like there is an invisible wheel of dumb shit and people just spin the wheel and say and do whatever it lands on...just spin the wheel..."

"Notice how the these loudest people never run for office because they know their nonsense will get voted down, but online and in the media they can float nonsense and be supported or they can just say, "in my opinion" to free themselves from consequence." I said.

"I think a lot of this canceling and censorship is racist and sexist." William said.

"And you'd be thinking correctly." I stated.

"More people die from the cold than the heat. They can't even handle an evolving climate." Michael said. "Through schools, the media and medication the number of insane has grown so large that they can engage coalition politics. Subservient groups can only join if you adopt a set of values, which is why all of these groups despise each other.

"If they don't agree with the studies or the research; they'll say it's not valid. They just keep moving the mental health goal post or sanction violence. They tend to attach themselves to ideologies that are impervious to reasonable discussion.

"Here's the thing…those people did write that, they did pass that, they did earn that, they did perform that, they did accomplish the mission, they did build that, they did endure that and they did risk that and now here you come trashing it... We are only able to accomplish the things we've accomplished because of our grandparents and parents; we are only as free as we are because of our forefathers; they shouldn't be vilified now.

"Some of the things they did may have been unfortunate, immoral, maybe even criminal, but were it not for what they did we wouldn't even be here. These people shouldn't be tore down decades and centuries later, or long after they are dead. You can recognize the positives and the negatives in a person, life isn't an all or nothing proposition. They did what they did so we could be great you don't have to like it.

"I can't cancel someone because most of the time it's canceling someone for same things our grandparents and parents did. Instead of just admitting that they are afraid or that they need to work on themselves they would rather someone else be the problem."

"How can people not comprehend that censoring and labeling people into silence, maintaining poor schools and putting people in jail for profit, color or race is actually killing people." I said.

"They don't want to understand it." Anthony said.

"I concur, you Caesar loves human more than ape, face fukka." Brandon stated.

"Republican's with afros." William stated looking at the TV.

"It must be election season. That's when entertainment news media talks about Black Men." I said shaking my head. "The veneer of caring lends them political power. Political parties aren't the same but the results at the bottom are similar, because both political parties serve capitalism, not the people. Most of society's problems come from capitalism and both parties want to preserve it, making them both right wing.

"Capitalism is an immoral system that requires a certain percentage of the population to be unemployed, and another percent to be in servitude."

"So basically, we are going to have the same political outcome no matter who is in power." Brandon said.

"Pretty much, specific black leaders that control black media and black culture use it to shake down white institutions. It's always the same plan: Target groups, surveill groups and manage groups, then undermine, co-op and then recontextualize whatever movement the people are being drawn to. They did all of this marching, protesting, getting beat on, boycotting and when you finally get heard and look at the nonsense they are producing."

"I guess all the ludicrous stuff that came before just didn't go far enough. The Sambos on the right are upset with Sambos on the left but they are both Sambos." Anthony said.

"When Dr Martin Luther King said that the US government 'owes black folks a check' and the dream he had that day, 'turned into a nightmare' the psychological dogs were unleashed. The passive controlled King could be a figurehead. The radical King could not be." I said.

"It's crazy... there's no other way to describe it". Michael said.

"All you need to know is that if it generates money capitalism will encourage it." Anthony said.

"Sometimes I be on one, but you know how messed up in the mind I would have to be to go on social media to bash another person. You know there seems to be a lot of obviously insane people that are heads of states and corporations." William said.

"Sometimes the powers that be allow things to go haywire." Anthony said.

"Come on now, those are accidents." Michael stated.

"Secure systems get breeched, documents, conversation and emails get leaked, something that always works, just fails, and glitches stop holiday travelers from traveling and no one gets fired and the system they have been talking about for years just happens to be ready… They always have the bailouts ready. Utilizing bank collapses as controlled demolitions, these planned accidents and glitches never seem to benefit the customers… You profit more for selling the hope, the dream." Anthony said.

"Corporations are just responding to the outrage." Michael said.

"See corporations and politicians get scared when the public is unafraid. They have to move people towards one thing and away from other things. People just can't be told the truth. The truth is so damn unbelievable and so horrifying that people will literally lose their minds. They could be living on an island, fishing every day and your leaders will tell you there's not enough water and you'll be saying, yeah there isn't enough water we need to do something." Anthony continued.

"How are they getting away with this?" Kyle said.

"Due to decades of bullshit, there are now just enough idiots willing to show their ass for free, there are just enough idiots willing to die to defend the wrong things and enough idiots whose behaviors and thoughts can be manipulated. There are people who specialize in the polarization of imbeciles." Anthony responded.

"None of this is new." I offered. "People have done dumb things for a long time. Only now you can record it and spread it, and sometimes that emboldens others to do dumb things. You can't fault people for not having the capacity to reevaluate their beliefs, for not being able to see beyond themselves?"

"Yes I can." Anthony began. "They can't imagine themselves as anything but eternally threatened, and that makes them dangerous; they believe they are spouting logic. Like Michael said they aren't applying science correctly and they know it. Most people aren't creative or talented... they're just good at copying. They believe the groupthink. They will only believe official reports; they won't even believe their own eyes. They won't believe their own memory until its part of an official report. Large proportions of people have grown up thinking stupid things are good, and now stupid things have actually become normal.

"Everyone seems so certain of their beliefs, their positions." I said. "I believe that there is a very real possibility that we are all wrong, maybe that's why people cling to beliefs and positions so long. We don't want to have to start over; we don't have to throw it all away when that's probably what we should do. Those echo chambers are created by their unwillingness to budge.

"They care more about the people on reality TV than their own relationship. I see them typing away and liking other people's realities, while theirs falls apart. They complain about children that were created somewhere between contempt and lust."

"I just want to job that I don't hate." Jerome mockingly said "Okay, take your ass to school, learn a trade, deal with that job until you can get another job get and shut the hell up."

"They're unassailable because of their history." Brandon said.

"Damn that... I assails." Anthony stated.

"But that's why they always bring up their personal designation and who they are affiliated with..." Kyle said.

"It's cowardice." Anthony said.

"Some people just don't know who they are." Michael said.

"And some people do." I responded.

"Most people are just upset because other people can actually express how they feel. That's why they hate-watch, hate-post, hate-type and hate-follow....thinking about how they can't really express their true thoughts and feelings." Anthony said.

"Look how easy it is for people to say, Tom Cruise is crazy but not the people he's dealing with..." I said.

"Brainwashed..." Anthony responded.

"He's not doing what we are doing, he must be crazy and we have to make the people see that..." I said.

"Religions are probably behind that." Brandon said.

"Most people are agreeable so they're really easily influenced." Michael stated.

"Controlled..." Anthony added.

"Or that." I said.

Of course Anthony is right. I was accustomed to fighting for every morsel, opportunity, job and every inch that I got. It was surprising for me to see people who didn't have a record, who had never been locked up and who didn't have any real baggage, not fight for every morsel, opportunity, job or even their rights. Freedom is priceless, just ask someone who doesn't have it.

In fact most people showed a lack of courage unless they were in a group. The reason they offend so easily and so often is because they don't know what they should be fighting for and what they should be fighting against. They are looking for someone to trust, searching for someone they can believe in that will tell guide them. Most have never had their freedom taken from them, so from my point of view they are taking so much for granted. By not trying, not seizing opportunities; they are allowing people to run over them... this actually bothers me.

The View From Inside

Tonight, everyone came armed with information and their best quips. Pizza was being eaten, fingers were covered in buffalo sauce and cups were filled with various concoctions. William's play list had my walls vibrating and every now and then we would belt out familiar song verses.

"Your cell phone gets time from GPS satellites that pre-corrected for Einstein's General Theory of Relatively because they are in different gravitational fields." Michael explained.

"...because any concentration of matter and or energy will curve the fabric of space and time. There is a duality between space and time." I added.

"It's interesting that most people that work in the government have backgrounds in psychology." Michael said. "Although skills are transferrable we physicist, chemist, biologist and other scientist almost never work in our field. Most of the time we are working on projects that have nothing to do with our expertise."

"Yeah, none of that explains why I keep kicking y'all's ass in this game." Kyle said.

"Kyle, with your three hours of freedom you just gotta drop by Nic's..." William said

"What you saying...that his apartment is a bar... Nic's on 14th." Kyle said.

"Sometimes it is..." I said, laughing.

"Who's your favorite artist?" William said.

"God..." Anthony replied.

"The Neanderthals will tell on you quick, no offense Kyle." Jerome said.

"None taken." Kyle said as he pulled out a notepad and wrote something down.

"What are you writing down, you police ride along face fukka?" Jerome cracked at Kyle. It was good to see those two vibing again.

"I see you are still staying in shape." Michael said to me.

"I got to..." I said.

"You can't eat zingers and lose weight." Michael said.

"You're eating a zinger right now..." William said.

"I know, these zingers are good." Michael said, smacking his lips.

"You fat face fukka." William said.

"Potato chips are bad for you... hand those to me." Michael said.

"Yousa Potatoes Au Gratin face fukka." Brandon said slurring.

"What happened to that fine ass mixed girl you came through here with a few months ago?" Anthony said to William.

"Dominique..." William responded.

"The one that smelled like orange blossoms...that was you... I knew one of our representatives was on the scene." Jerome said.

"Shawty, cheeked up ... I bet it's like butter." Anthony said, making a cupping hand gesture.

"I can't believe it ain't..." William said with a smile on his face. "Yeah, she got that yum. yum-yum and she's not on psyche meds or antidepressants."

"Man, you lucky." Brandon said.

"Not so fast most psychotic breaks happen in a person's twenties. She's a psychology major...right... so watch out." I said.

"What do you mean?" William responded.

"Most people choose professions that affected them as children, psychology, criminal justice, modeling, social work; professions that may indicate unresolved issues. It's not hard to see how a person would seek a position of power or a career to help them understand their own mind."

"She was a psychology major, now she's a brand rep." William said.

"A brand rep... I wear a lot of brands. You can get paid for doing that?" Kyle asked.

"You can't," William said laughing "Dominique puts on a freakum dress and on Friday and Saturday night she spends a few hours in bars and clubs. When someone offers to buy her and her girlfriends a drink, she has them buy alcohol from whatever company she's representing that night."

"What do you mean?" Kyle said pushing the pause button on the video game.

"When someone offers to buy her a drink she says, yes and the brand of the company she represents. The funny thing is that she doesn't even drink alcohol."

"And that's a job..." Kyle said.

"She makes about $1,000 every weekend..." William said. "She's Dominican and comes from a middle-class family."

"Sounds like an asset to me." I said.

"Remind me not to buy them anymore drinks in clubs and bars..." Brandon said.

"If you gettin' sum on a regular you not buyin' drinks in the first place." William said looking at Brandon.

"Oooo." We all laughed.

"B...b...but....but... you da one... with da..." Brandon stuttered.

"Just hold the L..." I said patting Brandon on the shoulder.

"She is a twelve on the attractiveness scale. She could ruin my life and I wouldn't complain." Anthony said. "Somebody would hire that even if that is incompetent."

"Are you still dating her?" Jerome said.

"What do you mean?" William asked.

"I think she's out your league bro..." Jerome said.

"There's always one..." William responded.

"One what?" Jerome said.

"Hater." William said.

"You don't really have a job, I mean pushing all those buttons on a computer and posting videos, is not a real job." Jerome said.

"If you get paid to do it, it's a real job." I interrupted.

"She's too fine for you. You gotta share her fam." Jerome said.

"If she's too fine for me, she's way too fine for you..." William fired back

"You selfish bro... You know you get your heart broken easily. You ain't tryna win." Jerome said while downing another drink.

Kyle neatly rolled up his silver controller's cord and sat it next to him. Then he pulled out another controller, this controller turned electric blue once it was plugged in. "Who wants a shot at Drogon?" Kyle said, looking around the room. The hypnotic glow of this controller caught everyone's attention; even Michael stopped shoving things into his mouth.

"A new challenger approaches!" Michael said, reaching for a video game controller.

"Maybe you haven't been keeping up on current events but we just got our asses kicked, pal!" Brandon said to Michael.

"Don't rapid jab." Jerome advised.

"If you come over here and put your hands on a controller part two of my killin' spree will begin on your ass." Kyle said as they started playing.

"You don't drive, you ride share everywhere." Anthony said to William.

"So."

"So, you one time at band camp face fukka, need a vehicle, a scooter, a skateboard... something." Anthony said.

"You vehicle shaming me..." William said. "Remember the big break up I had?" William said to me as he played Steve Winwood.

"Of course I remember, you were over here for two days whining and getting angry at love songs." I said.

"When she told me that she wanted to break up; my heart never beat fast, I couldn't speak. What made it so bad was that she told me that she loved me, but she wanted to be with other people. I didn't realize that all of those stupid little arguments we had were signs that we weren't mature enough, that we were scared. Scared to be this close, too afraid to be vulnerable; we were scared the way love scares most people. Everything I said or did somehow injured her. I was confused." William said.

"She might have been afraid that you were going to break up with her, so she did it to you first." I said.

"My heart felt like it was melting." William said grabbing his chest. "I felt like all my choices had been taken from me. I was this close to ending everything. Do you remember what you said to me?"

"If you play 'I've Been Thinking About You' one more got damn time I'm going to ask you to leave..."

"After that…"

"*We need heartbreak. Whether it is the heartbreak of I hurt myself, or my body doesn't work the way I want it to any more, or the I thought this would make me happy heartbreak we need to go through heartbreak to get better ourselves. There is no insight without the heartbreak.*" I said recalling the conversation.

"As a former friend-zoned person, I can co-sign that." Michael said. "Life is going to hurt you; how you use that pain is up to you. You can spend a week sending 400 text messages or you can spend that week choosing to make yourself better.'

"Nic, I was wallowing in sorrow wishing that I could have done things differently and you said…"

"That is the same as wanted to be someone else. You can't undo something wishing you had done something differently without an altering all the good things about you, all the little pieces that make up who William is. If you changed that one little thing, the relationship may have lasted another month or until the next argument but what happened is what happened. Relationships change you on your journey to being an evolved version of yourself.' I repeated what I said to him.

"What you said and how you said it cut straight through to me. That day, I resolved to win-win-win no matter what and that's what I'm doing, focusing on what matters…me. When I was younger my motivation for getting up in the morning was tied to pussy. Now I stack dat cheese and stay focused on where I am going." William finished.

"And you wouldn't have this new focus, this new direction without the…" I said.

"Heartbreak…" William said fist bumping me. "I had never hurt like that before. I had to put in the work. I let go of the things I can't control. One thing I have learned is that if y'all broke up for good reasons don't let her come over talking about needing closure."

"Why?" I said.

"Because it's not dollar bills, it's the mind-state that's ill. And she'll come over at one in the morning wearing something form-fitting that you've never seen her in and you haven't seen her in weeks…" William said as the music pounded behind him.

"…keep going…" Brandon encouraged William to continue.

"...her lips shimmering, smelling delicious, looking tasty, with no panties on her wet, freshly waxed coochie and her mind dialed up to full freak. And you'll bounce your meat off her ass but once you're done, you'll be like I can't be doing this... There's never no in-between... We either niggas or King. We either bitches or Queens." William finished.

"I hear ya tryin' to be like Mos Def..." Brandon said.

"Yeah, Mos Def-i-nitely Vulgar." I said laughing.

"She was unrighteous anyway." William said.

"You signed up for the terms and conditions..." I said.

"That I did... that I did. Every time I bust a nut, I say I'm gonna change." William said laughing.

After we laughed, William played songs that made our eyes light up as soon as we heard them.

"I make it whistle like the Andy Griffith theme song." Brandon exclaimed, clapping his hands together.

"What do they say about going full retard?" I said to him. William was sobering up but Brandon was really starting to feel the effects of the alcohol and marijuana.

"Is this the man who wrecked the buffet at the Haro Club this morning?!" Brandon mockingly said.

"Is this what happens when you collect spores, molds and fungus?" William asked.

"You go halfway in and make her earn the rest." Brandon stated.

"This guy..." Anthony said.

"Some people like their fries dark skin and some people like their fries lite skin ya feel me." Brandon said.

"I'm tired of you!" Jerome yelled, pointing at Brandon.

"Here he comes with the dumbassery." I said.

"I'll freak you right, I will. I'll freak you right, I will. I'll freak you right, I will. I'll freak you like no one has ever, made you feel... Yyeeaahhh!" Brandon performed an ear splitting, inebriated, voice cracking rendition of this classic ballad which was sacrilegious.

"No!" William shouted with his eyes wide.

"Please stop." I said.

"I'm just sayin'." Brandon muttered.

"You lucky I'm sort of Christian." Jerome said still glaring at Brandon.

"Man we getting' older quit pretending that y'all still out here Supermannin' these hoes." I said to Brandon.

"Your soul is mine!" Kyle said to Michael.

"Is it hot in herre?" Michael said still playing the video game with Kyle.

"Nic you remember when we did those calculations..." William said.

"You mean when we estimated that you spent $5,000 a year dating..." I said.

"Five grand!" Anthony said. "Per person..."

"What the hell are these ladies eating... rent?" Jerome said incredulously.

"Nic, open up a window." Michael said.

"Damn, I got you taking off your coat and opening windows..." Kyle said, pushing all of the buttons on his controller.

"I'm sweating over here." Michael said wiping his forehead.

"Losses are heavy to carry." Kyle remarked.

"That's what happens when you're getting your ass beat." Brandon said.

"That's the perspiration of loss..." Jerome said.

"When the real you is wack as hell there's always money, clothes, make-up and movements to enhance you." I said. "Knowledge, skill and talent can help lower the cost of dating but..."

"Five thousand, it blew my mind too." William said. "That was the day I started investing more into myself. I have been able to book bigger guests and better DJs, which earns me more money. I'd rather work towards my goals, jack off and not have drama. Any drama and I'm out..."

"You just leave..." Brandon said.

William nodded his head in the affirmative.

"What kind of answer is that?" Anthony asked.

"Nic, would you say that disrespect is an answer?" William asked.

"I would." I responded.

"I'd rather put energy into something that benefits me. In two or three years I'll be close to earning six figures and anyone who partnering for the journey is getting left... straight up." William said.

"You sure is talkin' a lot of smack with your Right Here Waiting, Should've Known Better ass." Anthony said.

"You always bring up old shit. I ride share and I buy environmentally kind products. I'm doing my part, you rollin' around in that big 6000 SUX, backfiring out all kinds of pollutants…"

"What?!" Anthony stated. "Is the US military doing their part? Are nations that wage war doing their part? Are cruise lines and deforesters doing their part? Is NASA doing its part? Is industry doing its part?"

"Honestly, no they aren't." William responded.

"Industry is forcing the individual do their part… All of you culture shifting, depopulating, gluten free, urban foraging, almost hamburger eating, climate refugee just consume lies for breakfast. I bought that car because I wanted it. No ad, no government program, no amount of shaming is going to push me into spending my money to save an environment that has already been lost.

"Y'all paying top dollar for subpar eVehicles to make yourselves feel better; I don't have to do that. Y'all are not better than anyone else, in fact y'all worse for believing the bullshit. You can spend your time and money eating things that don't cast shadows and plant-based foolishness, so you can proudly beat your chest and say you are doing your part, if you want to. Are the rims big? Do it ride good? Lean back, right hand on the pinewood." Anthony said.

"You know if you can't drive, just say that. We'll clown you no doubt but at least it's honest." I said to William.

"Whateva." William uttered.

"Michael, you lost again… I told you that Kyle is unstoppable." Jerome said.

"You got 10 buttons on that controller and you just smashing the B button." Kyle said.

"I almost had him this time." Michael said getting up. "I was one button away."

"You just over there losing." Brandon said laughing.

"Shut up. You lost too." Michael said.

"Yeah but I didn't lose like you did. I can't stop the MVP of the league."

"Who leaves their job, drives all the way over here and decides... today I want to lose....who?" Kyle said mockingly.

"Your losses were inevitable, bound to occur that which cannot be avoided." William added.

As Michael put his controller down, everyone looked at him and just hunched their shoulders.

"As for Dominique, I figure that if she can get people to buy her and her friends drinks all night, she can get people to book tables." William said.

"How is that working out?" I said.

"We are in a testing phase. I prefer not to have my emotions played with anymore, unlike y'all." William said.

"Why are you even over here?" Anthony questioned William.

"I come over here because Nic has plastic straws." William replied while sipping his smoothie through a straw.

"Your heroes only exist on the screens, never meet them. You'll see they aren't in the political party you're in and that they are a serial gonorrhea spreader." Anthony said.

"Yo, is that a Black Bruce Lee action figure?" Brandon said, looking away from William and at the poseable character model that sat on my entertainment center.

"Sure is…" I said.

"Tight…" Brandon said picking the action figure.

"Don't drop it." I said.

"William, you always on yo smart phone. He's electric slidin' into DMs." Kyle said as he severed a head and ripped arms off in the video game.

"I'm just making sure the music mode stays on point." William responded.

"I hardly speak to the mother of my son." Kyle stated as he pressed the pause button on the controller. "She only speaks to me when she wants something… usually money. When I speak to my son, I'm on a time limit. His mother threatens to call the police on me for no reason. Jessica is always telling me to put my foot down, and every time I put my foot down, we end up in Family Court. Being here with y'all, here, is the only time I am listened to."

"If you are trying to get custody, you've got to go the full 100 yards with no blocking and no timeouts." I said. "That's why most dudes just fight for visitation. Most of these cases don't even go before a judge. If the mother manages to turn the children against you, fighting for custody is a lose-lose situation… Sometimes you got to let the kid go."

"Sometimes." Michael said puzzled.

"Letting a child go is the hardest thing you'll ever have to do." I responded. "If you do let a child go you better have a really good plan for coming back. I said.

"Fighting for custody with empty pockets is damn near impossible." Anthony said.

"My baby momma is trying to keep my pockets empty…" Kyle said.

"Exactly." I said.

"I've done everything I was supposed to do and then some. I've done for her kids, for her mom." Kyle said. "I pick up my son all the time. Family Court treats me like I'm not even human, like I don't have feelings. When I had two jobs, they were like why aren't you spending time with your children…"

Everyone in the room had a look on their face of knowing exactly what he was going through.

"Just stop…" I told Kyle.

"Stop what?" Kyle responded.

"Just stop," I repeated. "You can't put everything on her, you chose her."

"True enough…" Kyle said realizing his own responsibility in his selection process.

"They don't care if you never get to spend time with your child." Anthony said.

"Why?" Michael said.

"Because you left her…" Anthony said.

"If she didn't have my child, what she's doing would be harassment. What kind of protection do I have?" Kyle said.

"Asking for protection or to be treated fairly makes us look weak." William said.

"Bro, it's your male energy. Look at Brian McKnight, he called child protection services when he heard about an older cousin sexing his teenage daughter." Anthony said.

"I would have gone off too, so what happened?" Brandon asked.

"All the protection services did was inform the mother, who promptly cursed him out, blocked him from the family's social media pages and forbid the daughter from speaking to or seeing him." Anthony said.

"Damn that's messed up." Michael said.

"Because the father is concerned or has questions you want him out of the child's life, that's foul." Kyle said.

"She didn't want the questions and she probably didn't want the answers. She just wanted the money and any prestige that came from birthing his child." Anthony said.

"So basically, we've slipped into the dark side…" Kyle said.

"How do we change this dynamic of dysfunctional relations and damaged child rearing?" Jerome said.

"It's what society wants." I said.

"But why?" Kyle said.

"The same old why… money. Who has it; who is willing to spend it and how to control minds." Anthony said.

"Nic and I did an experiment pointing out instances where a white person did something or died and the media wanted the audience to know their life accomplishments and their back story. They wanted the audience to think there might have been foul play in their death or that they may have been justified in who they killed. When someone race died or did something the media reported it as possible gang ties or it was a footnote." Kyle said.

"Deep." Anthony said.

"Was that the day y'all were talking about how Darth Vader was Charles Foster Kane in the prequels?" William asked.

"The other one…" Kyle said.

"The one about how David took advantage of Goliath?" Anthony asked.

"That's the one." I said. "We were talking about how narrative is important and who is in charge of the narrative is more important."

"What do you mean?" Michael said.

"When you think of whiteness as more of an ideology, than a biological fact, you can see why a film like *Joker* was successful. The Joker isn't even super or special. It's a film about a crazy white people doing crazy white people things and getting celebrated for it." I said.

"To many he's a superhero." Kyle said. "He expresses the frustration within the young and confused.

"There is a genuine outrage and offense but when it comes to movies any sort of media; I know that corporate media are in the business of manipulating and exasperating people's actual reactions and legitimate concerns in order to maximize their business. Once you stop and ask yourself, am I really as upset as I think I am or am I letting the constant static from the biggest static producers on the planet trick me into doing their marketing for free, you might not be moved so easily.

"Batman is not super or special but the same rationale applies. Captain James Hook hates and fights Peter Pan because Peter Pan is an asshole that kidnaps children. Hook is doing what heroes are supposed to do, but according to the narrative Captain Hook is the villain." I said.

"Batman does represent many aspects of white identity." Kyle said.

"I like Batman." William said.

"Of course, you do. You like all the musty superheroes." Anthony said. "Black characters always have something covering their face or their electricity keeps everyone at a distance."

"...Batman, Batman you say." Brandon chimed in. "Seeing a 40-year-old man in a Batman suit isn't easy."

"I like X-Men because of the Martin Luther King and Malcolm X dynamic." I said.

"Right..." Brandon said.

"But they sanitized it by making them mutants. Mutants, although uniquely gifted, are generally weaker than the original." Michael said.

"What does it mean when you go out on a date and she doesn't order anything but she keeps taking food off your plate." Jerome said.

"It's not cute and she doesn't really want to share food with you. She wants to control your food intake and she's testing your co-dependency. Tell her to order her own damn food!" Anthony responded.

"Brandon is in your refrigerator again eye-fuckin' your grapes." Kyle said.

"See he tellin' on everybody, that's your white coming out." Jerome said to Kyle.

"You're right it is." Kyle said laughing.

"There you go with your go tell it on the mountain ass." Brandon said tossing a few grapes into his mouth. "...You fruit bat face fukka."

"Leave my grapes alone..." I shouted.

"Sorry about the grapes..." Brandon said coming back into the living room.

"He's always sorry for eating someone else's shit." William said.

"He got a two year history of being sorry for eating other people's food." Jerome added.

For some reason, once everyone was in the living room I thought this was the perfect time to get up and sing and unveil some dance moves I had been working on. I got up and danced around with the confidence of Tony Manero.

"There are 88 keys on the piano, pick one and sit your ass down!" William snapped as he stared at me.

"Bru, you always somewhere poppin' yo ass." Anthony said.

"Sit yo Patrick Swayze, Billy Ocean, Do it for Lil Saint ass down!" Jerome jabbed.

"Nic, be over here being a private dancer and doing dumb shit like, The 14 Days of Valentines... Where he does something special for her for 14 straight days... making us look bad." William said frowning.

"Don't hate. I like to be ahead of the game." I said smiling.

"Dumb shit…" Kyle added.

"Right…right…" I said, sitting back down.

"What's that you're eating over there?" Brandon said staring at Jerome.

"A quarter pounder with cheese." Jerome proudly said unboxing his food item.

"… in a Burger King bag…" I skeptically said.

"They said I can have the burger my way." Jerome responded displaying his burger.

"Old girl was having nightmares about me cheating on her; she would wake up wanting to fight. I was like, baby don't believe those lying ass dreams. I broke up with her over 3 months ago, she still calls me every day. She changed her last name to mine. If the world were flat, I would literally jump off the edge just to get away from her ass. She told me that the relationship isn't over until she says it is…" Brandon said.

"That's because you're too nice when you are in a relationship," I said.

"Too nice…" Michael responded.

"I am always the gentleman…" Brandon replied.

"That's the problem. She feels like she put a lot of time into the relationship. Even if the relationship isn't working they don't want to just walk away from it. They need you to be an complete bastard so they can outright hate you." Anthony said.

"Man, dats crazy…" William said.

"I'm a nice guy but I gotta see that ass in 3D." Brandon said.

"Women aren't really attracted to nice guys." I said.

"Saying that you're a nice guy, is like saying I'm lame, don't like me." Anthony said mocking Brandon.

"I had to keep telling her to respect my boundaries..." Brandon said.

"I'm gonna stop you right there...You out here tellin' people to respect your boundaries?" Jerome said.

"I like it when money makes a difference but it doesn't make them different. I don't want to get hurt, so they have to take it easy on me. Y'all know I wear my emotions on my sleeves..." Brandon fired out.

"No disrespect but I'm gonna say something disrespectful... No one is 100% masculine or feminine all the time, but what you are talking about is some bullshit." I said.

"I told y'all he pulling them outta the discount bin... This is an intervention." Michael said.

"Do you like washing dishes and folding clothes too." Jerome laughed.

"Fuck what you niggas be talkin' about, you're opinion doesn't count, what I'm doin' is the only thing that matters." Brandon stated.

"Man, you super simpin'. You sound like a whole ass Drake song..." I said.

"For real..." William said laughing. "You're probably cryin' about your problems with jumpoffs...I bet your journal is full of screams and tears."

"Like I said, everyone is entitled to their opinion." Brandon said.

"And if you don't want to hear everyone's opinion, keep your business to yourself." Anthony said.

"So, what yo sayin'."

"I'm sayin', you sound feminine." Anthony said.

"How so?"

"Dude, the way you framed it…" Jerome blurted out.

"And how did I frame it…"

"Moist." Michael said.

"Damp." Kyle said.

"You are talking like you need permission to have agency. You can't be telling people to respect your boundaries. If they are disrespecting you, they damn sure aren't listening to you either. And now you want to argue back and forth with us. I swear it's like talking with my little sister…" Anthony stated shaking his head.

"I just be expressing myself to them." Brandon stated.

"See there you go again." I said.

"If she crosses the line once, she's gonna do it again." Jerome said.

"You arguing for 3 hours during which you had to pull out a resume, power point presentation, an excel spreadsheet and a hand drawn diagram…explaining exactly where your boundaries are, for what? She'll never see your point of view. I'm not choosing that nightmare again, it's exhausting." Anthony stated.

"Y'all just can't handle the women I handle…" Brandon said.

"I don't want a woman I have to handle." I said. "I want my women to be my peace. Raise your standards, treat yourself better."

"All I have to say is that every needless argument will make me like you less." William said.

"Whatever your boundary line is, they'll push it to somewhere else. You should know this already." I said.

"I'll keep searching for the one..." Brandon stated. "This is my journey."

"Brandon..." Jerome said

"What?"

"Brandon..." Jerome again said.

"What?!"

"Fuck you!" Jerome said.

Everyone's eyes met as we laughed.

"So Kyle, I hear that Jessica is the provider in the relationship..." Michael asked. Kyle slowly nodded his head.

"And y'all talkin' about me." Brandon stated.

"I don't know about that situation..." Jerome said.

"You ah midhusband..." Michael smirked at Kyle.

"I don't mean to laugh, but... I... I do mean to laugh." I said laughing.

"Talk like this is only going to make me show even less mercy." Kyle responded.

"Got em!" Michael said laughing. "You have to admit that one was funny…"

"Losing allows you a lot of time to think up jokes." Kyle fired back.

"Y'all making this harder than it is supposed to be." I said.

"For real tho…" Anthony said.

"If your girl is the kind of person that doesn't care about North Korea, China or Houston and they somehow keep changing the conversation back to them, move on. Life is moving, you don't have time to be waiting on an adult to get their mind right that's like raising a child." I said.

"The consequences for their choices are lowered while your choices are legally taken from you." Anthony finished.

"My money, my choice." William stated as he changed songs.

"For real, there is a strategy involved in having sex, the angle, the position, the rhythm." Kyle said putting in another video game.

"There's a certain level of skill a man needs in order to get a women. A woman doesn't need skill to get a guy." Anthony said.

"Can y'all tell Brandon that he needs to stop chasing strugglers. He won't listen to me." Michael said.

"I mean, I'm not going to wife-up a woman I don't respect, and most of the women I go out with are not respectable." Brandon said.

"Wait…What!?" Anthony said confused.

"You are not respecting yourself, more than them not being respectable." I said.

"What makes them not respectable?" Anthony asked.

"Because, they are after my money, my car, my potential… I don't respect that." Brandon said.

"We all need to make better choices." I remarked. "I know I do."

"Still, ain't nothin' like wild caught pussy…" Anthony stated.

"Right." Michael said.

"It's tightness is a reflection of dick size, so it's always real tight for me." Brandon stated.

"Is that how you view it?" Anthony said.

"I stop listening when she starts telling me what she likes in bed." I said.

"Why?" William asked.

"Because she wants me to do the things other dudes did to her. I do what I do, not what an orchestra section of people before me did." I said.

"That makes sense, okay, what else…" William said.

"Go out on dates to museums, art fairs, picnics, walks on the beach, watch sunsets, go to Astro Skate, have fun but be smart."

"Oh my god he talked to me, he looked at me…can I just go from my door to the mail box without being objectified…" William mockingly said.

"Everyone gets looked at…" Jerome said.

"I know." William said. "Sometimes it's just not worth the risk."

"Sometimes it is." Michael said. "We have to allow some level of engagement, people have issues of that there is no doubt, but in order to find the best person for you, you have to be approached. Do you know how many women broke my heart? Do you know how many godless she bitches I had to dick down? Do you know how many pumps I wasted before I ran into the love of my life?"

"We can't all be military veterans, poetry reciters or scientists." William said dismissively.

"But you can be yourself." I said.

"That's easy for you to say. Women just come over to your place and take all of their clothes off." William said.

"Well…you don't have a place, you have a room..." I said.

"Fair enough." William said.

"What, you need help with your stroke too." Anthony said.

"See, now you goin' too far. I'm just saying that things are easier when you are fearless…" William said.

"It's not about being fearless, I know who I am. I don't play games. I'm just up front and I don't lead with money. I see options everywhere, but I don't mind going home alone." I said. "Rejection is okay. The word no doesn't hurt me. If you stay positive and work on yourself, people will be drawn to you."

"You doin' all the shit the ladies don't like." Kyle said.

"It's okay to care..." Jerome said.

"Fuck dude, do you want something real or do you want to spend two or three months just trying to get the panties—you not going to get both!" Anthony said.

"Cracking the EMT principle is hard." Michael said.

"Is that a new NASA program?" William asked.

"It's an old human one, which can apply to many things. It's a principle whereby men want as much sex for the least amount of energy, money and time." Anthony said.

"Principles don't apply to Nic." William said.

"It's hard being this damn sexy." I said jokingly. "In general, ladies want as much energy, money and time for the least amount of sex. I'm just one of the guys they slept with that they can conveniently erase from their sexual history. They're not going to tell their boyfriends or husband about our wild sexcapades and I'm not going to say anything.

"I like romance and I believe that love is out there for me so I have to put myself out there. You might end up with the person you're not supposed to be with, and the sooner you recognize that the better. Running the dating gauntlet is daunting, it's a free-for-all. Some people will like you for you and some people won't. You just might get lucky."

"You can't just count on good looks and good genes; you will have to put somebody else's needs and wants above your own." Michael said.

We all sat in silence for a moment. William loudly sighed and then turned the music back up. Shantel called me and asked if I was chilling with my friends tonight, of course I was. She wasn't tutoring me anymore, so I told her I wouldn't be able to pick her up, and she said she understood.

"The best thing about America is that you don't have to travel all over the world to fuck third world bitches." William said.

"Shut your Mr. Backseat ass up." Jerome responded.

"You shut yo ass up!" William fired back. "Who are the 5 best club promoters that you know? Think about it, William, William, William, Bill and Liam which is short for William." He said while closing each extended fingers.

"Every day I hear people complain about nerve pain, viral encephalitis, gout, Crohn's and all sorts of problems that I could have but wasn't controlled enough by advertisements to go to the doctor for them." Anthony said chewing on a licorice root. "I just shake that it off and keep going. I'm not going to be programmed into giving doctors monthly dividends. Why can't people die slowly and naturally without them finding six or seven other conditions when you only went in there for one?"

"How else could universities, pharmacies, the healthcare industry, the pharmaceutical industry and medical profession be sustained if people couldn't be convinced to do things?" I said.

"I know right, it's not like they tryin' to save us and keep us around." William said.

"It's all experimental even the over the counter medications." Anthony said.

"Now y'all sayin' that health care is a scam." I said shaking my head.

"You look like you eat ass." Jerome said to Michael who had a mouth full of sponge cake.

"What does someone that eats ass look like?" Michael said smacking is lips.

"You nigga." Jerome laughed.

"You got me on that one, but see that's what I'm saying y'all always talking that macho male stuff...I ain't even gon' front...I'm a screamer." Michael said.

"What you mean, you ah screamer?" Jerome asked.

"Yeah, the neighbors don't hear my wife, they hear me. I'm the one screaming. I be like…Joan, Joan…Joan!" Michael screamed.

"Bruh, you almost made me drop my drink." Anthony said, laughing.

"This guy…" Jerome said glaring at Michael.

"When you are on your back you don't have to chase the orgasm so much." Michael said with a serious look on his face.

"That's like saying she fucked herself with your dick." I said.

"It is none of my business, but since you are telling everybody your business… I'm making it my business. You are being submissive in the bedroom too?" Anthony said, shaking his head.

"I'm a power bottom." Michael replied confidently.

"Why do I have to listen to him say these things?" Jerome said in frustration.

"I'm not going to be the guy that wants to love you more but can't because I'm afraid that if I bring the real me out, you'll leave. So I'm screaming, moaning and a lot of other things." Michael said.

"Props." I said to Michael.

"Certain animals do kill for fun that's a misnomer. Snails kill a lot of people every year. Did you know that malaria has killed half of the people that ever lived?" Brandon said randomly. "Nature doesn't have a dark side."

"How you know all this shit?" William asked.

"Performance enhancers in college—Adderall, Marijuana." Brandon replied.

"My son's mother said she'll always choose the child over the daddy." Jerome said.

"They think all this drama is some kind of game." I said. "You have to invest in your relationship. You have to value the other person. The bottom line is that your relationship doesn't own you, you own it. You have to cultivate relationships; don't expect everyone to be an adult."

Married With Children

"Local Hero Goes Wrong!" The headline read. I wasn't a hero; at least I didn't think so. People didn't think of me in this way because I played basketball in high school. They thought of me this way because in my teens, I ran errands for the elderly, volunteered at shelters and Black people mattered to me long before it was fashionable or profitable.

Every day the courtroom was filled with supporters because everyone knew that all I did was defend myself. I wasn't really concerned about my own safety and I fought back only when my 11-month old daughter was attacked. See, I was raised wrong because I wasn't in the habit of just allowing children to be abused.

It wasn't that long ago, but it was still a different time. It took me a long time to realize that what had occurred was part of something larger. I was removed from the home and I became the swarthy boogeyman they claimed we all were. Sometimes, I still wonder how was a 20 year old new parent supposed to know that race, gender and politics would converge to force them to do the wrong thing?

Knowing too much, yet not enough is a strange place to be. Somehow society knew before I did that I would not be a proponent of making ourselves dumber on purpose. I would not distort the meaning of things for capitalistic gains. That I would toss away stereotypes and unpacking the baggage associated with gender, race, social movements, politics, and sex. I would not go along to get along. I would challenge narratives. I would follow a different path. I would not follow the curriculum. I would listen.

None of us introduced ourselves by our accolades or accomplishments. These often random people gave me pure thoughts and emotions and their honesty guided me away from a hardening heart. People came here because they wanted to be here. They gave me insight, humor, friendship which motivated and pushed me. I gave them a place to be, something to belong to and the security of someone actually listening to them.

Theories and icy pragmatism aside, the best stories and tales come from poor people, who also by far have the most sex. Poor people don't have to wonder if their friends are only around because of fortune and fame. These weren't scripted lives; these lives were full of mistakes. Between these walls I brought together and managed converging disciplines, voices and personalities.

These weren't exactly the Munk Debates but they were more honest. These points of view came from people on the ground, people in the thick of it. These weren't academic, journalistic or political discussions. Through such discourse we were able to receive information that is often held tightly behind pay walls, degrees and social structures.

The promise being that the many pitfalls of life might not be avoided, only made softer. The only way to learn and grow was not to be blinded by friendship. My friends were flawed, high vibration people. We didn't hold back with each other, that's the only way the truth can be obtained.

I wasn't the kind of hero society was looking for. I would not parrot the same talking points that come from those same disingenuous, anti-intellectual, instinct flattering, criticism groups that stifle actual discussion and replaces complicated nuance analysis with binary arguments where you just shout slogans back and forth and dismiss something sight unseen because it seems like or you've heard it before.

I learned my lesson. Doing the right thing isn't always the smart thing. I still couldn't allow children to be abused. So, my policy became that any child or person that needed help and I could provide it I would, but from a distance. In ways big and small we are heroes to our children. Sometimes being a hero is a punishment.

"These people, their kids and their dog are both on anti-depressants. They are standing in long lines for cell phones. All of this nonsense is why I moved on to better things." Michael said.

"What do you mean?" Kyle said.

"If you find a quality woman you better marry her because you're beating the odds." Michael said. "After I got married the shemons stopped attacking. Our bond spiritually protects us. Marriage, for me is stable, predictable. We develop as individuals while coming together as a unit. It's not easy. "

"I'm not going to risk my life for some chick that doesn't suck dick." William stated.

"So you are just going to eat all the apples…" I said laughing.

"You're not going to get a high quality woman with streaks in your drawers anyway." Jerome said laughing at William, who just smirked at him.

"It's hard to be with someone when what you have to deal with doesn't matter to them." Anthony stated.

"My wife is inspirational. We enhance each other." Michael said. "I don't mind watching those shows with her. I don't want to think when I get home. I do enough thinking at the office, so I'm a follower when it comes to most things. I want the packaged and commercialized stuff."

"Michael, your kid is about a year old... right. I told you raising a child wasn't going to be as hard as you thought..."

"You were right. The shit is harder." Michael responded.

"Harder..." I said.

"My whole life is changed. No doubt, I love my son and just watching how quickly he learns is really amazing but I rather work more and for my wife to work less, that's all I'm saying."

On the weekends I occasionally saw men with their children, but hardly ever on the weekdays. At these gatherings, we shared a lot on how to deal with the mothers of our children, visitation and the courts. The gathering brought others into the support system, others who could move things forward. I hoped my efforts would encourage more men to contribute to a possible infrastructure that would support all of us having our children around more... but it didn't.

I expected a few attempts from them to have their children move but there were none. Most guys have their kids only on the weekend because it's hard changing your whole life when you don't really have to. My friends would occasionally bring their children by my house but it wasn't anything regular.

I did things because I had to. I saw the problems in society and in the community before most people. I am the way I am, but I am not special. Pride is the devil, everyone is different. Michael enjoys being married and anyone can see that, but the truth is that he was just as scared as we were but he trusted that he made the right decision."

"I'm thinking of dating outside my race, and not for the clout, but because inside my race they are mentally and physically trying to kill me..." Anthony said.

"When things go wrong the first thing the average Black woman is going to do is separate from the Black man." William said.

"Dealing with Jessica's baby daddy was rough in the beginning. Remember when we were all about to roll over that fool's house... Now that I work part time things are actually working out." Kyle said.

"If things are working out so much why is your Mr. Mom ass always in here kicking everyone's ass in video games?" Jerome said.

"Pent up hostility..." Kyle said.

"You Hyrule face fukka..." Brandon fired out.

"You overcorrected." I offered.

"Maybe." Kyle responded hunching his shoulders as he picked up the controller.

"Stop dating hoes. Date 402s." Brandon said.

"What... four ohh twos." I enquired.

"Yeah 4-0-2s, almost hoes, that's all that's left." Brandon stated.

"Brandon you're one to talk." Michael said.

"I don't know what you talkin' 'bout, I get box." Brandon confidently replied.

"But you are constantly violating the cardinal rule; if you can't lift her, you can't be with her." Michael said.

"I'll just say...don't knock it until you've tried it." Brandon fired back.

"Oh, we've tried it and we knockin' it." Jerome sarcastically said.

"I exercise to increase my options." Brandon said "But like I sayin' I had to bounce from my last relationship. I couldn't take the abuse anymore." Brandon said.

"When a full-figured woman puts hands on you, you feel it." I said.

"I've been hit by women since I was born." Brandon said.

"Who hasn't…who hasn't…" Anthony stated

"JJ never gets hit." Jerome said confidently.

"Stop lying…" I said.

"That's what I'm going to tell everybody." Jerome said smiling.

"I'll never again ignore the emotional and psychological abuse because of attractiveness ….never." Anthony said.

"It's not funny! Who likes getting hit?" Brandon said. "I mean, why hit someone because they don't agree with you? Why grab the steering wheel while I'm driving? Why?"

"For the senseless, things don't have to make sense. One time I said something my daughter's mother didn't like and she wouldn't let me see my daughter for three months. That shit hurt like hell. If she had my child she doesn't need to physically hit me, I mean she still hit me but she didn't need to. Now, if any of us sees or hears abuse we are not only going to talk about it." I stated as everyone silently nodded in agreement.

"When you get married you stop singing, because the party is over." Anthony said.

"Example?" I said.

"How many hip hop, R&B, rock and pop are about the joys of being married?"

"Hardly any." I responded.

"Think about it, there are decades of music about wilding out, playing, freedom, infatuation, friends, buying bullshit, irresponsibility, drugs and hooking up; marriage is supposed to be the opposite of all of that." Anthony said.

"Look if you want romance, be romantic. You want love— be loving. You want respect— be respectful. I want to be a better husband and a better father; Anthony and Jerome, you both know that's a constant process. I have a good partner and I like being married. I still get hit, but not as much." Michael said.

"Oh that's right, you married that cutie who was always acting like she needed help." Jerome said.

"...believe me, it was no act." Michael responded. "Nic, you were right when you said that what you want usually isn't what you need. I am glad Joan and I chose each other. We close on that rental property in two weeks. Pretty soon, she'll be able to stay home and raise our children."

"Children..." William said.

"Joan is pregnant..." Michael said.

"Y'all expecting again..." Anthony said. "You just getting in deeper and deeper."

"You big dummy!" Jerome said imitating Redd Foxx.

"Y'all hatin' on me because I graduated college before I started my family."

"That has nothing to do with it." Jerome responded.

"Congrats, man." I said, giving him a crisp high five. Brandon and Kyle enthusiastically hugged Michael.

"Coongrats…" William sarcastically said.

"Don't be jealous." Michael said.

"Jealous of what?" William responded. "You Lieutenant Worf face fukka."

"A lot of people think the infertility issue is on the woman's side but a lot of the fault is with the man. Some men have a difficulty with impregnation, and it goes beyond low sperm count, illness, injuries, chronic health problems or lifestyle choices." Anthony said.

"So, we should consider ourselves lucky." Jerome said.

"I got da good meat. God did his thing when he made me; I'm sure I can make it happen." William said confidently.

"Not everyone can procreate and you won't know until it happens." Anthony said.

"If all you have is a big dick then you really don't have much." I said. "See, the universe knows to give a person a delivery mechanism with less or more length to better complete the delivery. Some of us need to deliver the package right in the mail slot and some of us can toss the package down the street and it still gets delivered. Sometimes it's not about how many, it's about spermatic aggression and intelligence."

"You're not wrong." Anthony said.

"Having children one after the other is the best way to go." I said patting Michael on the back.

"I don't know if I could even get married again. These women out here talking about wanting to be a wife, but they not even a good girlfriend." Jerome said.

"You're the one who is always buying some woman a ring..." Anthony said to Jerome.

"Those aren't engagement rings, they are be quiet rings." Jerome said, putting his index finger to his mouth.

"Go ahead and get married, as soon as you do something wrong, she'll throw you away." Anthony said.

"High fructose corn syrup is good." Brandon said gulping down his drink.

"You're not adding to the conversation." I spouted to Brandon.

"I love, love, I'm just bad at it." Brandon blurted out.

"These ladies will tell you that they can have any man they want. If they put it out there not many would turn it down, but that's not the same as having any man." Anthony said.

"You have to get with someone you can vibe with emotionally, socially and financially." Michael said.

"They say they want you to communicate, but that's only as long as you are agreeing with them." Jerome responded. "When they say they want you vulnerable, that's exactly what they mean."

"Yeah, you want sexy, demure and intelligent but you have to settle for fat, loud and opinionated." William said smirking.

"When we were dating she only half paid her bills and her credit was terrible." Michael said.

"So now it's all good..." I said.

"Everything is the same, except I'm paying the bills and repairing her credit while trying to stop her from spending me to death." Michael responded.

"And there it is…" Anthony said smacking his lips.

"I ain't sayin' she's ah gold digger…" William stated.

"There's a cost to everything." Michael said. "She's a good mother to our son. Besides, I was tired of all these women objectifying me. I was tired of being repeatedly violated. I am a human being. I have feelings. I'm not just here to please a woman. When I wake up I'm not thinking about sex. If I get it get it. If I don't, I don't."

"I bet you can't even get hard no mo..." Jerome said.

"I lose an erection every time I get a bill." Michael said smiling.

"Erections aren't unlimited, you need to conserve them." I stated.

"Are you actively turning down ass?" William said to Michael.

"I can't help it if my wife finds me attractive. She says good sex gets rid of headaches and made her monthly cramps go away. She wants me empty when I leave the house. She comes home and gets on the treadmill. So sometimes I have to not give in. It's good to regulate yourself." Michael said.

"But you turnin' down ass tho." William said.

"Michael, you've been married for two years now. I know you've hooked up with one of those women in the lab. I know you handling dat…" I said.

"I'm really not, but those lab coats do hide bangin' bodies. Most people in these fields don't pick up social cues well so your career is at risk if you mess with them." Michael answered.

"Word…" Brandon said.

"Your wife is five years younger than you and you'll die five years before her, so she's going to get the house, the money, the pension and still be young enough to enjoy her life when you're gone." Anthony said.

"You got to get them younger than you because the older ones might be ran through, have bad habits and a head full of bullshit." Bandon said.

"If you want a good mate that's college educated; well guess what… they might be ran through. Having someone to share your life with is great. For me it was worth the risk… I just can't…" Michael said.

"Have a real opinion…show emotions…do what you want to do…" Jerome quickly said.

"Y'all supermen everywhere except at home, naw! I can't accept that my ceiling is Lois damn Lane…" William said.

"You n-words need to stop. Give and take goes a long way in a good relationship and I have a good one. Ummm, Brandon, we have to get going." Michael said, watching Brandon almost fall over while drinking another smoothie.

"You have a curfew too." Anthony said and everyone laughed.

"You got them dick hard pills?" Brandon asked me

"Are you having issues?" I said.

"I didn't say I was having issues, I said do you have some."

"90% of the time if you change the person you won't need the pills." I smiled.

"You remember Denise…" William said.

"Vaguely...oh... She's the one with the...and the... I remember her." Brandon said making hand motions.

"Homegirl that dresses like a tomboy..." Michael said

"She doesn't dress like that anymore...she's bad." Jerome said.

"So, what happened?" Michael said.

"She was over here about a month ago tearing into them about their relationship problems." William said.

"Y'all need to be torn into." Michael said. "Y'all don't need a to-do list; y'all need a stop-doing list."

"You always over here tellin' people what to do. You, and I'll form the head face fukka." Jerome said to Michael.

"That's right and when my kitchen pipes get clogged I'll give your Handy Manny ass a call." Michael fired back.

"Was William snickering and asking for nut milk when she was here?" Kyle asked.

"Nope." Anthony said.

"Nut milk?" Brandon asked.

"He means almond milk; he just likes to say nut milk." I responded.

"But it is nut milk... almonds are nuts..." William said, defending himself.

"We know..." Anthony said.

"And it is funny..." William said.

"We know..." Anthony said.

"So what you sayin'?" William asked.

"He's commenting on how the nature of even the most uncouth changes when soft legs are around." I said.

"Well, almonds aren't nuts they are drupes. Most nuts have a hard outer shell. Mangoes and peaches are drupes as well..." Brandon said.

We all just stared at William and he slowly put his head down.

"You just had to ruin it..." William mumbled.

"Sometimes you have to teach the people who teach you." Anthony said.

"You could have just let me have it." William solemnly said.

Michael got closer to William and started looking at his smart phone.

"Hey, you can't be looking at my DMs." William said to Michael trying to shield his smart phone from Michael's eyes.

"What's that?" Michael said to William.

"Research..." William said looking at his cell phone.

"You wrong for watching that kind of nakedness..." Michael said.

"If they didn't put it out there I wouldn't be able to look at it." William said.

"...What website is that?" Michael said.

"Naw, you're a happily married man." William responded.

"I'm married, I ain't dead." Michael stated.

"She's just another pervert masquerading as an exhibitionist. I don't know why society allows these ladies to get away with flashing everyone?" William asked.

"Because women and men like seeing woman barely dressed or naked, no matter the psychosis behind it." I answered.

"True enough." William said.

"You wouldn't consider Bugs Bunny or Wil E. Coyote as being half naked, have you seen the cartoon these children are watching?" Jerome said.

"Didn't they say your son is on the spectrum, he has the Tism?" Kyle said to Jerome.

"No, the school said he might have ADHD," Jerome said. "What he has is soft porn teachers in front of him and titties and fat asses in his pocket. Even if he doesn't look at it, he knows it's there. I had the teacher move his desk to the front of the class and I've taken his smart phone."

"They have too many options…" I said.

"Work is too hard for this upcoming generation. They get traumatized from having a video game taken from them." Anthony said.

"When a blogger uses racially or gender coded language or says, this is what a real man would do, what real black person would do or they start talking like they have a PhD in the field that's how I know they are full of shit." Kyle said trying to hand Anthony his phone.

"No thanks." Anthony said. "I'm not the type of nigga that'll type to niggas…for what. Here's a video of me, watching other people watching other people. They gon' tell the Internet on you. Google is your research team. People sure do have it hard on the Internet."

"Going outside is expensive." William said.

"Shit, because of these stay-at-home kids corporations have made staying inside expensive too!" I said.

"Research shows that there is a correlation between cases of attention-deficit disorder and the proliferation of cellular phones." Michael said.

"Right." Kyle said.

"Man, fuck all dat you don't need a report and you don't need a study… just look at what they are doing, we in da middle of a damn zombie apocalypse. They don't look like the ones in the movies and shows, but it's them." William said in obscure way.

"There can only be zombies if there's a market for them." I said looking at William. "I'm not in the eye scan here, finger print there, put my family's DNA online crowd, but I do see the inherent danger in such things. Progress means that you have to step where you've never stepped before, but should we allow digital targeting to drive people's morals, values and beliefs? I have been on the outside looking in and I want to guide myself."

"Some people would call that convenience." Michael responded.

"Is it…" I responded.

"What agencies have access to this convenience?" Anthony said. "What if fully embracing technology means submitting to outside control?"

"I'd still do it." Michael replied.

"We are nerds but that doesn't mean that I have to look the other way when stores change layouts just to make customers stay in stores longer." I said. "I don't like having non-standard sizing charts for clothes. I don't appreciate how they add loading screens and inflating wait times just to build trust. I'm not a big fan of paying full price for unfinished things that have to be updated every couple weeks.

"I don't support the government influencing thoughts and behaviors. And excuse me if I don't play along when corporations keep the price the same, shrink the package and claim it has less sugar or fat, of course it does. It doesn't matter if it is a printers, coffee maker, operating systems or razor everyone knows you don't make money off the console; you make money from the games.

"There are certain are characteristics in certain people which allows them to be moved from one new thing to the next new thing. That shit no longer works on me. There is always hoopla over this latest technological offering like its special but it's just a car and those are just lights. All money and technology put into vehicles; marketing them with incredible safety features, but none of those feature have prevented accidents or deaths. For now, at least, the overlords are human. Lord help, us when we get locked out by electronics, chastised by automated responses and shot by robots…" I said.

"It's efficient. It's just a nudge towards what people would likely to choose." Michael said.

"Would they…" I said.

"When you really start looking at it, everything isn't always as it appears. Computers don't protest, an automated kiosk doesn't protest, robots don't protest." Kyle said.

"Innovation means less dependence on workers. Efficiency means they're getting rid of old methods for newer, faster, cheaper methods. All of it means layoffs." Michael stated.

In the middle of the music and conversations, Brandon started grunting, making guitar sounds and making rhythmic noises with his mouth while he waved his hands as if he were conducting an orchestra.

"Bro!" I said frowning.

"What the hell are you doing?!" Anthony said.

Brandon just started the rhythm over as he got closer to William. William cut the music off and looked intently as more guttural sound emanated towards him.

"I am making the sounds of the song I want to hear." Brandon said.

"Just say the lyrics or use the Internet—dumbass. You must not be smokin' the same thing we smokin'." Jerome said.

"This song doesn't have any words and I don't know the name of it. I know the rhythm so I'm making the sounds." Brandon answered.

"Do it one more time…" William asked.

Brandon made the noises again as William nodded his head. William picked up his phone typed on it for about ten seconds, sat back and then Art of Noise's 'Beat Box' came out of the speakers.

"That's it!" Brandon yelled.

"How is this possible?" Michael said in disbelief.

"How the hell did you do that?" Anthony asked.

"Don't know." William nonchalantly responded.

"Man you better than Alexa." I said. "You Black Alexa."

"Balexa." Jerome laughed.

"That shit was fuckin' amazing." Anthony said still shaking his head.

I silently smiled and look at those assembled. We each had our moments of brilliance. It dawned on me that there were systems in place that intentionally sought to subdue this kind of brilliance, to tame the information, to sanitize, to kill and to incarcerate it.

I started to believe that the long sought after solutions to diseases, famines and many of the world's problems are locked inside of brains that are locked away, brains that would never see the light of day, brains locked inside of poor schools, brains that won't make it home tonight, brains that can't read or write, brains that are right now being bombed out of existence, brains that are being altered, brains that are being abused, brains that are overlooked, brains that are barely hanging on in places you never thought to look, in places you would never go.

There seemed to be forces actively working against this kind of knowledge, this kind of off-curriculum education, unkind forces, forces that lacked appreciation for humanity; forces that had a greater appreciation for enslavement, servitude and anger.

"Man, I still don't know how you did that shit." Michael said still in disbelief."

"Because I was inverted." William smiled while moving his hands together.

Space Exploration

"To the window, to the wall!" We sang.

"Y'all hear that?" William suddenly said. "Yo…Nic, your neighbors think you're selling dope…"

"Motherfucker I am," I replied blowing out smoke.

The apartment fell silent as we heard rustling outside my apartment window. Anthony quietly got into his ready stance.

"What's got you spooked; you ain't afraid of no man." I said to Anthony.

"There's something out there waiting for us, and it ain't no man." Anthony dramatically replied.

"I think Wrinkles the Clown is outside yo door." Jerome said, putting the lighter down.

"Zombies!" William said throwing his hands up in frustration.

An outline appeared and then there was a subtle knock at my door. It was Shantel, she had someone drop her off. She came in and sat in her usual corner of the couch. I introduced her to Kyle, Michael and Brandon. I was a little annoyed that I might have to drop her off.

"How are the Magic doing?" Jerome asked, trying to change the conversation.

"What are the Dolphins doing?" Kyle asked.

"Michael, we should probably get going." Brandon announced after looking at his watch.

"If you have a sugar daddy aren't you a prostitute?" William asked undaunted.

"No." My Ex-Tutor answered.

"But..." William said with wide eye curiosity that bordered on naiveté.

"Damn, read the room!" Anthony replied.

"But, is the word pet just another word for slave?" William said as he started to pack up his things.

"You don't expect your loved one to be murdered by police over a welfare check call." Jerome stated to change the subject.

"Will some cops might taze, assault, strip, starve, steal, freeze, plant evidence, use excessive force and murder and then lie about it like a criminal gang? Yes." Anthony said. "You have incompetent, rule breakers and criminal elements in every job, not just in law enforcement. People think police are just supposed to run into gunfire. When someone gets an award for being a hero there is usually only one person on that stage... what was everyone else doing during the incident? You can I have all the weapons and all the training in the world but when you actually get shot at your thinking changes.

"These dumbasses think it's cool to throw rocks at the police. The police have a hard job. That being said, I've done two tours of duty but the most I've ever been afraid was the night the police pulled me over near Overtown. Three officers' surrounded me all with their guns drawn and I'm supposed to be concerned about them being afraid of me..."

"When your last line of defense is a camera on your phone, society is in trouble." Michael said.

"I still can't believe they acquitted those cops..." Shantel said.

"They usually do." Jerome said.

"Fuk dat shit you talkin' Nicodemus has helped everyone in this room." Kyle stated without turning away from the video game. "Shit he saved my life twice."

"And he ain't never asked for anything in return." William said.

"Our presence has begun to deter crime in this area, little kids aren't running around unattended. Families can have safe events together. Kids aren't dropping out of school and I can't remember when the last shooting was." Anthony said.

"Nic's a good dude." Michael said.

"It's fucked up how they did you for protecting your daughter." Jerome said. "If I had known you back then I would have protested like I did for McDuffie..."

"I told you mandating that the police wear cameras would not prevent crime or stop abuse. From the very inception that idea was always about providing more content." I said to Anthony.

"And you were right." Anthony said nodding.

"From a world away people can be monitored in their home, when they step out their front door, in their car, while they're walking, talking and shopping, while they're having sex, or taking a shit." I said. "Being born, dying, all of your worst moments captured with or without your consent and you still believe we have the right to privacy.

"Cameras are everywhere and what we have been told is that this is for our protection. No, they're for our monitoring. Cameras are everywhere airports, law enforcement, federal government. They sold it to the public by saying these devices will make us safer, but that's just one phase.

"It is what it is, but still we have real neighborhood watches in effect and real information being spread. None of this is about me, it's about the programs Jerome brings to the community, the resources Anthony provides, the hiring Denise is doing and the connections William is making and of course the brains of Michael, Brandon and others have, it has to be a group effort."

"What about me?" Kyle said as I passed him the blunt.

"You are raising the children the right way and not contributing to the shit we are fighting against, that's good enough." I said. "When and if you can do more you will. It has taken a long time just to get people in this neighborhood to care about their future and to see how much they impact others. Still, there's a lot of work to do and that's where the children come in. They'll run for office and they will fill elected positions, they'll create new laws and new training. They are the change we are working for."

There was a loud honking outside. It was Jessica and children. Kyle quickly grabbed his things fist bumped everyone and hurried out into the night.

"You could have at least turn the TV to the Miami Heat game." Jerome yelled after Kyle walked out.

"Turn the music up." Anthony said to William.

"Damn, I always have to battle no see ums when I get around here…" Anthony said swatting at a flying insect.

"No See Ums, it's time for us to go." Brandon said, quickly grabbing his coat.

"Let me get another one of them cigars before y'all head out." William said.

I fist bumped Michael and said, "Get us off this rock."

Michael smiled, straightened his suit, he grabbed my forearm and pulled me close and whispered, "Unfortunately, the only way people are getting off this rock is through virtual reality." And he slowly walked to the door.

"It was nice meeting you." Shantel said to Michael and Brandon. Michael looked at Brandon and said, "...to the casino..."

"To the strip club..." Brandon responded licking his lips. "I only wanna asses set to smother you."

"I don't know how you get free lap dances." William said.

"Intelligence is sexy and don't worry about how I get free lap dances. Ya no-account, bush-whackin' barracuda face fukka." Brandon said laughing.

"Next gathering we not invitin' those that shave with Nair." Jerome said.

"You just mad that I don't hang out with your Christmas decoration stealing ass..." Michael said smugly.

"Don't lock the bottom lock." William yelled. "Why you like to lock everybody in when you leave?"

"...And don't invite those dudes that dwell in the sewer." Michael fired back as he and Brandon left my apartment.

"It's not the sewer it's the Department of Sanitation... dumbass." Jerome said. "Nic, I almost forgot, I put ten sand bags behind your apartment." Jerome said on his way out. "Michael, come back here so I may brain thee…"

"Yo, Anthony, can I get a ride to the crib?" William said grabbing his back pack.

"Let's go… I told you that you need a car. Stay up." Anthony said fist bumping me on his way out.

"I appreciate y'all for coming thru…" I said as they left.

Certain things men just can't say in the presence of a woman especially if she's the only woman in the room. Shantel again asked if she could sleep on the couch. Shantel was small and quiet; she just blended in. I often forget that she was even here. She had been non-tutoring me for about a week and a half. I didn't mind if she spent the night as long as she didn't cramp my style. Shantel being around, at least made me think about math. If I aced the math final, I'd barely pass algebra.

I was asleep in my bedroom when I felt something touch me. I open my eyes and tried to scan the darkness. My room was so dark that not even moonlight filtered through. I couldn't make out what it was and before I knew it, my dick was sliding back and forth on a warm tongue.

I pushed the darkness, but it changed angles and sucked me harder. Fright wandered my through intoxicated fog. Although intense, I couldn't make out the shape. The more warmth I felt the less of a nightmare it became. I squirmed and my warm juices exploded out. Normally, people that don't take pride in their work stop sucking at this point, feeling that the goal was accomplished or that now it was their turn.

The dream slowly sucked down the remaining juices. I quickly fell into resting mode; I was sleep before I rolled over. The following morning, I quickly got up and rushed into the living room. Shantel was sleep and still in the same position on the couch. Could I have been trippin'? I wondered.

I showered, got dressed and woke Shantel up. I took her home, it was a quiet ride. I'm not going to say anything about it that's for damn sure. A few days later she called me and asked if she could come chill. I said, "Yes." Once again, in the middle of the night I felt that same dream. It was Shantel. She was on top of me sucking to her little heart's content. This time she looked at me while she did it. It was dark but I could see that she didn't have on any clothes. I reached down and touched her thigh.

Her skin was different. It wasn't smooth, but it also wasn't bad. She hopped into the bed and shoved my erectness inside her wet pussy. Her fissured nipples stood at attention as she rode me like I was one of those mechanical bulls at a bar. Here's the thing, her coarse skin next to her soft wetness produced an unusual feeling. She orgasmed in that position and then she bent over and let me pound her into another one.

Two days later she called again, this time I was prepared, with a new box of condoms. The gathering ended early, so I could entangle with my ex-tutor earlier. Shantel no longer needed to assault me in the middle of the night. She told me that she was on the Depo-Provera shot, so it was on and crackin'. We fucked until another wave of orgasms hit her, then she went into the living room and curled up in her usual spot on the couch; this was a good thing because I had a booty call on the way.

My later night rendezvous was with the nurse I had reconnected with through social media. She had begged to come over. When she arrived I quickly ushered her little Cuban ass into my bedroom. My dick was, I can't believe I'm fucking this bitch, level hard. I don't know how Shantel slept through all the encouragement moans and booty clapping sounds.

When the Cuban nurse left she was too tired to look around my house. She never saw Shantel sleeping on the couch. Shantel didn't seem to care that women were coming by for midnight exercises. Sometimes after a woman left my house, Shantel would come into the bedroom and suck me as if to say the other girl didn't do it right.

The other night Shantel licked me until I was rock hard and then she spread her ass cheeks, breathed in deeply and eased me inside her eczema encircled anus. She pushed back as I pressed forward, going deeper. She sat on top on me with her back to me, leaned back and started bouncing. The friction, the different skin textures confused my body's signals, in a good way.

Her ass was tight and it cradled my penis. She turned so I could rub her. Every time I touched her, her ass tightened around me. "Oooooo, stay in there," she pleaded as we progressed to the doggy-style position. I thundered away as her fat ass welcomed more of me. I endeavored to see how deep it was. I adjusted my angle and came down as deep as I could go, she gasped. I slowly turned to get my balls flush against her sphincter. This was new space and I was now an asstronaut. Shantel started breathing again and she began applying pressure of her own.

How deep was it? Bottomless.

When I was ready, she brought me out of her, got on her knees, sucked me and rubbed herself. My penis was so far down her throat that when I came she didn't have to swallow. My muscles spasmed as her tongue coaxed out my warmth. That was the first night I gave her head; I'm good at that.

The folds of skin next to the eczema were really sensitive, once I discovered this I could quickly make her orgasm. She even liked quickies. At one gathering she asked me to come into the bathroom, under the pretense of something being broken. Once the door was closed she let all of her clothes drop to the floor. I was ready to give her head, but she didn't want me to lick anything.

She marveled at how I grew. It was like a magic trick; her eyes would get wide and dance with delight every time it happened. Having power over this magic trick thrilled her. Shantel wanted me inside her ass. You're probably thinking that I'm a freak anyway, but the truth is I had never done this before. The elders always told us youngsters that from time to time, you can be this freaky with your girl, but you have a problem when she starts asking for it. I still don't know what that means.

Lost in the System

Two months had passed since Shantel started and then stopped tutoring me. I failed Algebra and I watched the ashes of my burning dreams fall around me. On the way home from work I reevaluated if I was even cut out for higher learner. I would have to retake the class; damn here I go with the financial calculations again.

I completed the medical repair technician program, so my schedule changed. There was less of a need for my path to cross Shantel's. As the days went by we spoke less often until I lost track of her. Still, I was better off than when I started, as I was somewhere between celebrated and being discarded.

Two weeks after I became a full time medical repair technician, four cops busted in my apartment and started asking me questions, none of their questions applied to me. Nichole was crying, she didn't know what was going on. She called my mother, who promptly came over.

Apparently, the police had stopped by my mother's house earlier that day.

'Where is your son?' the officer had asked my mother.

'I haven't seen him in a while' my mother told them.

My mother, thought her son was into something illegal and she was being protective. The issue was that I parked my car at my mother's house, which I occasionally did. Nichole and I walked eight blocks to my apartment. The engine was still warm; so the police knew my mother was lying. Her lie caused their police antenna to go up and they started to look for anything I could fit the description for, which was everything. Anyway, right now they are in my house telling me they have more questions for me down at the station.

"Officers, officers you said you were looking for me. I'm right here where I'm supposed to be. I have my daughter here. I'm in my pajamas. Sergeant Egam you just ran a check on my ID and everything checks out, right, so I can come down to the station in the morning…"

"You're going down to the station now," Sergeant Egam said.

My seven-year-old daughter cried as I was shackled. I calmed her down by lying. I said, 'baby girl, go with grandma and I'll see you in the morning'. I leaned down and Nichole hugged me and I told my mother where my keys were. I have had many encounters with the police but this was the first time they actually busted into my home.

Three weeks before the police busted in my door. I was driving to work when a police car pulled in close behind me. I hadn't done anything and I always keep everything above board, insurance—check, car registered—check, but still my stomach tightened, my breathing became shallow and waves of panic rose inside of me. The police only followed me for a minute before they turned, but I was sweating. I pulled my car over and got out. My heart was beating fast, my pupils dilated, my throat constricted; it was as if I was being choked. I paced as I took deep breaths and tried to calm myself. Why was my body reacting like this? Why was my mind doing this?

I spoke to a few friends and all of them had various physical reactions to police officers following them around. I had to express this, so I sat down, opened up the computer and wrote my feelings down. I was a member of 93rd Street Community Baptist Church. The church had a scholarship fund and had asked for essays from prospective college students.

I banged out four gut wrenching, heart string pulling pages about this one-minute experience and I turned it into the church. When anxiety grabs a hold of you it's confusing, scary. Once I knew what it was and why it happened. I was able to do something about it. I started to meditate and utilized different breathing techniques that I could pass on. I had wrote the paper for therapy, I didn't think I would win. The next week the church called me in for an interview. It was Tuesday and I put my Sunday Best and went to the meeting.

I smiled and sat in front of the church board; they had serious looks on their faces. They asked me biblical questions, piece of cake, I had been groomed to be a pastor, but that's a story for another time. I nervously sat there as each church board member asked me about my life. The mood of the room changed when they talked about my essay. They related to me that all of them had similar experiences, but they had never seen it articulated in this way. They said that I was an important new voice that more people needed to hear. I smiled and nodded, I don't really know how to take praise. I mean, criticism I got a handle on, but praise was so rare that it was strange to me.

The following Sunday, I was in church and was called up to the front and the pastor announced that I had won a $1,000 scholarship. I was shocked; I don't even go to church regularly. When I got home I put the check in my cabinet. At first I thought, did I deserve the money and then I started thinking about my parties. There was enough to have some really great gatherings and maybe even take a little trip, which brings me back to the police busting through my door.

"Since we are just going to the precinct for some questions, can I ride in the front seat so I don't look like a criminal to my neighbors? These handcuffs hurt, could you use the twist ties?" I asked on the way to the police car.

"No, no." the officers said as they put me in the back of the police car. They took me to the police station. When we got there they fingerprinted me, took photos of me and they booked me. They never asked me any questions. They put me in a cold nasty cell, with a hard blanket, a toothbrush and a roll of notebook level tissue paper and a small motel bar of soap. I wanted to cry but I was around mixed company. The next day, I kept yelling until they told me how much my bail was. My bail was $1,000.

When I finally got my phone call, I called my mother. I told her where the scholarship check was. I told her to cash it and come bail me out. She said no. She didn't want me to lose that money, especially since I hadn't done anything. Normally, this is a reasonable assessment but not having done anything hasn't always played out well for me.

I needed to get out of here now for several reasons; my job being one, the other was my thoughts of *not again*. I spent the day repeatedly calling my mother urging her to cash the check, she eventually bailed me out. I was arrested on a Friday night and was released Monday morning at 2 a.m. I walked outside of the jail and lay in the middle of the parking lot and I cried for ten straight minutes.

I could have cried for another ten minutes.

I walked home, took a shower, ate breakfast, rushed my daughter to school and went right down to the college registration office. I had survived the onslaught of gang violence. I should have died any number of times but I didn't. I stayed out of trouble, worked hard, but something needed to change. I started going to school full time. I begged, borrowed and I petitioned to get into the classes I needed.

Going to school was tough and it was made worse because I couldn't get financial aid because the younger me messed that up. So the older me had to pay for school and pay back the financial aid money that 20-year-old me fucked off.

I went to school early and often. I mean, if you're paying for your classes why not get the most out of them. Most young people get financial support; so they just take frivolous college courses so they don't get kicked out of their parent's house. I was in school to work and learn, so professors loved to have me in class.

I got up at four in the morning and went to class, I was at work by eight, then back to school at two in the afternoon, then back to work at six in the evening and I was home by ten, in between those times I managed to drop off and pick up my daughter. It was a lot but I don't see the sense in complaining or posting about it, I just had to get it done.

I never received a court date from my arrest. After, two months I went down to the courthouse. I gave the clerk my driver's license and asked, "What am I being charged with?" and "When is my court date?"

"Sir, we have no record of your arrest," the clerk responded.

"What!" I stated. I paused for a moment and then I looked at the clerk and said, "Well, where is my thousand dollars?"

The clerk stared at me, lowered her glasses and said, "Mr. Johnson, just be glad you're out. Next!"

I could have easily turned to a life of crime. I believe the law and order crowd would have liked for me to do that, they expected me to do that, they had been waiting for me to do that, why else would they make everything so damn hard. Why else would they put systems in place to cultivate and foment the attitudes that slammed doors in my face, taken away every opportunity and denied me almost every job I was qualified for. The law and order crowd doesn't see human beings. They only see yes and no. How do you move forward if all people see is your mistakes?

293

It's amazing how suicidal thoughts decrease the more you volunteer and the more you have a sense of purpose larger than yourself. How was I to stay positive and maintain my dignity when I am treated differently and discriminated against by my history and by the way I looked? Why else would such an unjust system be allowed to operate without oversight? My spirit was defeated but I was raised wrong and I couldn't and I wouldn't ever again give anything the satisfaction of having control of me.

If I'm free then why don't I feel like it? Was I to just go on living my life, no harm, no foul, play on? Do I just swallow the resentment, allow injustices in my presence and remain silent while others go down dark paths? Do I buy into the dream? Could I start over with a new dream, one of my own creation, a better American Dream?

I couldn't have survived all of the things I've survived and not believe. In my life I felt the hand of some force at work, I had always felt it. It was apparent to me that there was some kind of divine intervention in my life. All of this was no coincidence, it couldn't be. I could feel God's presence. I had to do more. Society had no problem throwing people like me away. For me, one thing was clear, simply surviving would not be enough.

I had to change myself and I had to take these ideas and solutions outside of these walls.

Raised by Wolves

When got out, I blew in just as fast and just as furious as Hurricane Andrew had. I was living young, wild and free, if you were a bodybuilding chick—let's go. You're taller than me—let's go. Your favorite color is blue let's go—two times. Some of the coming together was practice and exploration to see exactly what I liked and wanted, but a lot of it was plain old weakness. Often I had sold myself to the lowest bidder.

I fucked rap chicks, gamer chicks, business suit chicks, cosplay chicks, scientific method chicks, goth chicks, ratchet chicks, PhD chicks, model chicks, earring through the nose chicks, minister chicks, boujie chicks, librarian chicks, reality show chicks, plus size chicks, AKA chicks and lesbians. I even fucked the police. Everyone has weaknesses and having weaknesses doesn't make you a weak person. I shouldn't have been with most of those ladies, but those are stories for another time.

As Nicole got older she began to call and spend more time with me. She had become so much of an advocate for me in her mother's house that I now had her full time, I worked full time and I was in school full time. Even with the second guessing and self-doubt became more responsible and I actively put out more positivity. Some of my gatherings changed into voter registrations and community events. Just before my second year of college I got engaged to beautiful, smart, funny, successful woman. We were in love; we brought the best out of each other.

One month into the excitement of being engaged. King was born. Shantel was King's mother; she didn't even bother to tell me that she was even pregnant. I didn't find out until her sister called me saying that Shantel was sick in the hospital. When I went to visit her I was handed a baby.

King's birth was an unknown situation; I knew things were going to be ever harder for me. I ended my engagement shortly after King's birth. I did not feel it was fair to my fiancée's eight-year-old daughter Summerish. I didn't want to end the engagement but I had to. It hurt and it hurt a lot, but raising my son should not be a hindrance in their lives and that was a good reason for me to hurt.

School helped me mentally recover from that shock and just like that math suddenly clicked for me. Math is actually easy once you realize that all the numbers are connected. My grades were great as I finished my second year of college. King had just turned one and that's when Kimberly Williams, my ex-girlfriend from 8 years ago, out of nowhere hit me with a child support order. I was like what the actual fuck! Eight years ago, she told me that Matthew wasn't mine, the court ordered DNA tests say Matthew is indeed my son.

That's three children and I wasn't 30 yet. Things were tough, real tough. I had steep hills to climb. It didn't matter if it was 8 years ago or yesterday, I made my bed and I had to lay in it. It didn't matter how many children I had. I had to drop them off and pick them up from school and I had to be on time doing it. I had to go to work. I had to pay the bills. No one is going to save me, listen to me whine about my upbringing or applaud my rage against social stratification. No one wanted to hear about my excuses, my reasons or my trauma turned into hate. I was firmly entrenched in urban thermal dynamics, but I had to keep moving forward. I was going to have to put in the work.

It was pure undiluted willpower that made me take not only Fall and Spring sessions, but I also attended Winter and Summer sessions. I routinely took 12, 15, 18 and sometimes 21 college units so I could finish as fast as possible. I cleaned the house when I didn't feel like cleaning it. I got up and ran when I don't want to. When I didn't want to study, I studied. I dug deeper and pushed past my limits to make the road forward less jagged.

I was paying child support for Matthew, Nichole and King. Matthew and Nichole were close in age. I was literally scraping by. When I needed new shoes I wouldn't buy them, until I was able to get all the kids shoes. The same went for clothes. I dealt with not having until we all could have. People never have enough because they don't know what enough is. In this way I turned wants into needs. This stopped me from just buying things when I wanted them…It forced me to plan more and to think of more creative ways of getting from Point A to Point B.

I spent a lot of time with all of my children. They all knew and spent time with each other. My focus was on my children and college. After everything that had and was happened college became one of the easier things I had to do in life. I maintained a B average.

I didn't sleep much and I powered through Community College and earned a degree, but the coach couldn't hire me. Here's the thing about going to school and having to pay your own tuition: it showed me what I was capable of, it made me appreciate my limitations, and it taught me how to adapt. I no longer fit in nice neat boxes, yet all I could do is fight for now.

I knew there was a possibility that my children could grow up and never know me, never be close to me. I couldn't allow that to happen. The only resource I had was time, so if I had to jump through hoops, so be it. The narrative couldn't be left up to anyone but me. If I could help it, my children would never think of me as a deadbeat.

I worked full time and I worked around the neighborhood helping people. I did whatever I needed to do to make ends almost meet. At your job employees are fighting, stealing, conspiring, robbing, lying on and intimidating people, sexing, having mental breakdowns and creating cultures of abuse and everyone by default was terrified of me. The funny thing is that things ran smoother when I was around. When I came to work, I was on time, I worked and apparently I boosted the morale of those I work around and my bosses liked that. It does suck being the only sane person at work.

One summer day after work, I went to my mother's house. As I pulled up, a thin manila folder colored child was sitting on my mom's porch. I parked and walked up to porch and that's when Eva Maldonado came out of my mother's front door.

"Hi Nic, this is your son," Eva said in an off-handed way.

"What in the actual fuck is going on?!"

"This is your son. Aaron, say hi to your father…"

The little boy looked up at me and said "Hi".

I angrily looked at Eva and sternly said, "We need to talk!"

Aaron sat on the porch and played with his toy cars. Eva and I went into my mother's house. She explained to me that when she found out she was pregnant, she panicked. She had a boyfriend at the time, which I didn't even know about. When she told her boyfriend that she was pregnant, he moved them to Oregon. She said she knew Aaron wasn't his baby, but she never told her boyfriend that.

As Aaron got older his skin got darker and this started to cause problems with her boyfriend and at school. Eva decided to come back to Florida when Aaron asked her, "Why don't I look like them?" Eva said that she wanted him to understand who he was, where he came from and his heritage.

"This is all fucked up! You've hurt a lot of people…" I stated.

"I was scared," Eva said.

Some people believe that being afraid is all the excuse they need to do or not do anything. It had been about six years since I had last seen her. Here's the thing about Aaron, I didn't know if Oregon was wilderness or if Eva is just a fucked-up mother because Aaron behaved as if he was almost feral. He cursed, he said whatever he wanted, whenever he wanted to say it. He picked his nose and ate whatever he pulled out. He randomly threw things, he hit people and he did not respect authority. He even growled when angered.

"Why did you bring this kid to me broken…" I asked her.

"I don't tell him no." Eva said, getting into her truck.

"What do you mean you don't tell him no."

"I'm his mother and I don't tell him no. I let him have whatever he wants."

My head was filled with a lot of thoughts and all of them were 'This bitch is crazy!' For a brief moment I felt bad for the guy who had cared for and thought Aaron was his son for the last 6 years. Did Eva just up and leave that guy as well? Is that guy looking for Aaron and Eva? There were more question marks surrounding Eva than there are on The Riddler's shirt.

Eva and I went to court and the court ordered DNA test came back, ninety nine percent my seed. The judge told me, 'I don't care if you and your daughter sleep in a car or on a park bench'. I thought that was a pretty fucked up thing to say. The support order was in place. My goal was to get to know Aaron, for him to get to know me and to integrate him into the family. Aaron was smart; he wouldn't do the same thing he got in trouble for twice. I could see myself in him and it was a small victory just convincing him that he wasn't Mowgli.

Eva told me that she didn't want a relationship with me; she just wanted her son to be American. That's a hell of a thing to want, I thought. Even with all the well debated problems present in America, this place is something Eva would lie, steal, deceive and cheat for. Nothing I did was for her; everything I did was for Aaron. Whenever I thought about how she had done all of this I became furious inside, but in order to move forward I let go of what was because I had to focus on what is.

"I'm a survivor. If I were a gazelle, I'd just trip the slowest gazelle and gallop away." Anthony stated, entering my house. This was his way of announcing himself as he came into my apartment. "That's why Father 'Happy Hands' Flanagan could never catch me. Now the church is saying that he needs our prayers…"

"Put the garbage in the composter." I told Anthony.

"Remember fine ass Angela you used to date, her breath stank to high hell…" Anthony said, sitting down.

"Oh god, don't remind me. Talking to her was like talking to her ass. I had low standards but they weren't that low."

"Things could be worse…"

"How?"

"You could have had a baby by dookie breath Angela."

"Naw."

"She was fine though."

"She was, but her halitosis beat Certs, Binaca, Tic Tacs, Spearmint, Doublemint, Big Red, Breath Assure, Mentos, Life Savers, Listerine triple action and a different diet..."

"Rotten inards..."

"It made my knees weak. I was like where is her dad, where is her mom, where is her family? Her fineness made me think that I could power through it... Whew wee." I said, shuddering just thinking about it. "And she was in everyone's face just talking and talking... I had to abort the mission, I couldn't see it through."

"It didn't last long." Anthony said.

"It lasted longer than it should have." I responded. "No amount of beauty of is worth that."

"She had a good head on her shoulders and she was going places..."

"It wasn't to the dentist... Not overlooking it..."

"At least you found out why she was single." Anthony said laughing.

"You sure are laughing real hard over there... What about that Malaysian girl with the West Indian ass you were dating that sucked her thumb?"

"Lisa Raye..." Anthony said, rolling his eyes.

"Remember we found her OnlySluts page. When she put on her hijab she got four times the views. Her mom had an OnlySluts page too."

"When she started talking to me, I thought her family was going to disown her. I thought I was going to bring dishonor to her family."

"Hey, some people would say that you sold your body to the government and you didn't get paid as well as she does from OnlySluts..."

"It's easy to say bullshit like that in a time of peace. Am I supposed to thank sex workers for their service... If you look at it that way, everyone is selling their body.'

"Military service is a sacrifice no doubt."

"Her breath was no walk in the park either."

"She was cute though."

"Not that cute."

"Wild times...sir... wild times..." I responded sighing.

"So a kid just showed up on your doorstep..." Anthony said looking at me.

"Pretty much..." I said in a depressed tone.

"So not only are they choosing to keep the baby, they're also choosing not to reveal the pregnancy... that's a new branch of Catholicism right there."

"Bruh... It's straight Days of Our Lives status over here."

"You just resettin' the clock. You just keep scoring. You like 90% from the field..." Anthony said teasing.

"I know right and I stay ribbed for her pleasure..."

"I need to start calling you Nicodemus Cannon..." Anthony said. "You've come a long way from having a milk crate entertainment center, making gourmet meals from ramen packets and Nichole's mother showing up unannounced, barging into your house and raisin' hell on your lawn in front of your neighbors."

"I'll say." I responded "Every time I get a handle on things the bottom drops out from dumb things I did years ago…"

"We have to say no, more often to titties and ass and focus on bigger goals."

"Right." I said. "A lot of these young hot ones have that stuff you can't get rid of."

"The last thing I want is that stuff you can't get rid of, but still we have to consider more than body health, mental health has to be higher priority. I'm going to start excluding anyone who has a year's worth of salary as debt and anyone who hasn't invested time or money into personal devolvement, because those are the ones who want to get their mind right while they are in the relationship….damn that."

"I want to be committed; hooking up isn't what I want to be doing. I want love and to be loved. I can't do anything sexually I wouldn't sit down and have a conversation about. Treating people like casual sexual partners means, I'm treating myself in a causal way. I want understanding, I want a connection; I don't want pieces, I want the whole. When you want to be with one, being with many loses its luster. I want to get married."

"Married? I didn't say all of that! I know you coming up short moneywise." Anthony began. "Weaning off of pussy is harder than quitting drugs. You actually have to buy drugs and get a medical exemption to use it. If you are addicted to heroin, it's not at your job waiting on you to clock in. When you wake up in the morning, heroin isn't right next to you in bed. You didn't just meet it on the SunRail and be in the bushes an hour later injecting it. Cocaine doesn't wait until it gets late and then ask you to hit it from the back."

"Right. Opiates don't have you sit between its legs while it braids your hair."

"Heroin isn't just out here looking for a good time."

"Cocaine ain't rationing out its high."

"Meth isn't unexpectedly showing up at your house in the middle of the night."

"Taking a chance on a relationship might not always end well, but it's probably better than being addicted to drugs." Anthony said laughing.

"I will not be shamed for my perceived proclivity for productive generosity." I said. "Besides, I have a big appetite."

"A lot of people have a big appetite they can't always eat though."

"I know how easy it is for someone to lose everything, how everything can be taken from someone, so in light of that…I do enjoy myself. I appreciate women. I mean if I'm going to do it; I'm going to do it. I get it poppin'."

"You're supposed to. You did everything right and you lost everything, so I get it. A lot of children grow up without the balance of being shown how to use and deal with emotions. They grow into people who need to feel something and sex is immediate gratification. I'm not saying that happened to us, but we have become too comfortable having meaningless sex. Sometimes the roster just falls into your lap.

"We are not the best looking dudes in the world, but we have qualities that make us desirable. A lot of dudes would be happy to have relations with one woman a year, even the married dudes. For most dudes, ladies ain't just falling out of the sky— it's not happening."

"What do you mean happy with one woman a year?" I asked.

"Again, I'm not taking about us; no doubt we get our strokes in. I'm over half a million stokes in."

"Half a million, that's a lot of spiritual unification… you ah slut."

"Hey, I was in the military, I'm rolling like thunder under the covers. You're near that number too… what's your excuse?"

"Only four of my half million strokes resulted in pregnancy." I said attempting to feel better about my situation. "It's not just sex, it's the vibe, the connection, how we rock together. You can't be vulnerable with everyone because they'll obviously take advantage."

"Trust but verify."

"We out here grinding."

"It's not luck."

"We good at being hoes... professionals…Straight pum-pumocide."

"A lot of dudes are two kids, four vacations, hundreds of dinners, tens of thousands of dollars and countless hours invested in relationships and are nowhere near even a thousand strokes... that's crazy to me. Most dudes can't breed and not just because they are unattractive, it's because they don't have meaningful skill sets and they don't know how to interact with people. The ones that are afraid to admit it will never change, they'll just get angrier. At least the people who watch anime, read poetry and have a little dog are trying to seem interesting." Anthony finished.

"Having your own place and looking like you have yourself together helps." I said.

"That it does."

"I'm just saying that having multiple sexual partners has a way of ruining you, it changes your perspective. It's not that the pussy wasn't good, the conversations weren't good enough for me to stay. I need more." I said.

"Who you tellin'? They hug you and the next thing you know you are in a relationship and won't even know how. Hugs are dangerous. I had two kids with a succubus so I can't be too hard on you. We fell for the bullshit, but we have to do better."

"That's for damn sure…" I said as we fist bumped each other.

In the quiet times I could still see the dream but it was now torn, battered and faded. From the outside I appeared well put together for a single person, but I was nowhere near marriage ready. I had already dated down so dating up was the only place I could go. Somehow even with 4 children my dating options increased.

Most of the ladies I dated, I could not in good consciousness afford to keep. I dated differently, but no matter the job, the education, the background, the political affiliations or race the results were the same, insecurity, plotting, lying and a general insanity that I had seen before. All relationships require you to lose some sanity to maintain them; I am discovering more and more that the sane thing to do is alone.

I was busting my ass at work, at school and as a father. So at the risk of being considered ghetto sometimes I had to bring Nichole to school with me and sometimes I took my her to work with me, sometimes I even had my two sisters with me. I didn't have a baby sitter so I did what I had to do. My new dream was to be the best father I could be, so none of this was an inconvenience.

Eva and Aaron moved about an hour away to Belle Glade, which is more violent than North Miami was. I had Aaron every weekend. One night he called me and while I was speaking to him, there was a loud commotion in the background.

"What's going on over there?" I asked him.

"My mom and her boyfriend are fighting again…" Aaron responded.

"…again…"

I got in my car and I drove out there. Eva didn't even live where she told me and the court she lived. I wandered around Belle Glade for three hours trying to find where she lived. A week later she showed up at my house.

"What the fuck happened!"

"We're always fighting and throwing things, you know how I am. I have a temper. Oh, he's black too…"

"Who's black?"

"My boyfriend."

"What the fuck does that have to do with anything…"

"Aaron has a black man in the house…"

"I don't understand…"

"You don't have to."

"All of this fighting has to stop. Maybe, Aaron should spend more time with me."

"Just try to take my son and watch what happens."

"I didn't say I was taking him. You said it's hard for you to find a job because of you immigration status. His older sister lives with me; his grandmother is nearby…"

"…Try and take him, if he even stays over your house an hour longer than he's supposed to I'll just take him to Mexico. You know I'm from there, you'd never find us and you'll never see him again."

"I'm not trying to take him. I just want what's best for him. I don't want him in any kind of danger. Aaron was scared the night he called me…"

"…Just try and take him…" Eva stammered. She didn't say another word. She gave me an obviously fake smile and got in her truck. Aaron hugged me and they drove off. That was the last time I saw Aaron.

It took a lot of time and translating but her aunt told me that Eva had moved back to Oregon to live with her mother. I tried contacting her; I tried sending Aaron mail, but none of it worked. I told the courts that Eva had disappeared, but they would not give me her last known address and they wouldn't tell me where they were sending the garnishments.

The DA's office refused to help me find them. They said it wasn't kidnapping and that it was a privacy issue. I thought I had rights regardless of my gender, but I didn't. There would be no Amber Alert. For a year I searched for Aaron by occasionally dropping her dad and aunt's house to see if there was any word. I would ask them if there was any way I could see Aaron— if there was a way, they didn't share it with me. Then after three years, three days and fourteen hours Eva called me.

"I hear that you are looking for me." She said.

"I was looking for Aaron."

Eva let me speak to him, it was around Christmas time and Aaron was 10 years old. I got their address and I sent him a Christmas care package. Plans had been made for me to go to Oregon, it never happened. Eva disappeared again, but the money kept coming out of my checks. The courts didn't care that she was keeping Aaron away from me. They didn't care if his homework was being done or if he was headed for college. They didn't care if his mind was stable. Aaron had two parents only on paper.

I came up with a plan: every six months, I filed a petition for support modification. This meant that Eva and I had to go to court, present documents and talk about money and how much time was being spent with Aaron. I went to the courthouse, but Eva didn't show up. They allowed her to call into the court. After the financials were discussed, I told the judge that I wasn't actually there to lower the amount of the court order; I just really wanted to talk to my son. Under pressure from the judge, she allowed Aaron to talk to me.

In this way, I got to talk to Aaron for about five minutes every six months. The first time I did this; there wasn't a dry eye in the courtroom, including mine. That was the first time the child support people didn't make me feel like I was the enemy.

Eva was terrified of being deported back to Mexico. For a person not to be deported you can apply for citizenship, ask for asylum, marry an American or have a baby born in the United States. Applying for citizenship can take years, asking for asylum requires that you meet certain criteria, marrying an American runs counter to prevalent agendas, having a baby was a quicker and easier way of doing this, it also relaxes global and social biases.

The babies born in the United States that keep people from being deported are called "Anchor Babies". Anchor Baby is often used as a political immigration term. It can also be the way one is tied to a person, a culture, a heritage or to rights. A baby can prevent you from going on that trip, from staying out late and from taking that job. There are anchor marriages, anchor families, anchor jobs, anchor businesses, anchor political affiliations.

The children I had anchored me in place, but it also forced my character and skills to development in unique ways. Aaron was an anchor baby. His birth prevented Eva from being deported, but his birth did not make her a citizen. Eva still had not applied for citizenship. She was off the grid and able to cross borders whenever she wanted; Aaron was her get out of deportation free card.

Whenever Eva didn't like the rules, or she felt she might lose control, she moved somewhere else. She'd start a new life a new with a new identity. She'd move to a place where no one knew her, where no one knew them. Eva didn't have Aaron because she loved me, she didn't hide him from me because she loved him, and she didn't say Aaron was another man's child because she loved that man. We were all simply resources for her to use.

Maybe Eva never loved our Blaxican child, maybe she did, but would she have loved Aaron if his birth hadn't provided her with refuge, money, validation or purpose? Of course she would answer yes, followed by, how could you even ask such a question, but the truth is that no one will ever really know, not even Aaron.

Maybe Eva thought she did me a favor by running. There is no telling what kind of nonsense she might have put me and my family through had she actually been around, maybe it was better that my love went to other kids and families. I won't make excuses for her but I didn't have a choice in the matter.

Eva moved away from tough questions and she manipulated everyone around her, even Aaron. Is that love? Why did she hide him? Why did she move every time someone started asking questions? These are questions best left for Aaron if he ever wants real answers.

I couldn't teach Aaron the importance of believing in himself. I couldn't show him the love I had for him. I couldn't show him how to focus on school. I couldn't teach my son about his West African roots. I did the only thing I could; send him care packages. My mother put in a bible and gifts, his sister added photos to the packages I sent. I included clothes, a store-bought cell phone and cell phone gift cards. I thought that would allow me to speak to him. When Eva found out I had been calling him she got rid of the cell phone.

I just hope he's okay.

www.ingramcontent.com/pod-product-compliance
Lightning Source LLC
Chambersburg PA
CBHW060948120726
47910CB00002B/533